"I thought I'd stay for a while," Zack said.

Lizzie gasped. "But that wouldn't be proper…" The thought of having Zack on the farm was disturbing.

She became unsettled when Zack put her in the focus of his dark gaze. "I'll send for my *mudder*—and my sister Esther," he said easily. "The three of us can stay there comfortably."

Lizzie felt a feeling of dread. "But—"

"Not to worry, Lizzie Fisher." He flashed her a friendly smile as he buttered the muffin. "I'll head home and then accompany them back to Honeysuckle. I won't be moving in without someone as chaperone."

But that wasn't all that concerned Lizzie. She couldn't help but wonder how long he—they—would be staying. Why did he want to stay? She'd never met her mother-in-law or any of Abraham's siblings. What if they didn't like her? What if they judged her incapable of managing the farm and decided she was no longer needed?

Could she bear to be parted from her children?

Because, in her heart, they were *her* children, although she hadn't given birth to them.

What would the future hold?

Rebecca Kertz was first introduced to the Amish when her husband took a job with an Amish construction crew. She enjoyed watching the Amish foreman's children at play and swapping recipes with his wife. Rebecca resides in Delaware with her husband and dog. She has a strong faith in God and feels blessed to have family nearby. Besides writing, she enjoys reading, doing crafts and visiting Lancaster County.

Books by Rebecca Kertz

Love Inspired

Lancaster Courtships

The Amish Mother

Lancaster County Weddings

Noah's Sweetheart
Jedidiah's Bride
A Wife for Jacob

The Amish Mother

Rebecca Kertz

HARLEQUIN® LOVE INSPIRED®

Recycling programs
for this product may
not exist in your area.

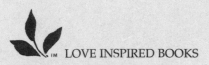

LOVE INSPIRED BOOKS

ISBN-13: 978-0-373-87986-1

The Amish Mother

Copyright © 2015 by Rebecca Kertz

www.Harlequin.com

Printed in U.S.A.

In my distress I cried unto the Lord,
and He heard me.
—*Psalms* 120:1

For Maggie, Ellie and Ainsley with love

Chapter One

Lancaster County, Pennsylvania

The apple trees were thick with bright, red juicy fruit waiting to be picked. Elizabeth King Fisher stepped out of the house into the sunshine and headed toward the twin apple trees in the backyard.

"You sit here," she instructed her three youngest children, who'd accompanied her. She spread a blanket on the grass for them. "I'll pick and give them to you to put in the basket. *Ja?*"

"Ja, Mam," little Anne said as she sat down first and gestured for her brothers to join her.

Lizzie smiled. "You boys help your sister?" Jonas and Ezekiel nodded vigorously. *"Goot* boys!" she praised, and they beamed at her.

"What do you think we should make with these?" she said as she handed three apples to Jonas. "An apple pie? Apple crisp?"

"Candy apples!" Ezekiel exclaimed. He was three years old and the baby of the family, and he had learned recently about candy apples, having tasted one when they'd gone into town earlier this week.

Lizzie grinned as she bent to ruffle his hair. Ezekiel had taken off his small black-banded straw hat and set it on the blanket next to him. "Candy apples," she said. "I can make those."

The older children were nowhere in sight. Elizabeth's husband, Abraham, had fallen from the barn loft to his death just over two months ago, and the family was still grieving. Lizzie had tears in her eyes as she reached up to pull a branch closer to pick the fruit. *If only I hadn't urged him to get the kittens down from the loft...*

Tomorrow would have been their second wedding anniversary. She had married Abraham shortly after the children's mother had passed, encouraged strongly by her mother to do so. She'd been seventeen years old at the time, but she'd been crippled her entire life.

"Abraham Fisher is a *goot* man, Lizzie," she remembered her mother saying. "He needs a mother for his children and someone to care for his home. You should take his offer of marriage, for in your condition you may not get another one."

My condition, Lizzie thought. She suffered from developmental hip dysplasia, and she walked with a noticeable limp that worsened after standing for long periods of time. But she was a hard worker and could carry the weight of her chores as well as the rest of the women in her Amish community.

Limping Lizzie, the children had called her when she was a child. There had been other names, including Duckie because of her duck-like gait, which was caused by a hip socket too shallow to keep in the femoral head, the ball at the top of her long leg bone. Most of the children didn't mean to be cruel, but the names hurt just the same.

Lizzie had spent her young life proving that it didn't

matter that one leg was longer than the other; yet her mother had implied otherwise when she'd urged Lizzie to marry Abraham, a grieving widower with children.

Abraham had still been grieving for his first wife when he'd married her, but she'd accepted his grief along with the rest of the family's. His children missed their mother. The oldest two girls, Mary Ruth and Hannah, resented Lizzie. The younger children had welcomed her, as they needed someone to hug and love them and be their mother. And they were too young to understand.

Mary Ruth, Abraham's eldest, had been eleven at the time of her mother's death, her sister Hannah almost ten. Both girls were angry with their mother for dying and angrier still at Lizzie for filling the void.

Lizzie picked several more apples, handing the children a number of them so that they would feel important as they placed them carefully in the basket.

"Can we eat one?" Anne asked.

"With your midday meal," Lizzie said. She glanced up at the sky and noted the position of the sun, which was directly overhead. "Are you hungry?" All three youngsters nodded vigorously. She reached to pick up the basket, which was full and heavy. She didn't let on that her leg ached as she straightened with the basket in hand. "Let's get you something to eat, then."

The children followed her into the large white farmhouse. When she entered through the back doorway, she saw the kitchen sink was filled with dirty dishes. She sighed as she set the basket on one end of the counter near the stove.

"Mary Ruth!" she called. "Hannah!" When there was no response, she called for them again. Matthew, who was eight, entered the kitchen from the front section of the house. "Have you seen your older sisters?" Lizzie asked him.

He shrugged. "Upstairs. Not sure what they're doing."

"Matt, are you hungry?" When the boy nodded, Lizzie said, "If you'll go up and tell your sisters to come down, I'll make you all something to eat."

Jonas grabbed his older brother's arm as Matt started to leave. "*Mam*'s going to make candy apples," he said.

Matthew opened his mouth as if to say something, but then he glanced toward the basket of apples instead and smiled. "Sounds *goot*. I like candy apples." Little Jonas grinned at him.

Matt left and then returned moments later, followed by his older sisters, Mary Ruth, Hannah and Rebecca, who had been upstairs in their room.

"You didn't do the dishes," Lizzie said to Mary Ruth.

The girl regarded her with a sullen expression. "I didn't know it was my turn."

"I'll do them," Rebecca said.

"That's a nice offer, Rebecca," Lizzie told her, "but 'tis Mary Ruth's turn, so I think she should do it." She smiled at the younger girl. "But you can help me make the candy apples later this afternoon after I hang the laundry." She met Hannah's gaze. "Did you strip the beds?"

Hannah nodded. "I put the linens near the washing machine."

Lizzie smiled. "*Danki*, Hannah." She heard Mary Ruth grumble beneath her breath. "Did you say something you'd like to share?" she asked softly.

"*Nay,*" Mary Ruth replied.

"I thought not." She went to the refrigerator. "What would you like to eat?" Their main meal was usually at midday, but their schedule had differed occasionally since Abraham's death because of the increase in her workload. Still, she had tried to keep life the same as much as possible.

"I can make them a meal," Mary Ruth challenged. Lizzie turned, saw her defiant expression and then nodded. The girl was hurting. If Mary Ruth wanted to cook for her siblings, then why not let her? She had taught her to be careful when using the stove.

"That would be nice, Mary Ruth," she said. "I'll hang the clothes while you feed your *brooders* and sisters." And she headed toward the back room where their gas-powered washing machine was kept, sensing that the young girl was startled. Lizzie retrieved a basket of wet garments and headed toward the clothesline outside.

The basket was only moderately heavy as she carried it to a spot directly below the rope. She felt comfortable leaving the children in the kitchen, for she could see inside through the screen door.

A soft autumn breeze stirred the air and felt good against her face. Lizzie bent, chose a wet shirt and pinned it on the line. She worked quickly and efficiently, her actions on the task but her gaze continually checking inside to see the children seated at the kitchen table.

"Elizabeth Fisher?" a man's voice said, startling her.

Lizzie gasped and spun around. She hadn't heard his approach from behind her. She'd known before turning that he was Amish as he had spoken in *Deitsch*, the language spoken within her community. Her eyes widened as she stared at him. The man wore a black-banded, wide-brimmed straw hat, a blue shirt and black pants held up by black suspenders. He looked like her deceased husband, Abraham, only younger and more handsome.

"You're Zachariah," she said breathlessly. Her heart picked up its beat as she watched him frown. "I'm Lizzie Fisher."

* * *

Zachariah stared at the woman before him in stunned silence. She was his late brother's widow? He'd been shocked to receive news of Abraham's death, even more startled to learn the news from Elizabeth Fisher, who had identified herself in her letter as his late brother's wife.

It had been years since he'd last visited Honeysuckle. He hadn't known that Ruth had passed or that Abe had remarried. *Why didn't Abraham write and let us know?*

"What happened to Ruth?" he demanded.

The woman's lovely bright green eyes widened. "Your *brooder* didn't write and tell you?" she said quietly. "Ruth passed away—over two years ago. A year after Ezekiel was born, she came down with the flu and…" She blinked. "She didn't make it. Your *brooder* asked me to marry him shortly afterward."

Zack narrowed his gaze as he examined her carefully. Dark auburn hair in slight disarray under her white head covering…eyes the color of the lawn after a summer rainstorm…pink lips that trembled as she gazed up at him. "You can't be more than seventeen," he accused.

The young woman lifted her chin. "Nineteen," she stated stiffly. "I've been married to your *brooder* for two years." She paused, looked away as if to hide tears. "It would have been two years tomorrow had he lived."

Two years! Zack thought. The last time he'd received a letter from Abraham was when Abe had written the news of Ezekiel's birth. His brother had never written again.

The contents of Lizzie's letter when it had finally caught up to the family had shocked and upset them. Zack had made the immediate decision to come home to Honeysuckle to gauge the situation with the children and the property—and this new wife the family knew nothing about. His mother and sisters had agreed that he should go. With both Ruth and Abraham deceased, Zack thought that the time had come to reclaim what was rightfully his—the family farm.

He stood silently, watching as she pulled a garment from the wicker basket at her feet and tossed it over the line. He had trouble picturing Abraham married to this girl, although he could see why Abraham might have been attracted to her. But why would Lizzie choose to marry Abraham? He saw the difficulty her trembling fingers had securing the garment onto the clothesline properly. He fought back unwanted sympathy for her and won.

"You're living here with the children," he said. *"Alone?"*

"This is our home." Lizzie faced him, a petite girl whose auburn hair suddenly appeared as if streaked with various shades of reds under the autumn sun. Her vivid green eyes and young innocent face made her seem vulnerable, but she must be a strong woman if she could manage all seven of his nieces and nephews—and stand defiantly before him as she was now without backing down. He felt a glimmer of admiration for her that quickly vanished with his next thought.

This woman and his brother were married almost two years. Did Lizzie and Abraham have a child together? He scowled as he glanced about the yard, then toward the house. He didn't see or hear a baby, but then, the child could be napping inside. How did one ask a woman if she'd given birth without sounding offensive or rude? *My* brooder *should have told me about her. Then I would know.*

"I'm nearly done," she said, averting her attention back to her laundry while he continued to watch her. She hung up the last item, a pillowcase. *"Koom.* We're about to have our midday meal. Join us. You must have come a long way." She bit her lip as she briefly met his gaze. "Where did you come from? I wasn't sure where to send the letter. I didn't know if you were still in Walnut Creek or Millersburg or if you'd moved again. I sent it to Millersburg because it was the last address I found among your *brooder*'s things."

"We moved back to Walnut Creek two years ago—" He stopped. He wasn't about to tell her about his mother's illness or that he and his sister Esther had moved with *Mam* from Walnut Creek to Millersburg to be closer to the doctors treating their mother's cancer. *Mam* was fine now, thank the Lord, and she would continue to do well as long as she took care of herself. Once his mother's health had improved, they had picked up and moved back to Walnut Creek, where his two older sisters lived with their husbands and their families.

Zack had no idea how Lizzie's letter had reached him. Their forwarding address had expired over a year ago, but someone who'd known them in Millersburg must have sent it on. He still couldn't believe that Abraham was dead. His older brother had been only thirty-five years old. "What happened to my *brooder*?" She never mentioned in her letter how he'd died.

Lizzie went pale. "He fell," she said in a choked voice, "from the barn loft." He saw her hands clutch rhythmically at the hem of her apron. "He broke his neck and died instantly."

Zack felt shaken by the mental image. He could see that she was sincerely distraught. "I'm sorry. I know it's hard." He, too, felt the loss. It hurt to realize that he'd never see Abraham again. He thought of all the times when he was a child that he'd trailed after his older brother.

His death must have been quick and painless, he thought, trying to find some small measure of comfort.

He studied the young woman who looked too young to be married or to raise Abe's children.

"He was a *goot* man." She didn't look at him when she bent to pick up her basket then straightened. "Are you coming in?" she asked as she finally met his gaze.

He nodded and then followed her as she started toward the house. He was surprised to see her uneven gait as she walked ahead of him, as if she'd injured her leg and limped because of the pain. "Lizzie, are *ya* hurt?" he asked compassionately.

She halted, then faced him with her chin tilted high, her eyes less than warm. "I'm not hurt," she said crisply. "I'm a cripple." And with that, she turned away and continued toward the house, leaving him to follow her.

Zack studied her back with mixed feelings as he lagged behind. Concern. Worry. Uneasiness. He frowned as he watched her shift the laundry basket to one arm and struggle to open the door with the other. He stopped himself from helping, sensing that she wouldn't be pleased. He frowned at her back. Could a crippled, young nineteen-year-old woman raise a passel of *kinner* alone?

Lizzie was aware of her husband's brother behind her as she entered the house with the laundry basket. She flashed a glance toward the kitchen sink and was pleased to note that Mary Ruth had washed the dishes and left them to drain on a rack over a tea towel.

"Mary Ruth, would you set another plate?" she said. "We have a visitor." She was relieved to note that her daughter had set a place for her.

Mary Ruth frowned but rose to obey. Lizzie stepped aside and the child caught sight of the man behind her. She paled as she stared at him, most probably noting the uncanny resemblance of Zachariah to her dead father.

"*Dat?*" she whispered. The girl shook her head, then drew a sharp breath. "*Onkel* Zachariah."

Watching the exchange, Lizzie saw him smile. "Mary Ruth, you've grown over a foot since I last saw you," he said.

Mary Ruth blinked back tears and looked as if she wanted to approach him but dared not. The Amish normally weren't affectionate in public, but they were at home, and Lizzie knew that the child hadn't seen her uncle in a long time.

To his credit, Zachariah extended his arms, and Mary Ruth ran into his embrace. Eyes closed, the man hugged his niece tightly, and Lizzie felt the emotion flowing from him in huge waves.

"Zachariah is your *dat*'s brother," she explained to the younger children.

Chairs scraped over the wooden floor as they rose from their seats and eyed him curiously. Zachariah had released Mary Ruth and studied her with a smile. "You look like your *mudder.*"

"Why didn't you come sooner?" Mary Ruth asked. She appeared pleased by the comparison to her mother.

"I didn't get Lizzie's letter until yesterday," he admitted. "After reading it, I quickly made arrangements to come."

Mary Ruth nodded as if she understood. "Sit down," she told the children in a grown-up voice. "*Onkel* is going to eat with us. You'll have time to talk with him at the dinner table."

The kitchen was filled with the delicious scent of pot roast with potatoes, onions and carrots. Mary Ruth had heated the leftovers from the previous day in the oven, and she'd warmed the blueberry muffins that Lizzie had baked earlier this morning.

Her eldest daughter set a plate before Zachariah and then asked what he wanted to drink. Standing there, Lizzie saw a different child than the one she'd known since Lizzie had married Abe and moved into the household. It was a glimpse of how life could be, and Lizzie took hope from it.

After stowing the empty laundry basket in the back room, Lizzie joined everyone at the table. The platter of pot roast was passed to Zachariah, who took a helping before he extended it toward Lizzie. Thanking him with a nod, she took some meat and vegetables from the plate before asking the children if they wanted more.

Conversation flowed easily between the children and their uncle, and Lizzie listened quietly as she forked up a piece of beef and brought it to her mouth.

"Are *ya* truly my *vadder*'s *brooder*?" Rebecca asked.

"Look at him, Rebecca," Hannah said. "Don't *ya* see the family resemblance?"

Lizzie looked over in time to see Rebecca blush. She addressed her husband's brother. "You haven't visited Honeysuckle in a long time."

Zachariah focused his dark eyes on her and she felt a jolt. "*Ja.* Not in years. My *mudder* moved my sisters and me to Ohio after *Dat* died. I was eleven." He grabbed a warm muffin and broke it easily in half. "I came back for a visit once when Hannah was a toddler." He smiled at Hannah as he spread butter on each muffin half. "It's hard to believe how much you've grown. I remember you as this big." He held his hand out to show her how tall.

Hannah smiled. "You knew my *mam*."

He had taken a bite of muffin and he nodded as he chewed and swallowed it.

"How come we haven't met you before?" Matthew asked with the spunk of a young boy. "You didn't come for *Mum*'s funeral."

"I didn't know about your *mudder*'s passing," Zachariah said softly. "I still wouldn't have known if not for Lizzie. I wanted to come to see you and your family before now, but I couldn't get away." He glanced around the table. "Seven children," he said with wonder. "I'm happy to see that your *mudder* and *vadder* were blessed with all of you." He smiled and gazed at each child in turn. "How old are you?" he asked Ezekiel.

Ezekiel held up three fingers. "Such a big boy. You are the youngest?" He seemed to wait with bated breath for Zeke's reply, and he smiled when his answer was the boy's vigorous nod. He then guessed Anne's and then Jonas's ages and was off by just one year for Jonas, who was four.

"How long are you going to stay, *Onkel* Zachariah?" Rebecca asked.

"Zack," he invited. He leaned forward and whispered, "Zachariah is too much of a mouthful with *Onkel, ja*?" Then he shot Lizzie a quick glance before answering his niece's question. "I thought I'd stay for a while." He took a second muffin. "The *dawdi haus*—is it empty?" he asked.

"Ja," Mary Ruth said while Lizzie felt stunned as she anticipated where the conversation was headed. "'Tis always empty except when we have guests, which we haven't had in a long time…"

"Goot," he said. "Then you won't mind if I move in—"

Lizzie gasped audibly. "But that wouldn't be proper…" The thought of having him on the farm was disturbing.

She became unsettled when Zack put her in the center focus of his dark gaze. "I'll send for my *mudder*—and my sister Esther," he said easily. "The three of us can stay there comfortably."

Dread washed over Lizzie. "But—"

"Not to worry, Lizzie Fisher." He flashed her a friendly smile as he buttered the muffin. "I'll head home and then accompany them back to Honeysuckle. I won't be moving in without a chaperone."

But that wasn't all that concerned Lizzie. She couldn't help but wonder how long he—they—would be staying. Why did he want to stay? She'd never met her mother-in-law or any of Abraham's siblings. What if they didn't like her? What if they judged her incapable of managing the farm and decided that she was no longer needed? Could she bear to be parted from her children? Because, in her heart, they were *her* children although she hadn't given birth to them.

She had enjoyed a good life with Abraham. She'd worked hard to make the farmhouse a home for a grieving man and his children. *And Abraham appreciated my efforts*, she thought. Right before his death, she'd felt as if he'd begun to truly care for her.

"You don't have to worry about us," Lizzie said quietly as she watched him enjoy his food. "We are doing fine." Her hands began to shake, and she placed them on her lap under the table so that he wouldn't see. "There is no need to return. I know your life is in Ohio now."

Zack waved her concerns aside. "You'll be needing help at harvest time. It can't be easy managing the farm and caring for Abraham's children alone."

Lizzie felt her stomach twist. Zack, like everyone else, thought her incapable of making it on her own, and he'd referred to the children as Abraham's. She experienced a jolt of anger. Abraham's children were her children, had been for two years now.

Then a new thought struck her with terror. Zack was the youngest Fisher son. Wouldn't that make him the rightful heir to his family farm? If so, had he come to stake his claim?

Lizzie settled her hand against her belly as the burning there intensified and she felt nauseous. Was she going to lose her home and her family—the children she loved as her own?

She closed her eyes and silently prayed. *Please, dear Lord, help me prove to Zack that I am worthy of being the children's* mudder. When she opened them again, she felt the impact of Zack's regard. She was afraid what having him on the farm would do to her life, her peace of mind and her family.

Chapter Two

Zack had departed for Ohio the same day he'd arrived after making known his shocking intention of staying on the farm. After sharing their midday meal, he'd gone as quickly as he'd come with the promise to return, ready to move in with his mother and sister. Lizzie had no idea when he'd be back, but she and the children immediately went to work readying the *dawdi haus* the day after his departure. She would not have him feeling unwelcome.

"Did you hang up the sheets?" she asked Mary Ruth as the girl briefly entered the bedroom where Lizzie swept the wooden floor. She and Hannah had stayed home from school to help her get ready for Zachariah's return.

"Ja," her daughter said. "I did the quilts and blankets, too."

Lizzie smiled. "That's *goot*. We want to be ready for your uncle, *ja*?"

To her surprise, Mary Ruth grinned back at her. *"Ja.* It will be wonderful to have family here."

Lizzie nodded in agreement with Mary Ruth, but as her daughter left for the other bedroom with dust cloth and homemade polish in hand, she wondered what the

Fishers' stay at the farm would mean for her and her future.

The cottage had two bedrooms, a bathroom, a combination great room and kitchen, and a pantry. A covered porch with two rocking chairs and a swing ran along the front outer wall of the *dawdi haus*. Lizzie had always liked the little house and the comfort it offered guests and the *grosseldre*, or grandparents, for whom it must have been built.

Hannah and Rebecca entered the largest bedroom, where Lizzie continued to clean and prepare for their expected guests. "I wiped inside the kitchen cabinets and the countertops, Lizzie," Hannah said.

"And what about the pantry?"

"I helped Hannah carry all the jars you said to bring," Rebecca said. "Want to see?" There was an air of excitement among the sisters.

Lizzie studied the two happy girls and smiled. "*Ja*, show me." She followed Hannah and Rebecca through the great area to the kitchen nook on the other side.

"*Mam*," young Anne said. "Look how nice they are!"

The jars of tomatoes, sweet-and-sour chow-chow, peaches and jam appeared colorful on the clean pantry shelves. "You girls have been working hard." Lizzie smiled. "*Danki.*" She looked about and didn't see the two youngest. "Where are Jonas and Ezekiel?" she asked with concern.

"Outside with Matt," Mary Ruth said as she approached from the other bedroom across the hall from where Lizzie had been working.

Anne nodded. "They are pulling out weeds and dead things from the flower garden."

No doubt the boys were working, as per her instructions, to clear out the dried rudbeckia blossoms and stems. The flowers also known as black-eyed Susans created a beautiful display of bright color from late spring to mid- or late summer, but in the fall, seeds from the dead centers had to be spread across the soil to ensure next year's glorious display of gold and black.

"You have all worked hard on these today. I appreciate it. I couldn't have prepared the cottage without you." Lizzie noted with pleasure the smile on Mary Ruth's face.

"Is there anything else we need to do?" the girl asked.

"We'll go shopping tomorrow for supplies," Lizzie said. "And we can bake bread, put some in the pantry and freeze a few loaves for them. They are welcome to eat at the farmhouse anytime, but they may want to take some of their meals here in the *dawdi haus*."

"Ja," Hannah said. "It's a nice *haus*. It will be *goot* to see someone living in it."

Lizzie hoped so. "It's been a long morning without a break to eat. Are any of you hungry?"

"Ja!" the girls cried.

Matt entered the house with his younger brothers. *"Ja,"* he said, apparently hearing the last of Lizzie's words. "We're hungry. What's to eat?"

Lizzie thought for a moment. "What would you like? Hard work deserves a special meal."

"Pizza!" the youngest ones cried.

"Pizza," Lizzie said with surprise and a little dismay. Money was tight, but she could make a crust from scratch, and she did have jars of tomato sauce she'd canned earlier in the summer. She could make her own pizza sauce and top it with whatever cheese she had in the refrigerator, fresh green peppers and onions. She could make a second pizza with just the cheese for the youngsters who wanted their pizza plain. "Pizza it is," she said with a smile. "And then afterward, why don't

I make those candy apples I promised yesterday." The children wholeheartedly agreed to the plan.

As she and the children left the *dawdi haus* and headed toward the farmhouse, Lizzie felt as if they were a family for the first time since the tragic loss of her husband—their father. She experienced a lightening of spirit and hope for the family's future.

Later that night after the children were in bed, Lizzie went up to her bedroom, the room she'd shared with Abraham, and stared at the bed. Sleep hadn't come easy to her since Abraham's passing. Last night the worry over her late husband's family moving into the *dawdi haus* had caused her to fret into the early morning until, exhausted, she'd finally fallen into a fitful sleep not long before she had to get up to begin her day again.

She had a mental image of Zack as she'd first seen him. He looked like a young Abraham, only with dark hair and more handsome features. Not that her husband hadn't been good-looking. He had been, but she hadn't noticed that at first. She had married him at a time that had been difficult for everyone, a time of mourning for him and the children, a time of concern that she might have made a mistake in agreeing to the marriage.

But we found our way, Lizzie thought as she moved across the room. Time had healed Abraham's grief and his gaze had lost the sadness. Then he had begun to appreciate everything that she had done for the family—taking care of the house, doing the wash, loving his children.

They had married as strangers—he'd needed someone to care for his children after his wife had died, and she'd needed a life of her own.

During the first months of her marriage to Abraham, she had slept in the sewing room after quilting long into the night. She had produced some beautiful quilts by their first anniversary, when Abraham had invited her to sleep in the master bedroom. Afterward she had worked on her quilts in the evening instead, with Abraham seated nearby in his favorite chair while the children had played cards or read stories.

Since Abraham's death, she had gone back to quilting through most of the night until she'd fall into bed exhausted and sleep only to awaken early to begin her chore-filled days. She enjoyed quilting and everyone complimented her on her handiwork. She had recently sold one of her quilts at Beachey's Craft Shop, the money coming in at a time when they needed it. Ellen Beachey, the shopkeeper, had been gracious in taking her quilts and craft items so that she could earn much-needed cash.

She crossed to the sewing room off the bedroom and picked up one of her colorful quilt squares. Her mind reeled with emotion as she went to work. As she began to make tiny, even stitches in the fabric, she thought of Abraham and the children and how difficult their father's death had been for them, how hard it had been to lose their mother two years earlier. They were wonderful children, and she loved them.

Would having Zack and his family here help her relationship with the children or hinder it?

She paused, closed her eyes and prayed. *Please, Lord, help us to become a family. Don't let me lose everything I gained when I married Abraham.* A family. A home. Children who needed her.

Mary Ruth's and Hannah's sweet behavior would have made her feel at peace, if not for the knowledge that Zack would return soon and disturb the life she'd made for herself with the children.

Ah, Abraham, I'm sorry. 'Twas my fault that you're no longer with us.

Tears filled her eyes as she plied needle to cloth in tiny, even stitches. She recalled her husband's face and his eyes, which had eventually looked at her with more than kindness, with caring that had turned into love. In the months before he died, Abraham had begun to see her as a wife rather than a housekeeper and helpmate.

She sniffed as she set down her sewing and rose. She was tired. She undressed by candlelight, carefully removing the straight pins securing her dress, and got ready for bed. She brushed her hair, recalling with a smile when she'd brushed out her youngest daughter's hair earlier.

Her hip ached and she reached for the menthol and camphor salve to rub on the sore and swollen joint. The scent was strong, but she was used to it, welcomed it because any little pain relief was worth it. She could take aspirin or ibuprofen, but she'd used so much of it recently, she decided it was best to save it for when the pain became unbearable without it.

She moved toward the bed, pulled back the quilt and climbed onto the mattress. She heard a gentle knock on her bedroom door. *"Ja?"*

"Mam?" The door swung open, and her youngest daughter, Anne, peeked inside, holding a flashlight.

"Anne," Lizzie murmured. She waved her in. "What's wrong?"

Her daughter approached the bed. *"Mam,* do you think our *grossmama* will like us?"

Lizzie smiled reassuringly. "She will love you," she said, believing it to be true. "You are her granddaughter. All of you children are her grandchildren. Why wouldn't she love you? Love all of her *kins kinner*?"

Annie tilted her head as she regarded her with unusually grown-up eyes. "Will she love you, too?"

Lizzie smiled, unable to assure her when she didn't know. "You are worrying too much, Anne. They will come and all will be well."

The child smiled. "I am glad. I want us all to be happy together. It is time for us—you—to be happy."

Lizzie reached for the girl's hand, pulled her close. "I am happy," she said sincerely. "You and your sisters and *brooders* make me very happy."

"Even though Mary Ruth can be sharp to you?"

She nodded. "*Ja*, no matter what. I am happy with you all, and I love you."

Anne grinned and leaned over to hug her. "I love you, *Mam*."

Lizzie closed her eyes as she held on to her daughter. "I love you. You all are everything a *mudder* could ask for and more." She released her child to pat her cheek. "Now run off to bed. We've a busy day tomorrow."

Annie nodded vigorously and spun to race out of the room, pausing on the threshold to glance back at Lizzie. *"Danki."*

Lizzie raised her eyebrows in question.

"For being my *mam*," Anne explained before she hurried on and shut the door behind her.

Lizzie blinked against happy tears as she leaned to blow out the candle. As the room plunged into darkness, she relaxed and lay back against her pillow. She felt sleepy and hopeful for the first time in a long while.

The next morning she was up and ready to begin her day. Now that the *dawdi haus* was prepared for guests, she needed to clean the farmhouse. She made breakfast first, and soon the children joined her in the kitchen, ready to eat. Lizzie beamed at them as they sat down.

"Hungry?" she asked. "I made pancakes, bacon, sausage and eggs."

"It looks *goot*," Hannah said.

"It tastes *goot*." Matt had grabbed a piece of bacon and popped it into his mouth.

"Matthew, mind your manners and put some on your plate."

"*Ja*, Lizzie." Matt nodded, looking solemn, and then he grinned.

Lizzie laughed; she couldn't help it. The boy was looking at her with such delight that the pure joy of the moment deeply touched her. It was nice to hear laughter in the house again.

Her older children helped the younger ones get their food. Lizzie watched with fondness as Rebecca cut up little Jonas's pancakes for him.

This is what family is about, she thought. Had she ever felt so lighthearted when she was a girl? She couldn't recall laughing at the dinner table. Her mother had treated her differently than her siblings because of her disability. It was as if she'd been unable to accept that her daughter wasn't perfect.

"Anne, be careful with your milk," Lizzie warned without anger.

Anne set her glass down and smiled at her with milk-mustached lips. "When do *ya* think *Onkel* will be here?" she asked.

"*Onkel* Zack," Hannah corrected.

Lizzie sat down and filled her plate. "I don't know. Surely by next week."

"What else must we do to be ready for him?" Hannah asked.

Lizzie looked at her fondly. "I thought we should clean our *haus* next. We wouldn't want *Onkel* Zack, *Grossmama* and *Endie* Esther to see a dirty *haus*, would we?"

"Nay!" the children chorused. The family teased each other as they ate breakfast, and when they were done, Lizzie and her daughters rose and tackled the kitchen first before moving on to clean the rest of the house. She sent the boys outside to make sure that there were no sticks in the yard and the porch was free of any balls and play items. She'd asked Matt to check the honeysuckle bush near her vegetable garden to see if it needed to be pruned back.

Later that afternoon when the children were at the kitchen table enjoying a snack, Lizzie heard a car in the barnyard. She hurried toward the door in time to see Zachariah Fisher climb out of the front passenger side of the vehicle and then reach to open the back door. A woman alighted as Zack went to the trunk and waited while the driver met him. The Englisher lifted out two suitcases and set them on the ground.

She saw Zack exchange words with the driver. Then he and the woman approached the house. Lizzie stepped out onto the porch to meet them. She heard the children behind her, chatting happily after seeing who had returned.

Lizzie was startled to see him. She hadn't expected him back so soon. His gaze locked with hers as he drew closer. Her heart started to pound hard.

Chapter Three

He inclined his head. "Lizzie."

She swallowed against a suddenly dry throat. "Zack."

He drew the woman forward. Lizzie saw that she was older than Zachariah but not enough to be his mother. "This is—"

"Esther," Lizzie said with a smile. "Your *schweschter*." She was pleased to note Zack's surprise when she'd addressed his sister by name. "We're glad you could come and stay with us."

Esther's gaze warmed. "And you're Lizzie."

Lizzie nodded. "Are you hungry? May I offer you a snack to hold you until supper? There are cookies and apple crisp. The cottage is ready for you. I believe you'll be comfortable there."

"We all helped to fix it up for you," Rebecca said as she joined Lizzie on the front porch.

Mary Ruth and the rest of the children stepped out of the house and gathered behind Lizzie and Rebecca. Anne and Matt stood behind them, inside the door.

Esther smiled. "*Hallo*. So you are Abraham's children. My nieces and nephews."

Rebecca stepped forward. "Would you like to come in? Matt can put your luggage in the *dawdi haus* for you," she told her aunt. She glanced at her brother and, understanding, Matt came out of the house and approached.

"*Danki.* I wouldn't mind coming in for a bit," Esther agreed.

Zack captured Lizzie's gaze as he handed Matt a suitcase and picked up the other one. Her heart gave a little jump before it started to beat normally again. "I'll go with Matt," he said. "We'll be right back."

Esther nodded before she followed Lizzie and the children into the farmhouse. Once inside, she paused to study her surroundings. "Everything is the same, but different," she said.

Lizzie understood. She hadn't given much thought to the fact that Esther, Abraham and the rest of their siblings had lived here with their parents before their father's passing. As they continued through the house and into the kitchen, Zack's sister smiled appreciatively. "It smells wonderful in here."

Hannah smiled. "We baked today. Would you like some apple crisp?"

Esther shook her head. "We stopped to eat on the way."

"Tea?"

At Lizzie's invitation, Esther sat down at the kitchen table. "*Ja*, that sounds *goot*."

Lizzie studied her sister-in-law. Esther Fisher was a tall, attractive woman with warmth in her brown gaze and soft pretty laugh lines at the corners of her eyes and near her mouth. She wore a black traveling bonnet and a blue dress with black cape and apron. Her features were kind and full of character, and Lizzie immediately felt comfortable in her presence. She thought that she and Esther might become good friends once they got to know each other.

Memories assailed Zack as he entered the *dawdi haus*. His grandparents had lived here when he was a young child. They had passed on when he was seven in a terrible accident. A drunk driver had slammed his car head-on into their small open buggy as his grandfather drove *Grossmudder* and himself to Sunday service. That he and his family were in the buggy several yards in front of his *grosseldre*'s vehicle saved their lives, but Zack had gotten a good view of the awful scene. It had been a traumatic experience for everyone but most especially Zack.

As he followed his nephew through the house and into a bedroom, he noted slight changes to the cottage. There was no sign that his *grosseldre* had lived there. He sighed silently with relief as he set his suitcase in the closest bedroom and then followed Matt into the next room, where his sister would stay.

"Lizzie and the girls made up the beds and put stuff in the kitchen for you," Matthew told him. "They stocked the pantry and the freezer, but Lizzie said that you are *willkomm* to eat with us. She wanted you to have food in case you got hungry or didn't feel like coming over."

Zack studied the boy and nodded. "That is kind of her." He examined Esther's room, pleased how clean and comfortable it appeared. A lingering scent of lemon oil intermingled with the fresh air gently billowing the white window curtains. A quilt in soft blues, greens and cream covered the double bed.

"Lizzie made the quilt," Matthew said after apparently noting the direction of Zack's gaze. "She quilts a lot and makes wonderful things. She sells her quilts at Beachey's Craft Shop."

Zack couldn't help but admire the bedcover. The pattern and colors were striking, but plain enough to be used within their Amish community. He walked to the bed and ran a hand over the soft cotton in solid colors. "Beachey," he murmured. "Ellen Beachey's family?"

When his nephew nodded, Zack smiled. "They've owned the shop since Ellen was a child." He felt a softening inside at the memory of Ellen Beachey, remembering her as a young feisty girl. She was older than him by about ten years, pretty, but she'd been a handful to her parents, although she'd been respectful to the church and the folks within Honeysuckle. He remembered that she and Neziah Shetler had been sweethearts, but by the time he'd returned home for a visit, the couple had broken up. He wondered whom she finally married.

"Do you know she has a bright lime-green push scooter?" Matt said. "She rides it down the hill from her house to the main road and uses it to ride to the craft store."

Zack chuckled. "That sounds like Ellen." He envisioned her flying down the hill, her prayer *kapp* barely held on by bobby pins, her eyes bright with excitement. Following his nephew into the kitchen, he listened as the boy showed him the contents of the food pantry. "Ellen still works at the store, then," he murmured after he'd nodded approvingly at his food stock.

"Ja." Matt closed the pantry door and faced him. "We're glad you're here," the boy said. His expression became solemn. "We miss *Dat*."

Zack understood. "I haven't seen your *vadder* in a long time. I regret that I won't have the chance to see or talk with him again." He felt a keen sense of loss, but somehow, for his nephew's sake, he managed to smile. "But he is with *Gott*, and so is your *mudder*."

"You knew my *mam*?" The boy seemed eager to hear more about his parents.

"*Ja.* Ruth and your *dat* were married before my *vadder*—your *grossdaddi*—passed and we moved away." Zack recalled how difficult it had been for them, especially his mother, who'd loved her husband deeply and felt the terrible loss. When his father had died, his mother hadn't wanted to stay on the farm. She had moved with her younger children to Ohio to live near his eldest married sister, Miriam, who lived with her husband and children in Walnut Creek. His older brother, Abraham, had remained behind to run the family farm and build a life with his new wife, Ruth.

"We miss *Mam*, too," Matt said as they walked together out of the house and across the yard.

"She and your *dat* loved each other." Zack noted the boy's features so like his brother's. "You favor your *vadder*."

"I do?" Matt appeared pleased by the thought.

"*Ja.* You've got his eyes, yet you have a bit of your *mam*, too."

Matt blinked. "I— *Danki*." The whispered word held a wealth of meaning and gratitude.

"Let's go back to the *haus*. Lizzie and your *endie* Esther will be wondering why it's taken us so long."

Matt picked up his pace, and Zack followed, glad he had decided to return to Honeysuckle, if only to get to know his brother's children.

Zack pulled the screen door open and waited for Matt to enter first. He noted the difference in the gathering room as he headed toward the kitchen and the sound of laughter coming from the rear of the house. As he entered, he saw his oldest niece, Mary Ruth, chuckling at her little brother Ezekiel, who was grinning from ear to ear as the three-year-old put forkfuls of apple crisp into his mouth. "Ezekiel, slow down," his sister Hannah warned, "or it will choke you."

The boy stopped for a moment and blinked up at her. "But it tastes *goot*, and I'm hungry."

"Zeke," Zack heard Lizzie say quietly, "your sister is right. If you aren't careful, you will choke and hurt yourself. If you take your time, you will enjoy it more."

Zack watched with surprise as the little boy nodded and grinned in Lizzie's direction. *"Ja, Mam,"* he said, and then he began to eat more slowly, chewing his food thoroughly before swallowing. His brother's widow smiled at the child with affection, clearly pleased by his obedience.

Lizzie looked up then as if sensing a presence, saw him in the doorway and stood. "Zack," she said, her expression becoming shuttered. "May I get you something to eat? Some apple crisp—"

"It's *goot*, *Onkel* Zack!" little Ezekiel told him with a mouthful of the treat and a grin.

Zack shook his head. "We ate ourselves full on the way here."

"'Tis delicious." Mary Ruth smiled as she held up the plate as if enticing him to try it.

He had the sudden urge to grin. "Hmm. May we take two pieces to eat later?"

"Ja. I'll wrap them up for you." Lizzie cut two slices of the apple treat, set them on a plate and covered it with plastic wrap. She placed the dish within his easy reach. "Is everything in the cottage all right?" she asked almost shyly, referring to the *dawdi haus*. She sat down and cradled her teacup with her hands.

"Ja. It looks *goot*. We'll be most comfortable there." He saw that she looked satisfied. As he sat and waited for

his sister to finish her tea, Zack studied his late brother's wife. Dressed in a light blue dress with a full-length black apron, Lizzie was stunning. Her dark red hair had been rolled in the Amish way and tucked beneath her white head covering without a single strand out of place. Her green eyes appeared large in her pretty feminine face; her nose was well shaped and small, her lips pink and full. Despite her young age and obvious handicap, he could see why his brother had chosen to make her his bride. He looked away, startled by the direction of his thoughts.

"We should get settled in," he said.

Esther agreed. "*Ja.* The tea was *goot*." She stood and picked up the plate of apple crisp. "We will eat this later."

Zack rose and nodded his thanks. "We will see you tomorrow," he said. "It's been a long day."

Lizzie stood. "Don't hesitate to tell us if you need anything."

He followed Esther through the back door of the farmhouse and sensed Lizzie's presence as he stepped outside. He turned to see her standing in the open doorway. She locked gazes with him. He felt a tightening in his chest before she broke eye contact. The children pushed by her and stood in the yard watching as he continued to the *dawdi haus* behind his sister.

"*Onkel* Zack!" a young voice cried. Zack turned to face his young nephew Jonas. "Do you know how to play baseball?" the boy asked.

Zack smiled. "*Ja*, I used to play." But it had been years ago, when all of his family had been alive and living in the farmhouse.

"Will you play with us sometime?" Jonas asked with hope in his eyes. "Next visiting Sunday?"

"Jonas," he heard Lizzie say softly. "Don't be pestering your *onkel*."

He didn't know why, but the woman's words bothered him. "I'll play ball with you," he said, his gaze rising to Lizzie's face, "come next visiting Sunday." His tone and words were letting her know that he had no plans to leave the farm anytime soon. When he saw her blanch, he realized that she'd gotten his message, and he suddenly regretted it.

His attention went to the young boy whose eyes glistened with excitement. Jonas wore a big smile on his face. Zack flashed him a grin. He heard a little catch in someone's breath and turned to discover that it had been Lizzie.

He'd come to the farm to see how his brother's widow and children were managing and to claim his inheritance. If Abraham had been alive, he would have stayed in Ohio, knowing that the farm was in his brother's capable hands. He would have forgotten that his father had intended him to have the farm. But after learning that Ruth and Abraham were dead, Zack had decided the time had come to step in and take back what was rightfully his. Lizzie Fisher, his brother's widow, was a stranger to him and no blood relation to his nieces and nephews. He'd decided that he couldn't allow her to keep his brother's children or the farm.

But now, after meeting her and seeing the way Lizzie interacted with the children, he was beginning to rethink the situation. He didn't know what he was going to do, but he'd figure out something. The children loved Lizzie, he realized as he crossed the yard toward the *dawdi haus*. Somehow he must consider what was in the best interests of the children as well as the farm property.

Zack sighed as he reached the cottage and held the

door open for Esther. He would pray to the Lord that he would choose right for everyone. *Complications*, he thought. He hadn't expected this many of them.

Chapter Four

Lizzie woke up feeling ill. *I overdid it this week*, she realized. All the hard work she'd accomplished on the farm these past few days had aggravated her hip, and the resulting pain made her nauseous.

She'd been sick a lot since Abraham had passed on and she'd felt the stress of managing everything alone. Ever since Zack's first visit, she'd been afraid. Her fears had intensified after his departure. Now that he was back, she wondered if he was silently making decisions that would impact her life with the children. If he chose to claim the farm, what would happen to them? Could she somehow stop him? Would the fact that he hadn't come forward before now work in her favor?

Lizzie frowned. The children were Zack's family and had the right to live on the farm with him. It was she who had no blood ties. She'd married Abraham, it was true, but for most of their married life, she hadn't been a real wife...until the night before Abraham's fatal accident, when they finally had consummated their marriage. Lizzie had been so happy that night because she'd realized then that her husband had begun to care for her as a wife instead of just a housekeeper and babysitter.

If Abraham had lived, she thought, *we might have had children together.*

Children. Lizzie gasped. *I've missed one month.* She'd missed a month before. Her woman's flow was often irregular. She wasn't sure why, but skipping a period happened to her on occasion. Since Abraham's death, she'd been so busy caring for the children and the farm that she hadn't noticed until now.

She rose from bed. It was early; the children were asleep, but it wouldn't be long before they stirred, ready for breakfast.

A baby. She would love nothing more than to give birth to Abraham's child, to have his baby son or daughter. The child would be a legitimate and accepted member of the Fisher family. *My child would cement the bond between the Fishers and me.*

Her Amish church community accepted her right to the farm as the children's stepmother and Abraham's widow. But did Zack agree?

Lizzie settled a hand on her abdomen. *A baby.* She silently counted the days since Abraham's death. Within the next day or so, she would know for certain. Somehow she just knew she was carrying her late husband's son or daughter. But she would not tell anyone yet. She would save the news for the right moment. She couldn't allow herself to become too excited at the prospect until she was sure. But how could she not be hopeful? She would love to give the children a new baby brother or sister to love, the child of their deceased father. Perhaps Mary Ruth and Hannah would finally accept her.

A door squeaked as if it was being closed carefully. Then she heard the sound of someone moving about in the hall. Lizzie grabbed the flashlight from her bed table and turned it on. She then hurriedly donned a robe over her nightgown before, with light in hand, she peeked into the hall.

"Anne," she whispered as the light fell on the child outside her bedroom door. "Are your sisters up?"

Anne shook her head. The five-year-old wore her nightgown and carried her clothes as if she intended to dress downstairs.

Lizzie waved her into the room. "*Koom.* I'll help you get dressed and do your hair."

Annie smiled and hurried into the room that had once belonged to Lizzie and Abraham.

Lizzie lit an oil lamp, turned off the flashlight and then helped Anne out of her nightgown and into her day clothes. Then she reached for a brush and comb. First, she brushed her daughter's long golden locks. Then she combed, rolled and pinned the roll against Annie's head in the Amish way. Lizzie smiled as she worked. She enjoyed fixing the girl's hair; the simple action of brushing her daughter's hair soothed her.

"Why are you up so early?" she asked softly. There was barely a hint of dawn in the eastern sky.

"I woke up and couldn't go back to sleep."

Finished, Lizzie stepped back and turned Anne to face her. "Is something upsetting you?"

Annie was quiet for a moment. "*Mam*, will *Onkel* Zack marry you and stay with us forever?"

Lizzie froze in shock. "I— *Nay, dochter.* I don't know your *onkel* that well and he doesn't know me."

"But you can get to know and love each other." Annie gazed at her as Lizzie placed a prayer *kapp* on the child's head. "It is possible."

Lizzie worded her reply carefully. "I suppose it's possible, Anne," she said, pausing before continuing, "but unlikely."

"You miss *Dat*."

Lizzie nodded. "Your *vadder* was a *goot* man and a wonderful husband."

"You didn't know him well when you married him."

Lizzie swallowed before answering. "What gave you that idea?"

Annie reached up to lovingly pat Lizzie's cheek. "I heard Mary Ruth and Hannah talking."

Lizzie felt dismayed. She could only imagine what the two girls had said. "I was happy to marry your *vadder* because then his seven children—all of you—became mine. I love you all as if I had given birth to you."

"I remember when Ezekiel was born." Annie shifted to sit beside Lizzie on her bed. "*Mam* didn't feel well, and I heard her crying and screaming. I was afraid."

"I'm sure it seemed worse than it was, Anne. Giving birth is a natural thing. *Ja*, it hurts a *mudder* as it happens, but then the birth is a joyous thing, and she forgets all about the pain."

"*Mam* didn't," Annie said, startling Lizzie with her words. "She wasn't happy after Ezekiel was born. She cried a lot and *Dat* tried to make her feel better, but she didn't listen." Annie looked at Lizzie with confusion. "Why didn't *Mam* love us anymore?"

"*What?*" Lizzie said, taken aback by the child's revelation. "I'm sure that your *mam* must have loved you very much."

Annie blinked back tears.

"*Nay. Mam* didn't want us anymore. I heard her telling *Dat*."

"She was probably tired and upset. I doubt she meant it." Lizzie placed an arm around her daughter's shoulders. "I'm sure your *mam* loved you just as your *dat* did." Annie had overheard things that her mother never should have said. It upset Lizzie to realize that Annie was still hurt by the memory. Some women suffered depression after giving birth. They couldn't enjoy life or their babies. Was that the way it had been with Abraham's first wife?

"I miss *Dat*."

Lizzie nodded. "I know you do," she whispered. "So do I."

"*Onkel* Zack looks like *Dat*, only his hair is dark and he is younger."

Lizzie had noticed and told her so. It hurt her to know that Anne had suffered. She hugged her, put on a happy face and said, "Now, we should go downstairs to fix breakfast. Would you like to help make waffles?"

Annie nodded enthusiastically. "*Ja*, I like helping in the kitchen."

"I'll get dressed and then we'll go downstairs. I need to feed the animals first. Will you set the table while I'm outside?"

Annie agreed, and soon Lizzie and Annie went silently down the stairs to the kitchen. Lizzie took out the plates, napkins and utensils and gave them to Anne. Then she left the house and crossed the yard. She reached the barn as Zack was leaving it.

"Zack!" she gasped, startled.

"Lizzie."

"Is there something I can help you with? I've come to feed the animals and do the milking," she said.

"The animals have been fed." Zack studied her intently. "And your cows have been milked." He held up the bucket of milk she hadn't noticed previously.

"You did my chores?" she said politely, but she was silently outraged.

"I thought I'd help with the chores while I am here," he said. "You have enough to do caring for the children."

"I've been doing just fine since your *brooder* died," she told him. "And I've been managing well."

"Ja." His voice was quiet as he narrowed his gaze on her. "But it's time someone helps you with the burden."

Lizzie stiffened. "I don't consider the children or this farm a burden."

He nodded, looking thoughtful. "I don't suppose you do. But I'd like to work as long as I am staying here. Is that a problem? What would you have me do all day, if not help with the farm chores?"

Lizzie opened her mouth to respond and then promptly shut it. She sighed. She understood how he felt. "Fine. You may help."

His lips twitched. *"Goot."*

"'Tis not because I can't do it," she pointed out quickly.

Amusement gleamed in his dark eyes. "I never said it was."

Lizzie felt satisfied. She would try not to feel threatened just because he needed something to do.

"Will you and Esther come for breakfast? The children should be awake soon. Please join us."

He seemed to think for a minute as his gaze went toward the *dawdi haus*. "I don't believe Esther has eaten yet."

"I'll set places for you." And she left, her composure shaken by her confrontation with Zack.

Lizzie headed toward the house, her thoughts spinning in her head. Having the Fisher siblings on the property disturbed her peace of mind and threatened her place within this family. She shouldn't be alarmed if her brother-in-law wanted to do farm chores. Zack hadn't come out and said that he was here to take over the farm. Perhaps she should confront him and learn the truth? *But what if in the asking, I give him the idea he never had?*

Do I really want to know? Or must I first convince him that I can manage without help before he'll stop worrying and return to Ohio?

Lizzie entered the house to find that Annie had set the table, and Mary Ruth, Hannah and Rebecca had come downstairs to help with breakfast. The girls looked over as she entered the room with a smile.

"I'll be making waffles this morning," she told Mary Ruth. "Would you like some?" Mary Ruth was slow to answer, and Lizzie added, "Your *onkel* and *endie* will be eating with us."

Her eldest daughter looked pleased. "I'll get the butter and syrup."

"I'll help with batter," Hannah said.

Lizzie shot her a look of apology. "I promised Anne that she could help."

Hannah looked at Anne, who appeared as if she would cry if someone took away her job of batter making. She appeared to understand. "Can we have muffins, too? *Onkel* Zack likes your muffins. I can open a new jar of your strawberry jam."

"That's a wonderful idea, Hannah," Lizzie said.

Soon, each of the girls had a special job to do to help in preparing breakfast for their aunt and uncle. Matthew and the two young boys, Jonas and Ezekiel, entered the kitchen minutes later. "It smells *goot* in here," Matt said.

Lizzie, who was showing Anne how to stir the batter, glanced over her shoulder. "Zack and Esther are joining us."

Looking pleased, Matt asked what he could do to help.

As the kitchen filled with activity of her and the children working together, Lizzie felt grateful. If nothing else, Zack's visit had brought the family together to work without sadness, sulking or anger.

Zack and Esther arrived for breakfast, and everyone sat at the large kitchen trestle table. Lizzie, with Esther's help, set out the waffles and other breakfast items.

"Waffles!" Zack exclaimed with pleasure as Lizzie handed him a plateful.

"You like waffles, *Onkel* Zack?" Annie asked.

Zack grinned at her. *"Ja."* He took a bite. "These waffles taste especially *goot."*

Lizzie watched her daughter beam and felt grateful to Zack for making Anne happy. He looked over and winked at her, and she couldn't help grinning back at him. He had known that Anne had helped with the batter, and he'd wanted her to feel special.

Zack Fisher is charming. If she weren't worried about his motives, it would be very easy to fall under his charm. She wondered how it would have been if they'd met at another time and under different circumstances. She frowned. She had to stop thinking of such things. Having such thoughts was disloyal to Abraham and to herself.

The children were excited to eat with their aunt and uncle. They chattered nonstop, especially Matt, Hannah and Rebecca, who debated the merits of waffles with maple syrup versus waffles with warm, sautéed apples.

"I like warm cinnamon apples best," Hannah declared.

"Nay, there is nothing like *goot* maple syrup," Matt insisted. "Don't ya think, *Onkel* Zack?"

Zack laughed. "Don't ask me. I like them both ways. I'm not partial to either one. I like mine with honey, too."

A discussion ensued then on the merits of honey versus maple syrup.

Mary Ruth was quiet, Lizzie noticed, but when she caught her eldest daughter's gaze, the girl smiled at her warmly and Lizzie realized that Mary Ruth was simply content to happily observe her brothers and sisters with their aunt and uncle. The atmosphere was one of a big happy family, and it was at times such as this that she felt glad that Zack and Esther had returned to Honeysuckle.

When they had finished their breakfast, the older girls left to do their assigned chores. Soon they would return to the kitchen to help prepare food for the next day. The youngest boys scampered outside with Lizzie's permission to enjoy a few moments in the sun under Matthew's watchful eye. Zack excused himself to check on something in the barn. Lizzie watched him go, wondering what needed his attention.

"Tomorrow is church Sunday," Esther said after she and Lizzie had enjoyed a few quiet moments at the table. She began to gather up the empty breakfast dishes.

"Ja," Lizzie said as she rose to help. "'Tis to be held at the Thomas Stoltzfus farm." She gathered tea and coffee cups along with the children's milk glasses. "Do you know them? Thomas and Marybeth Stoltzfus?"

Esther thought a moment. "Their names are familiar but I can't place faces on them."

"You'll have a chance to visit with them after church tomorrow." Lizzie filled up a basin with sudsy water and began washing the dishes. Esther joined her at the sink with a dish towel and began to dry.

Zack peeked his head back into the kitchen, startling both women. "Isn't it church Sunday tomorrow?" he asked.

"Ja," his sister said. "We were just discussing this. Lizzie said it's to be held at the Thomas Stoltzfuses'. Do you remember them?"

Zack shook his head. "But it's been years. Seeing them may jog my memory."

"Do you need anything?" Lizzie asked, wondering

again what he'd been doing in the barn and now why he'd returned.

"*Nay*, I just came to check on tomorrow. I'll have the buggy ready in the morning," he said.

As he left again, Lizzie stifled a frown and went back to work. It wouldn't do to give her thoughts away to Esther… that she was beginning to feel as if he were taking over the farm without telling her. She had to talk with her brother-in-law soon. The uncertainty, the fear, was eating her alive, and besides, she had something on her side now…the tiny baby growing inside her.

The morning dawned bright and clear as Lizzie made sure all the children were ready in time for Sunday service. She gathered up the desserts she'd made for the shared meal afterward and went outside to set them in the buggy. Zack and Esther were already outside waiting for her and the children near the vehicle. When he smiled at her, Lizzie felt a funny feeling in her chest.

"*Goot* morning." Matt ran ahead and grinned at Zack, whose lips curved upward in response.

Lizzie inclined her head in greeting as she approached, carrying two pie plates. Zack surprised her when he reached for her plates and stowed them on the floor in the front seat. The children climbed into the back of the buggy that had been built specifically for Abraham's growing family after Jonas was born. Dressed in their Sunday best, the girls wore black full-length aprons over royal blue dresses, with black head coverings. The three boys sported white shirts, black vests and black pants, with black shoes and black-felt brimmed hats. Seeing her sons looking so like their uncle gave Lizzie a flash of memory of their family life when her husband had been alive. Sadness overwhelmed her and she closed her eyes, fighting the urge to cry.

Soon they were on their way to church services at the Thomas Stoltzfus farm. Lizzie found herself in the front, seated next to Zack after Esther chose to sit in the back. As Zack drove, Lizzie was overly conscious of him beside her. She experienced an odd sensation in her midsection. *The baby?* It wasn't her unborn child that made her feel this way, she realized. It was Zack sitting closely beside her. She watched his strong hands handle the reins with confidence. He was relaxed as he steered the buggy along the paved road toward their destination.

She wondered how the congregation would react when they saw her and the children with Zack and Esther. Abraham had been well liked and respected, and they'd known that he'd needed to marry quickly for the sake of his children. But Lizzie had always wondered what they'd thought about Abraham's choice of a crippled seventeen-year-old bride.

Months into her marriage to Abe, the community women had begun to stop by the farm to visit with her, often seeking her company during church and visiting Sundays. Apparently after seeing how hard she'd worked and the love she had for her new family, the community must have decided that Abraham had chosen well.

When her childhood friend Rachel Miller had married Peter Zook, who lived down the road, Lizzie had been happy and excited. She, Abraham and the children had been invited to the wedding, and Lizzie had been overjoyed to see her dear friend happy and in love.

Zack steered the horse into the Stoltzfuses' barnyard and parked at the end of a long row of family buggies. He got out and assisted Esther. The children scrambled out quickly in a hurry to see their friends. Because of her hip, Lizzie slid out more carefully and was relieved to be standing steady and on firm ground, before Zack had a chance to reach her side of the vehicle. She retrieved the pies from the buggy floor and nearly bumped into Zack as she straightened. She gasped, instantly aware of his clean masculine scent—a mixture of her home-made soap, fresh air and a manly smell that belonged only to Zack.

Silently, he reached to take the desserts from her. She passed him the cherry pie while refusing to relinquish the apple. Lizzie firmed her lips. She was more than capable of carrying pies! He must have read her expression, for he captured her gaze, his lips curving with amusement, before he turned his attention to his sister, who joined them with the dish of brownies she'd baked yesterday afternoon.

How dare Zack laugh at her expense! She felt her throat tighten. She had handled the farm and the children since Abraham's death. The children continued to be clothed, fed and cared for. And she'd done it on her own, hadn't she?

She brightened when she caught sight of Rachel, who looked over and waved. Lizzie grinned and raised a hand in greeting, watching Rachel's gaze shift to Zack beside her as they approached. Her friend raised her eyebrows in question, and Lizzie could feel herself blush as she reached the front porch steps and handed Rachel her pie before she reached toward Zack for the other one. She sighed when Rachel looked to her for an introduction.

"Zack, this is a dear friend, Rachel Zook. Rachel, meet Zack Fisher, my late husband's *brooder*."

Zack gave Rachel a nod. "Rachel," he greeted warmly.

Lizzie encountered his gaze and suddenly felt flustered. "Rachel and I grew up together. She recently married Peter Zook, who lives just down the road from us."

"I'm sure you're happy to have her close."

Lizzie gave her friend a genuine smile. *"Ja,"* she and Rachel said at the same time. Lizzie laughed, warmed again by Rachel's friendship. Rachel was the only person who accepted Lizzie limp and all. If not for Rachel's presence during her childhood, Lizzie would have been unable to endure the other children's ridicule.

She saw Rachel's expression change as her friend studied Zack. Confused, Lizzie shot Zack a look only to find him staring at her and not Rachel.

"Zack?" Amos Beiler drew Zack's attention away from her and Rachel. Lizzie sighed with relief. She watched recognition dawn in Amos Beiler's expression followed by delight as he and Zack shook hands. She stood as the two men exchanged pleasantries.

"Lizzie," Rachel whispered, drawing her aside. "He is beautiful! He looks like..." She didn't say Abraham's name but gave Lizzie's hand a squeeze. "Only he's better-looking."

"Rachel!" Lizzie gasped, feeling her face heat.

Esther came up from behind Zack to join Lizzie and Rachel. She'd been standing quietly, studying the church members chatting outside. Lizzie gave her friend a warning look and managed to compose herself before turning to her sister-in-law.

"Esther," Lizzie said with warmth, "this is Rachel Zook. She and I have known each other since we were children."

"It's *goot* to meet you, Rachel," Zachariah's sister said.

Her expression brightening, Rachel smiled. "It's nice to finally meet some of Abraham's family." Her smile faded. "I'm sorry for your loss," she said.

Esther nodded, her eyes glistening. "My *brooder* was a *goot* man."

"*Ja,*" Lizzie whispered, suddenly feeling the loss keenly. She blinked back tears. "He was."

Rachel put her hand on Lizzie's shoulder. "Things will work out, Lizzie."

Lizzie forced a smile as she turned to Esther. "I miss him," she said.

Esther's features softened. "You must have made my *brooder* a happy man," she said, surprising Lizzie. "You're a hard worker and you love the children."

"*Danki,*" she murmured, wondering what Esther would think if she knew the truth.

"Lizzie! Rachel!" Marybeth Stoltzfus exited the house. She widened her eyes when she recognized Esther. "Esther? *Esther Fisher?*"

Esther smiled. "*Ja*, Marybeth. 'Tis nice to see *ya* again."

"Come in. Come in," the woman invited.

"I've known Marybeth since I was a girl," Esther whispered to Lizzie. "But she was a Yoder then."

The women set their dishes in the kitchen and then proceeded to the room where church services would be held. It was a large family gathering room. Benches had been placed in rows on three sides of the room, with the fourth side-area set aside for the preacher and church elders.

As she slid onto a bench next to her daughters, Lizzie recognized her sons seated next to their uncle on the other side of the room. She glanced toward Zack only to find his bright obsidian eyes studying her. She felt an infusion of heat and quickly looked away.

Preacher David Hostetler stepped into the spotlight and began the service. Everyone stood and began to sing from the *Ausbund*, the Amish book of hymns. They always sang a cappella, their songs sounding like chants. Aware of her daughters' voices beside her, Lizzie joined in to sing praise to the Lord.

A slight movement to the right of her caught the corner of her eye, and Lizzie turned to see who it was. Little Anne slipped past her older sisters toward her, apparently wanting to sit next to her. Lizzie smiled and laid a hand on the child's shoulder, pleased that this daughter, at least, loved her unconditionally. Mary Ruth shifted over to allow her little sister more room and then smiled at Lizzie, above Anne's head, as if she understood. Sensing his regard, Lizzie realized that Zack had witnessed the exchange. She had no idea what he was thinking as he glanced toward Anne then her again, before he returned his attention to the preacher.

Lizzie's heart started to beat hard as she focused on the service. Did she really want to know Zack's thoughts?

Preacher David gave a wonderfully stirring sermon, which caught and held her attention. Inspired, she raised her voice as she sang when the time came for the *Loblied*, the second hymn. When there was a break in the sermon, she prayed silently.

Soon, church service was finished, and Lizzie rose and followed her daughters out of the room and into the kitchen. The men and boys stayed behind and began to rearrange the church benches and set up tables for the shared midday meal.

When she entered the kitchen to help with the food, Lizzie was suddenly surrounded and the center of attention as the churchwomen asked about Zack and Esther and Lizzie's family until Esther walked into the room. The women's excitement rose as they recognized her. Several of the church ladies offered their condolences to Esther on her brother's death. Others questioned her about other matters, curious to know where the family had been living and what they'd been doing during all these years.

The setup of the dining area was complete. The food was unwrapped and ready to serve. The women grabbed the dishes they'd brought and carried them over to the men. Later, when the men had eaten, the women sat with their children and enjoyed their meal. The men escaped into the yard to talk about the weather, their farms, the upcoming fall harvest and other topics that the men liked to discuss.

Lizzie picked up two plates from the food table and carried them back toward the kitchen. As she approached, she overheard two women talking about the Fisher siblings and the farm. She listened, unable to help herself. When she heard someone mention her name, she froze.

"I was surprised to see Zachariah and Esther. But then, I suppose that I shouldn't be. Young Zack is the rightful heir to his father's farm." The first woman's voice came clear and strong, and Lizzie recognized her immediately as Joanna, Wilmer Miller's wife.

"What about young Lizzie? She's been a fine *mudder* to Abraham's children. What will happen to her if Zack decides to stay on the farm?" Lizzie knew the identity of the second woman as Martha Yoder.

"Zack will see that she is cared for. He was always a *goot* boy—I doubt that has changed about him," Joanna pointed out.

"But the children—

"Zack and Esther are more than capable of taking care of their nieces and nephews."

"But Lizzie is their *brooder*'s widow!" Martha exclaimed.

"*Ja*, but Lizzie has a hindrance. Do you think she can

do everything that's necessary to keep the farm going *and* take *goot* care of seven children?"

"That kind of thinking is not the Lord's way."

"*Ja*, I know," Joanna admitted, "but too often things are as they are anyway."

The women's voices faded as they moved out of Lizzie's hearing. Their words still hurt her as Lizzie turned away from the kitchen, the leftover food platters in her hands forgotten, and nearly collided with someone.

"Lizzie." Lydia King stood before her, startling her.

"*Mam!*" Lizzie gasped, nearly dropping the plates in her hands.

Chapter Five

"What are you doing here?" Lizzie asked. "I didn't see you at church service."

Her mother rubbed her forehead with her fingers. "We just arrived. Went to service at the John Millers'. Then I thought I'd come see my daughter since she doesn't visit me often enough."

Lizzie stifled a growing feeling of irritation. She had lost her husband and she was dealing with the farm, the children and the house. Her family lived in another church district but close enough to come to her if they wanted, as they apparently had today. Before Abraham had died, she'd seen them often. Didn't her mother realize how much she had to cope with?

Lizzie managed a genuine smile. She loved her mother, although *Mam* had been less affectionate with her than with her brothers and sisters during her childhood. "'Tis *goot* to see you, *Mam*." She glanced behind her mother, looking for her family. "Did *Dat* come? And William and the others?" She referred to her siblings who still lived at home.

"*Ja*, the boys are here. Katie stayed at the Yoders' after service. She's interested in young Mark."

Lizzie was glad for her sister, pleased that Katie had chosen to find her own happiness.

"Lizzie, you cannot continue as you have been." Her mother regarded her with concern. "You need to find a husband, someone to help you with the farm and the children."

Lizzie disagreed. "My husband passed recently. I'm managing on my own. Did you forget that you were the one who warned me that if I didn't accept Abraham's marriage proposal, then I'd never marry?"

Lydia waved her daughter's concerns aside. "You've shown yourself to be a *goot* wife and *mudder*. Any man would be lucky to have you."

Stunned, Lizzie could only stare at her. Who was this person and where was her real *mam*, the *mam* who'd hurt her, perhaps unintentionally, with words that made Lizzie realize that her disability bothered her mother? She'd never felt as if *Mam* accepted her. *My limp embarrasses* Mam. It was obvious to Lizzie that her mother found it easy to love William, Luke, Katie and her eldest married daughter, Susie. *But not me—her crippled daughter.* Lizzie hadn't known her mother's affection during childhood, and she was afraid to hope for it now.

It wasn't that her *mam* wasn't a kind person, a godly woman who lived by the *Ordnung*—the rules and religious teachings of the Old Order Amish community. But whether *Mam* realized it or not, Lizzie felt as though she'd never quite fit in. If not for her brother William, who loved to tease her like he did all of their other siblings, she would have felt completely alone and detached from the family. When her mother had urged her to accept Abraham's offer of marriage, it had been William who had encouraged her to think about it hard and long and decide for herself what she wanted to do.

"You've lost weight," her mother said.

"I'm eating well. I've been busy."

"Are the children helping out?" *Mam* asked as she watched Lizzie's younger children playing in the yard through the window glass.

Lizzie nodded. "They are *goot kinner.*"

"I can come by to help—"

"I'm fine, *Mam*, not to worry." She smiled to take the sting out of the rejection. "We are finding our way together. We just need time."

"It's been two months," her mother pointed out.

"Not long since their *vadder*'s death," Lizzie insisted. She was glad to see her mother but wished that things would get easier between them. "You said that William was outside?"

"*Ja*, he's talking with *Dat* and your *brooder* Luke."

"I need to take these to the kitchen," Lizzie said, referring to the dishes she held. The memory of Joanna and Martha's conversation still stung. She hesitated, wondering if the two gossiping women were still inside.

"I'll take them," her mother offered surprisingly. "Go. Visit with your father and *brooders.*"

After considering her mother's smiling expression, Lizzie gratefully gave her the plates. "I won't be long."

Esther came in from outside. "Lizzie, I've brought the rest of your pie—" She stopped abruptly when she saw the woman at Lizzie's side.

Lizzie felt sure that *Mam* and Esther hadn't met. Did Esther sense tension in the air between her and her mother?

Lizzie smiled, but she could tell that her mother was curious; and she didn't want her *mam* asking questions. As Zack approached, Lizzie felt her stomach tighten when she saw her mother take a good long look at him.

"Who's this?" her mother asked, studying the young man. She frowned. "He looks like—"

"*Mam*, this is Zack Fisher, my late husband's *brooder*."

A gleam of interest entered her mother's hazel eyes. "You look like him," she told Zack.

Zack nodded. "You are Lizzie's *mudder*." He eyed Lizzie and turned back to smile at her *mam*.

Mam nodded. "Lydia King," she introduced herself.

Afraid of what her mother might say, Lizzie flashed Esther a pleading look.

"Lizzie, Ezekiel is tired and wants to go home. Perhaps we should leave." Esther gave Lydia an apologetic smile.

"*Ja*, we should go home," Zack agreed. "We should tell the children to wait in the buggy." But still he didn't leave.

Lydia's eyes widened. "You're living at the *haus*?"

"They're staying in the *dawdi haus*," Lizzie said, embarrassed by her mother's question.

"I see." The look in her mother's eyes gave cause for Lizzie's concern.

"We should go," Esther said, and Lizzie sent her a grateful look. "It's been a long day, and the little ones are tired."

Her mother's expression softened. "They are growing like weeds."

Lizzie smiled. "*Ja.*" Ezekiel entered the house, rubbing his eyes. "Time to leave, Zeke. Where is Jonas?" The little boy gestured outside. "Tell him and Matt and your sisters that we'll be leaving in a few minutes." She turned toward her mother. "I'm glad you came," she said softly. "It is nice to see you." She regretted that she wouldn't have time to catch up with her father and brothers, but she needed to go.

Her *mudder* nodded. "You'll come for a visit soon?"

"We'll try." She hesitated. "But I can't promise."

Mam seemed satisfied with her answer.

Lizzie was conscious of Zack waiting patiently beside her. "I'm coming."

He nodded, hesitated. "I'll wait for you near the buggy."

Lizzie watched as he stopped to chat briefly with the gathering of men near the barn before he continued toward their buggy.

She was startled when a hand settled on her shoulder. She turned and encountered her mother's gaze. There was concern, caring and something she'd never seen in her expression. *Affection.*

"I will see you soon," *Mam* said softly.

Lizzie nodded and then retrieved her empty dishes, before she said goodbye to her parents and siblings. Then she and the children joined Esther and Zack for the journey home.

As he drove home from church services, Zack noted Lizzie's silence despite the fact that the children loudly chattered about the friends they'd seen, with Esther interjecting the occasional question or comment. He shot his late brother's widow a glance. She stared out the side window, unaware of his interest. She looked vulnerable, pensive…alone.

As he turned his attention to the drive, he could still recall every little detail about her. Dressed in royal blue with white cape and apron and white head covering, she was a young, pretty thing. *Beautiful,* he thought, *not just pretty.* He immediately thought of her problem hip. Did it pain her often? She never complained if it did, and he respected her for it. He flashed her another look, but he couldn't gauge her expression.

Turning his gaze back to the road, he recalled watching his little niece Anne as she'd switched places because she wanted to sit closer to Lizzie during church.

Things were complicated. He didn't know why he'd thought he'd be able to return home, walk onto the property and easily assume control. He frowned, unhappy with his own arrogance. He'd taken a lot for granted when he should have known that the Lord often had other plans.

Since his brother's death, Lizzie alone had cared for the farm and his children. He was beginning to realize that he couldn't ask her to leave. It wouldn't be fair or right since she was his brother's widow. He would stay to help her, see how well she managed in Abraham's absence. Lizzie needed help with the harvest. And while the community would come to assist her, there was still much to be done beforehand.

And what about the farm animals? How could she, a young crippled woman, handle the farm, the animals *and* his nieces and nephews? She was only one person, a young, vulnerable woman. He wanted to stay in Honeysuckle, but he had to make sure that the situation was fair to all of them. Zack smiled as he thought of his nieces and nephews. They were lively and smart, and they belonged on the property.

Would Lizzie be happy if he kept the children? Maybe she would be happier without the work and responsibility that had been thrust upon her.

Nay, Lizzie wasn't Ruth. Despite her disability, Lizzie wasn't weak. She'd never willingly give up the children or the farm. And he was beginning to wonder if he wanted her to.

Zack steered the horse-drawn buggy onto the road toward the house. It was late afternoon, but with the shortening of daylight hours, it seemed as if it were early evening. Sunlight had faded to dusk. The air was filled with the rich scent of autumn, the chrysanthemums planted near the house, the fallen leaves from the tree in the side yard. As he pulled the buggy into the yard and parked near the barn, he was conscious of Lizzie sitting quietly beside him. Something stirred within him, telling him that he was beginning to feel more for her than he should. He firmed his lips. *More than a brother-in-law should feel for his late brother's widow.*

He climbed out, extended a hand to help Esther out of the vehicle and then started around the buggy to help Lizzie. But Lizzie refused to wait. She scrambled out of the buggy. He sensed when she tripped, heard her cry out with pain and then watched as she quickly stumbled to her feet. He rushed to her side, but she seemed composed when he reached her. He might have thought he'd imagined her fall, if not for his niece Anne, who had witnessed it from the backseat.

"*Mam*, are you all right?" the child cried worriedly.

"Lizzie." Zack's first instinct was to ensure that she was all right. His sudden urge to protect and care for her was disturbing. He allowed his gaze to make a thorough examination of her. "Are you sure you're not hurt?"

Chapter Six

"**I**'m fine." Lizzie managed to smile at her daughter without meeting Zack's gaze. She was embarrassed. The fall had jarred her ankle and hip, which continued to throb incessantly while she struggled to hide the pain. She didn't want to admit to Zack that she'd hurt herself. She didn't want anyone's help, least of all Zack's. Abraham had accepted that she could manage on her own. Why couldn't his brother do the same?

Trying not to let on that she was stiff and sore, Lizzie reached down to pick up the empty pie dish and turned toward the house. She lurched and would have fallen again if Zack hadn't reached out to steady her.

"You have hurt yourself!" he exclaimed, examining her with dark eyes full of concern.

"Nay," she assured him, but she could tell that he didn't believe her. She was startled by his touch. His fingers on her arm made her feel things for him that she shouldn't. She didn't want to think of Zack as anything but her brother-in-law, but she couldn't seem to help herself. "I should go," she said, relieved when he released her. She quickly gathered her composure. "I need to fix supper," she murmured as she turned and started toward

the house. She stopped suddenly and faced him. "Will you and Esther join us?"

After a quick glance toward his sister, who was entering the *dawdi haus*, Zack shook his head. "We appreciate the offer, but we'll snack later at the cottage." He offered her a crooked grin. "Seems like we've been eating all day."

Lizzie chuckled, relaxing, no longer embarrassed about her fall. "I know what you mean." She had enjoyed a helping of most items on the food table. She shifted uncomfortably when Zack continued to stare at her. "I'll see you in the morning."

She didn't wait for his answer but continued on, looking back only once briefly to see that the children were following her toward the house. Her arm tingled where Zack's fingers had been. Her face flamed as she regretted her clumsiness in front of Zack. So much for attempting to prove that she was capable!

Once inside the house, Lizzie worked to prepare a light supper for the children, relieved that Zack and Esther had decided to eat at home. She had to process her attraction to Zack. She'd never felt this way about Abraham— theirs had been a marriage that had begun in necessity and ended in a calm and quiet love. Her feelings for Zack mortified and embarrassed her—why did she react so strongly to him whenever he was near?

Lizzie froze in the act of slicing bread for sandwiches. Did he suspect that she found him handsome, that she felt drawn to him like a moth to a flame? Closing her eyes, she groaned. She hoped not. It was wrong to feel this way. She was his brother's widow, and her husband had been dead less than three months.

"*Mam*, can we have potato chips with supper?"

Lizzie pushed thoughts of Zack aside and forced a

smile for her four-year-old son. "*Ja*, Jonas, you may have potato chips," she said. "But it's important that you eat your vegetables and meat, too."

"But, *Mam*, I had lots of meat and vegetables today."

"True," she admitted with a smile. "But eat something other than just chips, *ja*?"

Jonas agreed with a grin. *"Ja."*

Esther wandered into the kitchen and went to the pantry. She felt shaken. When Zack had asked her to accompany him to Honeysuckle, she'd been curious enough to come. Memories had assailed her when she'd first stepped into the farmhouse...of her father and mother smiling at one another, of the laughter, love and family values that had been evident within the house when her father had been alive. She still felt the loss of her father deeply although it'd been thirteen years since he passed. *Mam was devastated when* Dat *died.* Esther had worried that her mother would never recover, but moving to Ohio to live near their sister Miriam had helped *Mam* to get through.

She was glad she and Zack were staying in the *dawdi haus*. There were memories here in the cottage, too, but they were of her *grosseldre*, fond recollections of her *grossmama* baking and filling the kitchen with the wonderful scents of her cakes and pies and muffins and biscuits. *Grossmama* had kept an immaculate house, sweeping the floors and polishing the furniture daily. Lizzie kept the *dawdi haus* neat and tidy. It seemed the same but yet different. *It's the lemon oil*, she thought.

Esther caught herself staring at but not seeing the pantry's contents. She shook herself from the past. She grabbed from the shelf the wrapped cookies that Lizzie had made earlier for them. There was also a colorful array of pint jars filled with jelly, jam and apple butter, along with quart jars of vegetables, peaches and sweet-and-sour chow-chow. And Lizzie had stocked the chest freezer with loaves of bread, meat and ice cream. She smiled. She liked her late brother's widow. Lizzie was younger than she'd expected, but it was obvious that she loved the children and the life she'd created for herself here on the farm.

Esther chose a jar of strawberry jam and set it on the kitchen table. Then she reached toward the counter for the rest of the bread that she and Zack had enjoyed previously. Next she took out two plates, a cutting board and a knife from a cabinet drawer. As she slathered jam onto two pieces of bread with the knife, she tried not to think too much about today's church service. But she couldn't get it out of her mind.

David Hostetler is a preacher. Had she ever felt more shocked to learn that the boy she'd once known was now a preacher? Never in her wildest imagination had it occurred to her the boy she'd loved when she was fourteen would grow up to become a church elder.

Her fingers shook as she transferred the bread onto a plate for Zack.

She had watched David as he'd preached the sermon and felt the heat rise to her face. He was still handsome, she thought, but now he had a beard like the other married men within the Amish community.

Who was his wife? David hadn't stayed for the post-service midday meal, so she didn't get to see or meet her. The preacher and his family apparently had to be elsewhere, which was probably a good thing. She'd been so startled to see him after all this time; she would have felt awkward in his presence.

Moving to Ohio after her *dat* died had been one of

the hardest things she'd ever experienced, leaving her friends…leaving David. Her *mam* had wanted to move, so there was no question that she'd stay behind. If she'd been given a choice, she would have chosen to stay.

"That wouldn't be fair to Abraham and Ruth now, would it?" *Mam* had said. "It wouldn't be right to intrude on newlyweds starting their life together."

At the time, Esther had reasoned that if she'd stayed in Honeysuckle, she could have helped Ruth with the chores. But her mother had disagreed.

In hindsight, she knew that *Mam* had been right. It wouldn't have been fair to her brother and his new wife if she'd stayed and moved in with them.

If life had gone differently, she might have married David, instead of becoming a twenty-seven-year-old spinster. She released a shuddering breath. She'd have to see David sometime, speak cordially with him and his wife. Was he happy? If so, then she would be happy for him. She closed her eyes, seeing the teenager he'd been—smart, hardworking, handsome. *He is still handsome.* And she had no doubt that he was still smart and hardworking. It was an honor to be elected preacher. His would be a lifelong commitment.

Whom did he marry?

Zack walked into the kitchen, drawing her attention away from her thoughts. "What have you got there?"

Esther smiled. "Just bread and strawberry jam. We had plenty to eat earlier, don't you think?"

Zack grinned as he reached for the plate she'd prepared for him. "I agree." He picked up a slice of bread, took a bite and grinned. "This is *goot* jam."

"Lizzie made it," she said, watching his expression.

"She did a fine job." His face gave away none of his thoughts.

"*Ja*, she did." Esther paused and then asked, "What are you going to do about her?"

He stopped eating, his bread suspended inches from his mouth. "I don't know." He set the partially eaten slice onto his plate. "Is there iced tea in the refrigerator?"

Esther nodded, then retrieved the iced-tea pitcher and poured two glassfuls. She handed one to her brother. "Zack—"

Zack sighed. "I don't know, Esther. I know she's a nice girl. I was surprised to learn that she was our *brooder*'s wife. I didn't expect him to marry again." He took a sip from his iced tea.

"Life is never as we expect it." She studied her brother with affection. "You came here because you found out that there is a strange woman in residence. And while she also happens to be our *brooder*'s widow, you thought you could come in and take away the farm and the children."

"*Nay.*" Zack sighed. "*Ja.*"

"But now you're having second thoughts because Lizzie and the children are doing well."

Zack frowned. "You think Lizzie is managing on her own."

Esther narrowed her gaze on her younger brother thoughtfully. "She may or may not be. I'm not the one to judge. You're the one who knows how to run a farm. You worked here as a boy before we moved, and since then, you've done enough chores on Miriam and Joshua's farm to understand what needs to be done." She took a seat at the kitchen table. "Lizzie is certainly challenged with that hip of hers," she said softly. She wondered how much the young woman had been suffering in silence.

"She is determined, I'll admit. I don't know that she'd tell us if she's hurting or if the work proves too much for her."

"And if she told you, then what would you do? Tell her that she'll lose her family, her home and the life she's built for herself because she's not worthy?"

"Who said she's not worthy of this life?" Zack said with a look that made Esther wonder just what he was thinking. "I didn't. And she loves the children. She's a *goot* mother to them. They love her, especially those little ones—Anne and Jonas and Zeke."

Esther controlled the urge to smile. Her brother's defense of Lizzie was telling. "What do you think we should do?"

Zack looked thoughtful. Esther looked at him as Lizzie might see him—young but older than she, handsome, capable, too attractive for a girl's peace of mind. "We'll continue as we are for now. I'll make sure that she can manage on her own, and then it will be up to *Gott* to decide about the future of Lizzie, the children and the farm...and us."

A good plan, Esther thought as she rose to put her dirty glass in the dish basin. She could feel something happening whenever Zack and Lizzie were together, and she could anticipate the struggle that would no doubt ensue once they identified their feelings.

Zack stared at his sister with dismay. He didn't like discussing Lizzie with her. This sudden and new attraction that he felt for her was upsetting. She was his brother's widow. He shouldn't be feeling this way.

What am I going to do? He wanted to stay, but he'd be hurting Lizzie if he took back the farm. And the last thing he wanted to do was hurt her.

He was at a loss about what to do with the farm and the family.

* * *

During the days that followed, Lizzie adjusted to having Zack and Esther in frequent company. The Fisher siblings were here, and although she had no idea for how long, she decided to make the best of the situation.

It no longer startled her to see Zack tending to the horses, repairing a length of fence that needed fixing or doing some other chore. While there were times when Zack looked at her long and hard, which made her uncomfortable, for the most part, theirs was an easy farmworking relationship.

Wednesday morning before dawn, Lizzie was feeding the chickens when Zack exited the cottage, sipping on a cup of coffee. He waved when he saw her and approached.

"You're up bright and early," he said as he reached her.

She smiled. "I'm hoping to get a lot accomplished this morning. I plan to pick and put up the last of the garden vegetables." She could freeze them or make chow-chow with the leftover green beans, corn, onions and red beans. Then she needed to get the baking done. She planned to make extra loaves of bread for him and Esther.

"I thought I'd take Rosebud to get her right-front hoof checked. I think it may need shoeing."

Lizzie nodded. She had noticed the sorrel mare's slightly uneven gait lately. It was so minor that someone else might not have seen, but apparently Zack knew horses well enough to note the difference.

Lizzie mentally calculated the cost of a new set of horseshoes. Fortunately, she had enough money. Ellen Beachey had stopped by the house only yesterday to give her the money she'd earned from selling another quilt. She'd sold some smaller crafts, as well—a patchwork apron, two hand-stitched purses and a couple of baby quilts—which had made her over five hundred dollars in sales. During Ellen's visit, Lizzie had learned that Ellen had a new sweetheart—or rather, an old one, according to Ellen—Neziah Shetler, who once had courted Ellen when she was nineteen before they'd gone their separate ways because they'd thought their differences were too great to allow for a future together. Neziah, who had gone on to marry someone else, was now a widower with young sons. He'd proclaimed his love for Ellen, telling her—and proving to her—that the differences they'd had in the past no longer existed. He was courting Ellen with the intention of marriage. That Ellen was happy was evident in her bright smile and glistening blue eyes. Ellen's happiness had been infectious, and Lizzie couldn't be more pleased for her friend.

Lizzie realized that while she'd been reminiscing, Zack had begun to stare at her strangely. Embarrassed at her woolgathering, she hurried to answer him.

"I've got money inside," she told him. "Let me know when you're ready to take the mare."

Zack appeared as if he would object, but then he must have thought better of it. "Her other hooves look fine. It's just the one."

He gazed at her for a moment longer until Lizzie shifted awkwardly under his regard. "I've got chickens to feed and the milking to do," she said.

"I'll take care of the horses and then check the fence line on the east boundary," Zack called out to her as she started to walk away. "I think some deer might have broken through. I saw hoofprints near your vegetable garden."

Lizzie halted and glanced toward the garden in the side yard. It was hard to tell from this distance if deer had disturbed her plants. There were still bell peppers, pumpkins, spinach and turnips growing. She didn't want her late crop ruined. It was bad enough the beautiful animals sometimes got into their cornfields. *Better the corn than my garden vegetables,* she thought. "It doesn't look disturbed."

"Not yet," he said, "but it will be if they continue to get inside the fence."

Lizzie knew that Zack was an early riser who enjoyed a cup of coffee at the start of his day. After finishing his early-morning chores, he would be ready for a hearty breakfast, usually about the same time that the children and his sister were up and ready to eat. They studied the garden in silence, Zack with his cup of coffee and she holding a pail of chicken feed. Lizzie was overly aware of him beside her. She'd come to appreciate his help around the farm, but given her attraction toward him, she wasn't entirely comfortable with the silence between them.

"I should get back to work," she said. She could feel her face heat when he captured her glance. To hide her reaction to him, she quickly turned to scatter some chicken feed on the ground.

"Is there anything you need in town?" he asked.

Lizzie gave the matter some thought. "Some groceries and fabric. An Englisher came into the craft shop and asked if I'd make a wedding quilt for her daughter. Ellen asked me if I was interested before she took a deposit. She told me to take my time to think about it."

Zack smiled. "You make beautiful quilts." When she raised questioning eyebrows, he explained, "The covering on Esther's bed. Matt told me you made it."

"*Ja,* an easy design, but the quilt serves its purpose." Lizzie wanted to escape before she said something she'd regret.

"Will you come to breakfast?" she asked.

He shook his head. "I ate breakfast earlier."

She was surprised to feel disappointment. "I'll see you later in the day, then."

He nodded and acted as if he, too, was eager to get away. "Let me know if you need anything. We can talk about going to town later."

"*Onkel* Zack!" Matt ran toward them from the farmhouse. "Can I come and help?"

"You want to do chores?" He exchanged amused glances with her over the boy's head.

Lizzie smiled. "You're up and ready to go early," she told her son.

Matt nodded. "I meant to get up earlier in case *Onkel* needed me before *schule*." The boy stared at Lizzie. "It's all right if I help, *ja*?"

"With the farmwork?" she teased, and Matt grinned at her. "*Ja*, help your uncle," she encouraged. "I'm sure he'd appreciate it. But don't forget about *schule*."

"I won't," Matthew replied with a grin.

Then it occurred to her that Zack might not want his nephew underfoot. She looked at Zack in question. "Unless you'd rather he didn't go?"

A strange look entered his expression as they locked gazes. "Of course he may come." He then addressed his nephew. "But, Matt, I must warn you—there's a lot of work to do." He stared at her. "Lizzie." She watched him turn and walk toward the fields with Matt.

"Zack."

Zack paused and turned as Matt waited for his uncle. "You know where to find me if you need anything," he said. "I'll send Matthew home in time to clean up for *schule*."

"*Danki*," she murmured as he left. Feeling unsettled, Lizzie fed the chickens, put away the feed bucket, then went into the barn to do the milking. As she stepped into the dark interior, she was assailed by memories of her husband lying at the base of the ladder to the loft on the left, blood pooling near his head on the concrete floor. Swallowing hard, Lizzie looked away and hurried toward the cow stalls. As she took care of the animals, she was able to put the memory at rest, at least, for the time being. She finished the chore and went back to the farmhouse. The children were awake and in the kitchen as she entered it through the back door.

"Breakfast?" she asked.

"Ja!" Jonas cried, and Anne and Zeke echoed him.

Lizzie decided the vegetable-garden work could wait until after breakfast and her household chores. Esther joined them for the meal and insisted on staying to help with the housework. Lizzie worked inside, pleased to have Esther's and the girls' help.

Mary Ruth, Hannah and Rebecca worked quickly and efficiently at their assigned chores, and Lizzie found herself able to get to her garden much earlier than expected. Anne and Jonas decided to help her pick vegetables. The older girls and Ezekiel had gone with Esther to the *dawdi haus*, despite Esther's insistence that there was nothing to do except bake cookies. Little Zeke had perked up at the mention of cookies. When he asked if he could watch the cookie baking, Esther had smiled and held out her hand toward him.

Lizzie sighed with pleasure as she raked the garden. She hadn't felt this lighthearted in a long time. She was grateful to have the whole afternoon ahead of her to do her work. If her day continued as well as it had thus far, she'd have time in the evening to relax and read a book or finish the baby quilt for her unborn child.

Now that she knew she was pregnant, she had to consult the midwife. She felt amazingly good for being in her first trimester. Her pregnancy nausea was similar to the nausea frequently brought on by her hip-dysplasia pain.

Would the weight of her baby aggravate her hip? It wouldn't matter if it did. The only thing that mattered was her baby. She cradled her belly, hoping, praying that everything went well with her pregnancy.

"Mam." A young voice broke into her thoughts.

"Ja, Jonas?"

"Look how many I got." He showed her the large stainless-steel bowl, which he'd filled to the rim with turnips and bell peppers.

"You've been a busy boy!" she exclaimed with pleasure. He'd been working at the opposite end of the garden.

He grinned back at her. "I'll put these in the house and come back to pick more."

Lizzie agreed and then eyed him fondly as he ran as if he couldn't wait to return to help her.

Could a woman ask for better children? she wondered, overwhelmed with love. Since Zack's arrival, the older children frequently helped her without her having to ask. She had mixed feelings about her situation. If life continued as it had been going, then she wouldn't mind her husband's siblings living on the farm indefinitely, although things might change if they decided to move from the *dawdi haus* to the big house.

When are you going to talk with Zack about his intentions toward the farm? her inner voice taunted.

"Tomorrow," she declared. She'd talk with him tomorrow and put her mind at ease. She closed her eyes and swallowed hard. At least, she hoped her talk with Zack would calm her fears.

Chapter Seven

On Thursday morning, Lizzie was in the yard feeding the chickens. It was still dark; the sun had yet to make an appearance, although there was a tiniest hint of orange in a cloudless early-morning sky filled with stars. She loved this time of day when the world was silent, and she felt a part of God's nature. There was no one around to notice her limp or judge her. No one to condemn her for the choices she'd made.

"Lizzie."

She gasped, startled. "Zack!"

He had approached silently. She hadn't expected to see him this early.

He stood within two feet of her. She could see his gleaming eyes and the crooked smile on his masculine lips. "I'm sorry I scared you."

She had placed a hand over her thundering heart. "'Tis all right." She managed to smile. "I'll live."

His smile turned into a grin. "I wanted to ask you if you'd like to run into town today. We could go to Miller's General Store or McCann's Grocery. If you wish, we can stop at Beachey's Craft Shop. Then we can eat at Margaret's and return home afterward."

It sounded like a wonderful outing. Margaret's was the local Mennonite restaurant on the main street in Honeysuckle. For some reason, the thought of spending a couple of hours with Zack brightened her day.

"I'd like to go, but what about the children?"

"The older ones will be in school, and Esther will be here to mind Zeke and Jonas."

Lizzie grinned. "And we'll be back before the others get home."

"Then it's settled?" he asked. "Shall we leave at nine?"

Lizzie thought of all she had to do and decided that she'd have plenty of time to get her morning chores done. The rest of her work could wait.

"*Ja.* That sounds fine," she said. "I'll be ready at nine o'clock."

Five hours later, cleaned up after doing chores and wearing a freshly laundered dress, Lizzie exited the house to find Zack had brought around the family's market wagon. It had been some time since she'd taken a ride in the vehicle. The climb up onto the seat was high and was hard on her hip.

She smiled at Zack as she approached while worrying that she'd make a fool of herself when she tried to get in. She skirted the buggy to the front passenger side and to her surprise Zack joined her there. Her heart started to pound hard as she met his gaze. Overwhelmed by how handsome he looked in his burgundy shirt and triblend blue denim pants with black leather suspenders, she tried not to stare. Zack reached into the back of the wagon for a plastic crate, which he set on the ground for her to step on. He then extended his hand to assist her.

His thoughtfulness pleased her. She placed her fingers within his grasp as she put her foot onto the crate and allowed Zachariah to help her into the wagon. "Careful now," he warned as he firmed his hold when she started to stumble. She blushed at the heat of his fingers.

"Danki," she murmured as he released her hand when she was seated. The memory of his touch made her nape tingle and warmth run up her arm.

He was silent as he skirted the wagon and climbed into the vehicle's driver's side. He picked up the leathers, then turned toward her. "Where should we go first?"

She thought for a moment. Her face warmed as he gazed at her. "Beachey's Craft Shop? It's the closest."

He nodded, and then with a click of his tongue and a flick of the reins, he steered Rosebud toward the main road.

"Mam! Mam!" a young voice called out as Zack drove the buggy down the dirt drive.

Lizzie glanced back. Little Zeke raced after them, waving his arms. "Zack, please stop. It's Zeke," she explained.

He immediately drew the horse to a halt. Lizzie wanted to get down and run to her son, but she knew that if she tried to climb down without help, she'd hurt herself.

Zack got out and met Zeke as the child ran toward the buggy. He scooped the three-year-old into his arms and brought him to her.

Ezekiel's eyes glistened with tears as Zack lifted him to a height where he was eye to eye with Lizzie. "What's wrong, Zeke?" she asked softly.

The child sniffed. "I wanted to say goodbye. I never got to say goodbye."

She reached out to tenderly caress his cheek. "You don't have to worry," she said. "We'll be back this afternoon."

"You will?" he asked, blinking rapidly as he gazed at her.

"*Ja*, of course—"

Zack hefted the child onto the front seat. "I'll tell Esther that he'll be coming with us."

"Would you like to come?" she asked Zeke.

Ezekiel nodded vigorously, his eyes suddenly bright with excitement. "Can I?"

"May I?" she corrected. She met Zack's gaze. "You don't mind?" she asked.

"Nay." He grinned as he reached up to tap on the brim of the boy's straw hat. "I'll be right back."

As she watched Zack walk toward the *dawdi haus*, Lizzie sensed something shift within her heart. His tenderness, consideration, and patience with Zeke stirred feelings within her that frightened her. He was the brother of her late husband, and while her marriage to Abe hadn't been initiated by love, Abraham had still been her husband and she his wife. She had no right to feel this way.

Zack was her brother-in-law. She couldn't—*mustn't*—harbor feelings for him other than friendship between one relative to another.

"*Mam*, you all right?" Zeke asked. Her son placed his hand on her arm.

She turned to him with a reassuring smile. "*Ja*, Zeke. Are you ready to go to town?"

The little boy grinned. "*Ja!* We're going to town," he chanted. "We're going to town!"

Zack returned from the *dawdi haus* and climbed into the driver's seat. He flashed Zeke a grin. "All ready for your adventure?"

"*Ja!*" Zeke cried, clearly excited at the prospect.

Beachey's Craft Shop stood on the public road. The Beachey family lived in the house down from the store on the crest of a hill. She saw Zack study the store as they approached. He and Zeke followed her inside and waited patiently while she spoke with Ellen, the Beacheys' daughter, who now ran the business for her aging parents.

Ellen smiled as Lizzie approached the counter. "Did you decide if you'll be making the wedding quilt for Mrs. Emory's daughter?"

"Did Mrs. Emory say how soon she needed it?" Lizzie asked. "It may take me a while to finish one of this size." Mrs. Emory wanted to give her daughter a quilt large enough for a king-size bed. Lizzie thought she might use the wedding-ring pattern with calico prints in soft pastels, colors that would look good in any room.

"Dana Emory's wedding is over a year and a half from now," Ellen told her. "You should have plenty of time. I have an idea what Mrs. Emory likes. She loved the last quilt you brought. I'll get it." She left the room, leaving Lizzie to wait patiently for her return.

English weddings were often large and took months of preparation, Lizzie realized. Many of the little details, such as flowers, the church and the reception, were important to them. *If the man I loved wanted to wed me,* Lizzie thought, *I wouldn't worry about such worldly things.* She'd simply be eager to become his wife.

She and Abraham didn't have a usual wedding. Their marriage had been about the children, not her and the groom.

While she waited for Ellen's return, Lizzie watched Zack and Zeke as they wandered about the store. She saw Zack bend to whisper something in her little boy's ear and saw Zeke's face light up with a big smile.

Ellen returned with the quilt that had drawn Barbara Emory's attention. "She liked these colors," she told Lizzie. "I told her that you wouldn't be able to use the same fabrics but that you could find printed material in similar colors." The colors in the quilt were blue, yellow and spring green.

Lizzie nodded. "*Ja.* I can do that."

"You'll take on the work?" Ellen named a figure that made Lizzie gasp and unable to decline.

"How can I say no?" Lizzie said with a chuckle.

"I told her that you'd need a deposit to pay for the fabrics and some of your time." Ellen smiled. "I wanted to make sure you got some money up front."

"That's wonderful." Lizzie grinned, pleased. *"Danki."* The money would come in handy. It would take months to make the quilt, but if she worked nights, she could have it finished well before the wedding. And then she'd be able to make other craft items.

She and Ellen had completed their business conversation about the Emory quilt when Zack approached with young Zeke.

"Ellen," he greeted. "It's *goot* to see you again."

Ellen stared at him a long moment. "Zachariah Fisher?" She blinked and then grinned when he nodded. "Zack, I haven't seen you in—"

"Years," he said with a pleasant smile. "Since we were children."

"You were a child anyway," Ellen said with a grin. "Is there something I can do for you?"

"Nay." He drew Zeke closer with a hand on his shoulder. "We're waiting for Lizzie," he said.

Compassion filled the woman's dark eyes. "I am sorry about your *brooder.*"

Zack inclined his head, clearly appreciating her sympathy.

Ellen then turned to Lizzie. "Do you think you'll be able to make a few aprons? They sell as soon as I get them in."

"Certainly," Lizzie assured her. It wouldn't take her long to stitch up a few.

The door to the shop jingled, and Neziah Shetler entered and approached the counter. Lizzie saw Ellen's eyes light up and a smile curve her lips. Lizzie shot Zack a look and saw that he, too, noticed the change in Ellen.

"We should go," Zack said. Lizzie nodded, figuring that Ellen and Neziah might want a brief moment alone. "Ellen, it was nice to see you again." Neziah approached the counter. "Neziah Shetler? Zack Fisher." He held out his hand.

Neziah smiled as they shook hands. "Zack! Welcome home. It's been a long time. You couldn't have been more than twelve when you moved away."

Zack nodded. "I was eleven."

Lizzie listened patiently and kept an eye on Zeke while the two men talked, catching up.

"It was *goot* to see you both," Zack said when it was time to leave. "I trust we'll see you again soon."

"Lizzie. It's nice to see you again," Neziah said.

"It's *goot* to see you, too," she replied with a smile. "Zeke, *koom.* We must finish our errands before your *brooder* and sisters get home from *schule.*" With her son standing by her side, Lizzie turned to her friend. "Ellen, I appreciate the work. Tell Mrs. Emory that she can count on me to make her daughter's quilt. I'll purchase some fabrics for her to approve before I start."

"That's a fine idea." Ellen placed the quilt on the counter behind her. "I'll talk with her when she comes in next week."

"Can we go eat yet?" Zeke asked. "I'm hungry."

"Zeke!" Lizzie scolded gently, but Ellen and Neziah only laughed.

Zack hoisted Zeke onto his shoulders and headed toward the door. Lizzie started to follow and then stopped briefly when she saw Dinah Plank, the Beacheys' tenant who lived in the apartment above the craft shop and worked for Ellen in the store. "If you'll take Zeke, I'll follow in just a minute," she told Zack.

"Dinah," Lizzie greeted. "How is the widows' group? I'm sorry I haven't been to a meeting in a while."

"No worries," Dinah said. "We're here if you need us, but I imagine you've been busy with your company." The older woman glanced toward the door. "That is Zack Fisher, isn't it?"

Blushing, Lizzie nodded and quickly changed the subject to the upcoming widows'-club lunch. She and the woman chatted a few moments, and then after bidding everyone farewell, she joined Zack and Zeke, who were waiting for her outside.

"Miller's General Store or McCann's Grocery?" Zack asked with a smile.

McCann's Grocery was the only food store in the center of Honeysuckle, and it had other items, as well, but fabric wasn't among them. Lizzie needed to buy fabric, and the best place for material was the general store. She knew it wouldn't take long to get to the store; it was just a mile and a half past Honeysuckle village proper. "Let's go to Miller's," she said.

Zack steered the horse down the road toward Miller's General Store and then parked the wagon in the side lot. The store was a large wooden structure painted dark brown with white trim and a white roof. Glass windows ran the front length of the store, displaying a hint of what Miller's had to offer. Zack climbed out, secured the horse to the hitching post and then came back to lift Zeke down from the vehicle before assisting Lizzie. He spanned her waist with his hands and lowered her to the ground beside him. Lizzie kept her eyes downcast, aware of the way heat rose from her neck upward and the sudden thunder of her rapidly beating heart. They walked toward the store, one on each side of little Zeke, and then entered through the automatic side entrance. Walking beside Zack and her little son made it feel as though they were a family. Lizzie bit her lip and fought to banish the dangerous thought.

They walked around the store together, making a game of who could gather the most grocery items on Lizzie's list first. Lizzie won since she knew the layout of the store better than Zack or Ezekiel. Afterward, Zack and Zeke checked the candy aisle while Lizzie went to the fabric section of the store, where she chose solid material to make new dresses for the girls as well as various calico samples for Mrs. Emory's approval. During his trip down the candy aisle, Zeke asked if he could have a chocolate bar. Zack looked to Lizzie for an answer as she approached.

"*Ja*, Zeke, you may have one, but you must hold it until after we eat lunch," she told him.

"I think I'd like one, too," Zack said. "How about you?"

Lizzie grinned at the boyish, expectant look on his handsome face. "Sounds *goot*. I'll have the same as Zeke."

Soon, they were back in the buggy, heading toward Margaret's to eat.

"I've only eaten here once," Zeke said as they headed inside the restaurant. "It smells *goot*!" He studied his surroundings with wide eyes. He wasn't watching where he was going and nearly tripped. Zack quickly reached out to steady him.

"Careful now, buddy," Zack warned, but Zeke only grinned at him and headed toward an empty booth.

Lizzie smiled as she and Zack exchanged looks as they sat down. She saw the amusement in her brother-in-law's dark eyes and she widened her smile into a grin.

"I'm so hungry I could eat a horse!" Zack exclaimed. His good humor cheered her like the warmth of the sun brightened a cloudy day.

Zeke looked at his uncle. "We can't eat horses, *Onkel* Zack. We need them too much. Who would pull our buggy or our plow?"

Zack laughed as he tugged off the boy's hat and set it on the seat between them. "I wouldn't eat a horse, Zeke. Horses are big, and I'm just saying that I'm very hungry."

Understanding, Zeke grinned, and then he told them he wanted a tomato-and-grilled-cheese sandwich. Moments later, Lizzie listened with a smile as the boy gave the young waitress his food order. Zack decided on a hamburger and French fries, while she chose a bowl of ham-and-lima-bean soup.

The conversation seemed to flow easily, and Lizzie enjoyed herself as she watched Zack interact with Zeke. She felt comfortable seated in the dining booth with Zeke and Zack seated across the table from her. She couldn't help but notice the startling resemblance between uncle and nephew. The time passed so quickly that she was startled when she learned that they'd been in Margaret's for well over an hour.

"Cake?" Zack asked Lizzie when the waitress had taken away their plates.

"Chocolate?" she suggested.

He nodded. "Is there any other kind?"

"Can I have a piece?" Zeke asked.

"*Ja*, you *may*." Lizzie grinned at her son. "Or would you rather have pudding?"

Zeke appeared to give the matter some thought. "Rice pudding?"

"If you'd like."

"Can I still have my chocolate bar?" the boy asked.

Lizzie studied him a moment. "*Ja*, you may."

Zeke beamed at her. "I'd like some rice pudding, please, with a bit of cinnamon," he told the waitress when she had returned for their dessert order.

Lizzie enjoyed her cake and the company of the two handsome males with her. She was sorry to see their outing end, but it was close to one thirty, and she wanted to get back to the house before the older children came home from school.

The journey from Margaret's toward home was a ten-minute drive past McCann's Grocery and several English as well as Amish homes. Pleased with their purchases and the meal they'd shared, Lizzie relaxed and enjoyed the ride. Her ease with Zack made her realize that it was time to talk with him about his intentions for the farm as soon as she could find a moment alone with him.

They drove past the craft shop, and Lizzie waved to Neziah and Ellen, who stood outside. They must have shared lunch together before Neziah walked Ellen back to the store. Zack steered the horse-drawn wagon along the main street until they were out of Honeysuckle proper, then past the hill that led up to the John Beachey residence. Spying Ellen's father at the base of the hill, Lizzie waved. "Afternoon, John!"

"Lizzie!" The old man smiled. "Who have you got with you?"

"Zack Fisher, John," Zack said.

"Ah! *Goot* to see you back in Honeysuckle. It's been a long time, *ja*?"

"*Ja!* It's a blessing to be home," Zack agreed with a smile. After exchanging a few pleasantries with Ellen's father, he then urged Rosebud forward, steering the mare into a turn onto the dirt drive that led toward the Fisher farmhouse and cottage.

"Jonas!" Zeke called as Zack pulled into the barnyard and climbed out of the wagon to help the boy before rounding to Lizzie's side of the vehicle. The door to the *dawdi haus* opened and Esther hurried toward them.

"Zack!" she cried, her expression worried as she approached. Zack helped Lizzie down from the wagon and turned to his sister. Young Jonas, who had run out of the house, hurried to little Zeke's side.

Seeing his sister's worried expression, Zack frowned. "What's wrong?"

"'Tis *Mam*. Miriam sent word that she fell and hurt herself." Esther sent Lizzie a look that begged for understanding. "She wants us to come home."

Zack's brow furrowed with concern. "*Ja,*" he agreed. "Did you pack our things?"

Esther nodded. "And I called for a car. The driver will be here any minute."

Zack met Lizzie's gaze. "I'm sorry—"

"Go," Lizzie encouraged. She extended an arm toward Jonas, who came quickly to burrow against her side. "We'll be fine. I hope your *mudder* is all right." She bit her lip. "Will you let us know how she is?"

He nodded. He then picked up Zeke, held him at eye level. "You will be a *goot* boy, *ja*?"

Ezekiel looked as if he would cry. "I'll be a *goot* boy," he agreed.

Zack smiled and set his nephew down. He turned to the four-year-old. "Jonas?"

"I will, too," Jonas promised as he snuggled against Lizzie's side. Lizzie raised her other arm, inviting Zeke into her embrace. Her youngest son ran and hugged her about the waist, glancing back toward his uncle with a look of sadness.

"Does *Onkel* have to leave, *Mam*?" he asked.

"*Ja*, Zeke, he has to go," she said, giving him a reassuring squeeze. The day that had begun so well was ending on a painful note as Lizzie watched Zack and Esther prepare to return to their home in Ohio.

Her talk with Zack about the farm and her baby would have to wait. The only thing that was important now was praying for Zack and Esther's mother—and her mother-in-law.

"Tell Matt and the girls I will be back to see them when I can," Zack said.

"I will," Lizzie promised, blinking back tears. Today she'd enjoyed herself in the man's company. Now she wondered when and if she would ever see him again. She'd feared his arrival yet now was sad to see him leave. Her children would be upset to learn that their aunt and uncle had left without saying goodbye.

A short time later, as she watched their hired car drive away, Lizzie felt her gut wrench with sorrow. She waited until she could no longer see the vehicle before she took her two youngest into the farmhouse. "They'll be back," she assured them with more confidence than she felt. Would they return to Honeysuckle or would the seriousness of their mother's accident keep them indefinitely in Ohio?

Chapter Eight

When they returned from school, the older children burst into the kitchen, pink-cheeked and bringing fresh air and excitement with them into the house.

"*Mam*, I'm going to the *dawdi haus*," Matt said. "*Onkel* Zack said I could help him with the horses." He tossed his schoolbook onto the table and glanced down at his clothes. "I should change first."

"*Ja*, and *Endie* Esther said I could help her make apple dumplings this afternoon," Mary Ruth added, seeming pleased at the prospect. "I'm sure she's waiting for us. Did she pick apples today? There are some nice ones left to be picked."

"*Nay*," Lizzie said quietly. "I'm sorry, but I'm afraid neither of you will be helping your *endie* and *onkel* today. They are not here." She studied them with compassion. "They've gone back to Ohio. Your *endie* Miriam called for them to come home."

Mary Ruth didn't believe her. There was a hurt look in her eyes that tore at Lizzie's heart. "*Nay*. They're in the *dawdi haus*."

"I'm sorry, *dochter*," Lizzie said gently, "but they left

earlier. Your *onkel* Zack said to tell you that he would see you again when he returns."

Mary Ruth blinked as if fighting tears. "They're gone?" She shook her head. "Truly?" She frowned. "*Nay*, they can't be."

"I'm sorry, Mary Ruth, but it's true. They left about an hour and a half ago." To her surprise, Lizzie felt the loss as keenly as the children.

"You're glad they are gone," Mary Ruth accused suddenly, her eyes darkening. "You never liked them. You didn't want them to come!"

Lizzie felt her throat tighten. Her daughter's words hurt. She had done everything she could to prepare for their visit and offered a warm welcome to Esther and Zack, despite the reservations she had about them coming to stay on the farm.

"Mary Ruth—"

"*Nay!*" Little Ezekiel sobbed. "*Mam* likes them fine. We went to town with *Onkel* Zack and had a *goot* time! *Mam* laughed and so did *Onkel* Zack!"

Her eyes filled with tears, Mary Ruth studied her youngest brother. "*Ya* did?" she said softly.

"*Ja*," Zeke said. "Tell them, *Mam*."

"Your sister—everyone—is upset because your *onkel* had to leave."

"He said he'd be back," Zeke said.

Jonas nodded. "He said that," the four-year-old agreed. "They didn't want to go, but they had to leave. *Endie* Esther said that their *mudder* hurt herself."

Mary Ruth met Lizzie's gaze, contrition in her hazel eyes. "I shouldn't have said that. I'm sorry."

Lizzie blinked and touched first one corner of her eye then the other to hide her tears. "We'll continue on as best we can as they would want us to." She managed to smile. "Maybe your *grossmama* will recover quickly, and your *onkel* Zack and *endie* Esther will return." She had an idea. "Girls, why don't you go to the *dawdi haus* and make sure everything's ready for them."

"Do you think they'll come back soon?" Rebecca asked somberly.

"If they can."

"How long do you think they'll be gone?" Matt was clearly upset to have learned that his beloved uncle had left Honeysuckle.

"That will depend on how badly your *grossmudder* hurt herself and how quickly she recovers."

"That could be a long time," Hannah said.

Lizzie nodded. "It could. But it could also be a short time. We should pray for the best and hope they come back soon."

Anne approached, placed a small hand on Lizzie's arm. "Everything will be fine, *Mam*. If it is *Gottes Wille*, *Onkel* Zack and *Endie* Esther will come back soon."

Lizzie nodded in agreement. She never expected to feel this way about Zack's leaving. She had regarded the man as a threat at first, but then he'd been so helpful and kind that she'd relaxed and accepted his help with gratitude and without reservations. As Annie had said, whether or not he returned would be determined by God's will. Until then, she would manage the house and farm while caring for the children, and she would pray that with the Lord's help she handled everything well for her family…and her unborn child.

The cramp came in the middle of the night. She gasped and sat upright, cradling her abdomen where the pain originated. Lizzie struggled to rise and barely had time to stumble across the room before she vomited into a basin.

Nay, she cried silently. *Please, Lord, not my baby.*

When she saw the blood on her nightgown, she started to cry. She knew without a doubt that she was losing her baby. And then it was quickly over. Lizzie realized that she wouldn't be having her late husband's child, the child who would have meant hope for the future. There would be no baby to show for her and Abraham's love, a love that had ended right after it had begun. While she worked at the bathroom sink to get the stain out of her nightgown, she tried to weep soundlessly so that she wouldn't wake the children. She pressed her hand over her mouth to control her sobbing gasps.

Gottes Wille, she reminded herself a short while later as she returned to bed. In the solitary silence of her room, she allowed her tears to fall freely.

She had been the only one who'd known about the baby. She'd been going to tell Zack about her pregnancy when they talked about the farm, but now the only thing she could confess was that she had lost her baby.

Lizzie placed a trembling hand over her lower abdomen and cried until she became too exhausted to continue. But sleep was a long time in coming, and the pain of her loss had settled deep in her heart as she cradled her empty womb.

The next morning Lizzie struggled not to cry or to alert the children that anything was amiss. Despite the knowledge that the pregnancy would have been difficult with her crippled hip, she had wanted the baby and been willing to endure anything to give birth to Abraham's child.

The older children were in school. Zeke and Jonas were in the yard, playing. Lizzie looked out the kitchen window and watched as the boys ran around in circles, laughing and chasing each other. The sight made her lips curve into a tender smile. She may have suffered a miscarriage, but she still had her late husband's children and she loved them. Seeing the youngest two having fun was heartwarming.

She washed the lunch dishes, then dried and put them away. Lizzie felt as if she were in a fog as she moved throughout the kitchen and the house, cleaning. The older children were due home from school in less than an hour. She half expected to look up and see them rush through the back doorway.

A sudden sharp cry broke into her thoughts, and her heart raced with fear. Lizzie ran toward the window to check on her sons. Her pulse beat harder. There was no sign of either Jonas or Ezekiel. Frantically calling them by name, Lizzie ran out of the house in her search to find them.

"Mam!" Ezekiel screamed as he flew out of the barn.

"Zeke?" She hurried toward him.

"Jonas hurt himself!" Her son's face was white, his lips quivering.

Nay! "How bad?" Lizzie asked as she ran with him into the barn. Jonas stood inside a few feet, staring down with horror at his bleeding hand. "Jonas!" she cried. "What's happened?"

Young Jonas had tears in his eyes as he met her gaze. *"Mam."* He began to sob out an explanation, but he was too upset; she couldn't understand him. Soon after talking calmly with Jonas and Zeke, she was able to discover what had happened.

"Calm down and tell me what happened. Speak slowly," she urged softly, "so that I can understand." She inhaled sharply as she saw all the blood, but she tried not to alarm the boys.

"It was one of *Dat*'s tools," Jonas admitted. "That sharp curved thing." He'd touched the sickle on the wall hook next to several other farm implements, Lizzie realized. "I didn't think it would hurt to make it swing," he cried.

Her first inclination was to scold him, but she knew that he'd learned a lesson that he might never have understood if he hadn't hurt himself.

"Let me see," Lizzie said. She gently took Jonas's hand in hers and hissed out in dismay. "Come with me." She picked up her four-year-old and hurried toward the house, checking to make sure Zeke kept up with her and Jonas, who began to cry loudly with hiccuping sobs.

Once inside, she sat Jonas in a kitchen chair, took out some clean dish towels and wrapped them around the wound. "It's all right, Jonas," she soothed. "I know it hurts, but *Mam* will help you. Hold still, Jonas. *Goot* boy!"

The other children arrived home in the midst of the madness.

"What's wrong?" Mary Ruth said with concern as she entered the kitchen. "What happened?"

Blood seeped through the towel. Lizzie flashed Mary Ruth a concerned look. "Your *brooder* cut himself. Matt?" she said. "Can you get the buggy ready? Jonas needs to see a doctor."

Looking worried and pale, the older boy nodded and left. "Hannah, can you get me some towels from the linen chest?" Lizzie asked. "Mary Ruth, if I wrap Jonas's hand, can you hold pressure on it until Matt brings around the buggy?" Her eldest daughter nodded.

She addressed Rebecca. "Take Anne and Zeke outside. We'll be right out. Anne, don't worry—Jonas will be fine. Zeke, you're a *goot* boy for telling me what happened."

She had examined the wound thoroughly. It was a clean slice to the back of Jonas's hand, extending around to the right side. The cut would need stitching, she realized. As she hurried the children into the buggy, Lizzie decided that it would be better if they stayed with someone until she and Jonas were finished at the doctor's office. Lizzie waited while the children got into the buggy and then climbed in and took up the leathers. She gave Mary Ruth an approving nod as the girl held her injured brother on her lap.

Where could she take the children? Naomi Beiler's name instantly came to mind. Naomi was the head of the local widows' group in Honeysuckle. The woman had been the first one who had come with an offer to help after Abraham's death. She had convinced Lizzie to attend the haystack supper last month while Naomi's daughter Emma kept an eye on the younger children. The supper was a fundraising event for Raymond, Mary Blauch's baby son who'd been born prematurely and was in the Children's Hospital of Philadelphia.

Lizzie decided to stop at the widow's house and ask if Naomi would watch the children until she could return for them later that afternoon. The children might not want to stay, but it would be less stressful for everyone if Lizzie didn't have to worry about them when her focus should be solely on Jonas.

"Where are we going?" Mary Ruth asked as Lizzie pulled into the gravel driveway alongside the widow's home.

"To see Naomi Beiler. I'm going to ask her if you can stay with her until Jonas and I are finished with the doctor."

"Nay," the girl objected staunchly.

"'Tis best for everyone," Lizzie said.

"Not me," her daughter insisted with tears in her eyes. "I want to come. I can help with Jonas. I'll hold him for you while you drive our buggy."

Lizzie drew the vehicle to a halt. "Wait here." She ran to the woman's house, explained what had happened and asked if the children could stay until after she and Mary Ruth had taken Jonas to the doctor. "I can use your help."

Naomi agreed readily. *"Ja.* I will be happy to watch them for you. They'll be fine here. Do what you need to do and don't worry."

"Danki," Lizzie said as she fought back tears.

She returned to the buggy and urged the children out of the vehicle. "Come. You'll be staying here with Naomi. Behave, *ja*? I'll be back as soon as I can to get you."

Rebecca and Hannah exchanged glances. "Is Mary Ruth staying here, too?" Hannah asked.

"Nay. Help Naomi with the children."

"We will," Rebecca promised.

"Anne, Matthew, hurry," Hannah said firmly but kindly. *"Mam* needs to go."

Lizzie was proud of her children as she watched as they stepped out of the vehicle, one by one, their gazes drifting briefly to their brother Jonas, who looked pale and lay whimpering within Mary Ruth's arms. As she drove toward the clinic, Lizzie was glad that Mary Ruth was there to hold and comfort Jonas.

"Lizzie!" Mary Ruth's cry immediately drew her attention toward her son. Blood had soaked through the double wrapping of towels.

Lizzie flicked the leathers to increase the mare's pace, and the buggy barreled down the road as fast as the horse-drawn vehicle was capable. As she spurred the horse on, the thundering of the mare's hooves on the road mirrored her wildly beating heart.

At last, the medical building came into view, and she pulled back on the reins to slow the mare before steering the buggy into the parking lot adjacent to the building.

She secured the horse and then took Jonas from Mary Ruth. They raced inside, glad to see that the waiting room wasn't crowded. Lizzie carried Jonas to the front desk and explained to the receptionist what had happened.

The woman took one look at the bloody towels, quickly picked up the phone and spoke to someone in the back of the clinic. A medical assistant appeared and escorted them immediately into an exam room. A doctor came in within minutes, and Jonas cried as the physician gave him a needle filled with numbing agent before he stitched closed the wound. When he was done, Dr. Jones told Lizzie that Jonas needed a tetanus shot.

"Farm tools carry germs," the doctor explained. "It's important that Jonas gets the injection."

It didn't take long for Lizzie to agree. The doctor bandaged Jonas's hand and gave him an injection. Jonas was given a lollipop for being a good patient, which he enjoyed as he preceded Lizzie outside. Mary Ruth, who'd left moments before, waited by their buggy, ready to help her little brother. She met Lizzie's glance, and Lizzie could only guess the girl's thoughts as she climbed into the seat next to her daughter and picked up the reins.

Lizzie was exhausted. It had been a long, tiring day after a sleepless night, and she looked forward to the hour when the children were in bed and she could crawl under the covers. But there was supper to fix first and homework to be done by her older children.

She felt responsible for Jonas's accident. If she had

watched the boys more closely, they wouldn't have slipped into the barn to play.

"Mam?"

Lizzie turned, surprised to realize that it was Mary Ruth who had spoken. Until now, her daughter had never called her anything but Lizzie. *"Ja*, Mary Ruth?"

"Danki for letting me come today," she said quietly.

"I'm glad you did." She regarded her with affection. "We'll pick up the others and go home. I think we've had enough of an adventure today."

Mary Ruth smiled in agreement as she glanced at Jonas, who lay against her with his eyes closed. They stopped at Naomi's first to get the children before they continued to the farm. Jonas was tired and ready for bed early. The pain medication the doctor had given him made him sleepy.

During the remainder of the ride home, Mary Ruth had regarded her with warmth in her expression. Lizzie had returned her smile. It had been a good day for the family despite all the terrible things that had happened, beginning with her miscarriage and ending with Jonas's injury.

Chapter Nine

Saturday morning Lizzie rose after a good night's sleep. Usually, as of late, she'd suffered long nights without sleep, but yesterday's drama compounded by several sleepless nights had exhausted her to the point where she'd finally been able to sleep without dreaming. Losing her baby was emotionally difficult as well as physically hard on her. Friday night she'd been so tired that she would have drifted off if not for her concern for Jonas. She had gone to check on her son several times, worried that he'd be in pain or cry out for her, but he had slept peacefully, helped by the pain medicine that Dr. Jones had prescribed.

She headed to the kitchen to make bread, muffins and cupcakes to take to the Peter Zook farm. Tomorrow was visiting Sunday. There was a lot to do. After turning on the oven to preheat, Lizzie couldn't stop thinking about Zack and Esther. They'd left the day before yesterday. Did they get to Ohio safely? How was their *mam*?

She measured the ingredients for a double batch of corn muffins. She stirred them together in a large stainless-steel bowl until the batter was the right consistency and then filled two muffin tins until each section was two-thirds full. Next, she pulled out and mixed together the makings for chocolate cake, setting the mixture aside until the muffins were done and cooling on a wire rack. Then she'd wash and reuse the tins for baking cupcakes. She cleaned up the kitchen, and when the muffins were ready, she set each one on the cooling rack.

She had just taken the cupcakes out of the oven when she heard a firm knock on the back door. Lizzie set the tin on a hot mat and went to answer it. To her delight, her brother stood on her front porch, wearing a silly grin.

"William!" She laughed, pleased to see him. "What are you doing here?" She held the door open and he stepped inside.

"I thought I'd visit my favorite *schweschter*," he said. William sniffed the air appreciatively. "Mmm. Something in here smells *goot*." His familiar face had always comforted her during her childhood whenever she'd felt unhappy or alone. She watched him examine his surroundings.

"What's baking?" he asked. With dark hair, brown eyes and a mouth that was quick to smile, William was a handsome man. The young women in their Amish community were frequently seen vying for his attention. He was five years her elder, and she wondered why he'd never found someone he wanted to wed.

"I made corn muffins," she said.

He glanced toward the counter. "And chocolate cupcakes."

She chuckled at his expectant expression. "Would you like a muffin or cupcake?"

He shook his head. "Wish I could, but I've got to get home. I needed to stop by to tell you that a call came to McCann's for you yesterday. John said he sent someone to tell you but no one was home."

Lizzie's heart skipped a beat. "Jonas hurt himself and I had to take him to the clinic." She eyed her brother eagerly. "Was it from Zack?"

"*Ja.* He left word for you that he and Esther arrived safely and that his *mudder* is well. She fell, but she's unhurt. They'll be coming back to Honeysuckle."

Lizzie put on the teakettle. "Are you sure you don't want *coffe* or tea?"

William looked longingly at the cupcakes cooling on the counter. "Can't. *Mam*'s waiting for her baking powder and flour."

"I understand," she said. "Take a muffin for the road?" She saw the gleam in his eyes and quickly wrapped up two muffins for him.

She walked outside to see him off, pretending an indifference to news from Zack. She waved to William as he left and then entered the house to finish food preparations for the next day.

Zack is on his way back to Honeysuckle. She felt nervous and excited. She'd planned to talk with Zack about the farm, but now that she'd lost her baby, she felt uneasy about the discussion.

Zack is a goot *man*, she silently reminded herself. She kept telling herself this over and over as she washed dishes and prepared to make a soup for tomorrow night's supper.

Rachel Zook paid an unexpected visit later that afternoon.

"What are you doing here?" Lizzie asked. "I didn't expect you to come with so much to do." She blushed. "I should have come to help you."

"You have enough to worry about," Rachel said. "I just thought I'd stop by." She eyed Lizzie a long moment. "You don't look well. What's wrong?"

Lizzie swallowed against a lump. She explained about Jonas's injury and their subsequent trip to the walk-in medical clinic. After Rachel had expressed concern and checked on Jonas in the next room, Lizzie found the courage to confide in her friend. "I had a miscarriage." She explained what had happened two nights past.

"Oh, Lizzie," Rachel said as she reached to place a hand over Lizzie's on the table. "I'm so sorry. Have you seen the midwife?"

Frowning, Lizzie shook her head. "*Nay*, I didn't think—"

Rachel raised her eyebrows. "Lizzie, you must see her. You need to make sure that everything…ah…that you are well."

Lizzie understood what Rachel meant. "I'll see her Monday if I can get away," she promised.

Her friend squeezed her hand. "Why don't you go now? I can keep an eye on Jonas and the children. I'll even do some baking with your girls' help."

"You don't mind?" Lizzie was grateful for her friend's offer.

Rachel smiled. "*Nay*, I don't mind." Her expression became serious. "Lizzie, you need to see the midwife, and you need to see her today. Will you go?"

"*Ja,*" Lizzie said, knowing her friend was right. "I'll go."

Lizzie was nervous as she drove to the midwife's. She felt terrible for interrupting the woman's Saturday, but Rachel insisted that it would be all right. As soon as she arrived, she realized that Rachel was right. She had no cause to worry. When Lizzie told the midwife about her miscarriage, Anne Stoltzfus was kind and sympathetic. The woman had sable-brown hair, a quick smile and a dusting of freckles across her small round nose. She was the same height as Lizzie, and the warmth in her direct gaze made Lizzie feel as if she'd done the right thing in coming. She waved away Lizzie's concerns about coming on a Saturday and praised her for listening to her friend.

When Anne was done examining Lizzie, she assured her that she was fine.

"I know this is difficult for you," Anne said. She suggested that Lizzie do something special in memory of the baby she'd lost. "It will help with your grieving."

"Like what?"

The midwife's expression grew soft. "Plant a tree? Do a craft or make a quilt? The choice is yours and only you will know or understand what it means."

Lizzie blinked back tears. "*Danki.* That's a *goot* idea."

Anne escorted her to the door and then followed her outside. "You will come to see me again? If you have pain or feel uncomfortable in any way, please come back."

Lizzie nodded. She was about to say goodbye when Anne caught sight of something that upset her. Lizzie saw what got her attention: there was a goat snacking on her garden plants.

"That old goat!" the midwife exclaimed. "Why can't Joseph Lapp mend that fence of his?" Anne stopped suddenly, looking contrite. "I apologize. My neighbor's goats are always escaping into my yard and my garden. What's so hard about keeping them penned up? All he has to do is fix his fence. I sell produce. I don't need those creatures destroying my tomatoes and pumpkins!" Shaking her head, she suddenly chuckled as if seeing humor in the situation.

"I'm glad you came, Lizzie." Anne accompanied her to her buggy. "Take care of yourself. Remember to come back for a visit if you need me for anything." She smiled. "Perhaps a checkup each year."

Smiling, Lizzie said, "I will." The woman's kindness warmed her heart and made her feel better. *"Danki."*

She left Anne's with the knowledge that her pregnancy had been terminated by nature and that there was no reason that she couldn't carry another baby to full term.

Except that my husband is dead, and I can't see myself marrying again. She had mentioned to Anne about her concerns about being pregnant with her hip dysplasia.

With a wave of her hand, Anne had brushed her concerns aside. "Advanced pregnancy with your medical condition might make things more challenging for you, but with care, I don't see why you shouldn't have a normal pregnancy and delivery. The only difference is that you may have to stay off your feet as much as possible during your last trimester, when you'd be carrying the most weight."

It was unlikely that she'd get another chance, Lizzie thought as she steered her horse-drawn buggy toward home. *Gottes Wille.* If *Gott* willed it then so shall it be. She prayed to the Lord for guidance and for strength.

During the ride home, Lizzie stopped briefly to pick up the fabric samples from Ellen that she'd left for Mrs. Emory's approval. She was pleased to learn that the woman had approved her choice of colors and quilt design.

"Do you have anything else you'd like to sell, Lizzie?" Ellen handed the fabric to her.

"I can bring in the few items I finished the other evening. I'll stop by with them within the next couple of days." Lizzie left then continued toward home. She arrived well before lunchtime. As she steered the horse toward the barn, she noticed a car parked close to the farmhouse.

Zack? Had he returned after only two days away? Her heart started to pound. *It is Zack!* She parked the buggy, climbed out and then wandered in his direction.

Her late husband's brother was talking with the driver of the car while Esther headed toward the cottage, carrying her valise.

Lizzie rounded the vehicle and he caught sight of her. She locked gazes with him as he ended his conversation with the driver. After the man got into his car, Zack closed the distance between them.

"Lizzie," he greeted with a smile. "It's *goot* to see you again."

"*Hallo*, Zack," she said. He looked good, too good, she thought, and she was pleased to see him.

"You got my message?" he asked.

Lizzie inclined her head. "*Ja.* How is your *mudder*?"

He sighed. "Much better, thanks be to *Gott*. She fell but wasn't injured as seriously as Miriam thought. I'm glad we went home to see for ourselves that she is well."

"You must be relieved." She saw him glance briefly toward the buggy. "I ran an errand." She held up the shopping bag with fabric she'd picked up from Ellen Beachey. "Mrs. Emory approved my choice of quilt colors and pattern."

"That's *goot*." He took off his hat and ran fingers through his dark hair. "I'm sure she'll be pleased. You do fine work."

She blushed at his praise. "Rachel is here. She stopped by earlier and offered to watch the children while I was gone. I'll be making lunch soon. Will you and Esther *koom*?"

"*Ja*, if you are sure it's no trouble. I'm eager to see the children again. I'll get Esther. It was a long ride, and I know she will appreciate the meal."

Zack headed toward the cottage, and Lizzie watched him walk away. He stopped suddenly and turned. Embarrassed to be caught staring, she felt the heat rise to her face.

She had missed him, she realized as she went into the house. She felt a nervous tightening in her belly. Now that he was back, there was no reason to put off asking him about the farm. Was there?

Chapter Ten

"*Onkel* Zack!" Matt burst into the farmhouse kitchen, bringing fresh air and renewed life with him. "You're back!" The boy beamed at him before he turned to his aunt. "*Endie* Esther, I'm glad you're home. We were afraid you wouldn't come back."

"*Hallo*, Matthew," Esther said with a warm smile. "It's nice to see you, too."

Mary Ruth, Hannah and Rebecca with Anne entered the house minutes later. They all exclaimed, clearly pleased, that their aunt and uncle had returned.

"How is *Grossmama*?" Mary Ruth asked with concern.

"She's doing well," Esther said. "Your *endie* Miriam worries. We were glad to see them, but it was time to come back."

"Are you going to stay?" Rebecca asked softly. "We like having you here."

Lizzie listened, eager to hear the answer, as she was glad to see them, too, even though she had no idea about their plans.

"We'll stay for a while, if all goes well," Zack said vaguely, giving Lizzie cause for concern.

Why did she have the feeling that she would be involved in his decision to stay or go?

"When did you get back?" Hannah asked.

"A half hour ago." He raised his iced-tea glass to show her that he'd been relaxing and enjoying the afternoon here in the kitchen. "We enjoyed a late lunch."

"Are they staying for supper?" Rebecca asked.

"Ja," Lizzie said. "They said they would."

The girl grinned. *"Wunderbor!"*

"We missed you," Anne said as she went to her uncle. "It wasn't the same when you were gone."

Matthew agreed. "There was no one to help do chores."

Zack eyed him with affection before he met Lizzie's glance. She blushed and turned away. "Girls, Matthew, don't you have some chores to do? Maybe you should do them now before supper."

"I did mine this morning," Mary Ruth said. "Then we helped Ellen at the store," she explained to her aunt and uncle. "Ellen minded Asa and Joel for Neziah today. I straightened the shelves and put out new craft items, 'cause Dinah wasn't there to help. Matthew swept the floor, but mostly he kept the Shetler boys busy and out of trouble. Then, after she closed the shop, Ellen bought us all ice cream."

Before Lizzie could ask more about the children's day, Ezekiel and Jonas rushed into the room, drawing everyone's attention. The younger boys had been playing quietly in their room.

"Onkel Zack!" they cried in unison, *"Endie* Esther!" They ran closer, nearly colliding with Zack's chair.

Ezekiel halted in front of Zack. "Can we go to town again?"

"Ja, Zeke," he said with a gentle smile. "Soon."

"Can I come, too?" Jonas asked, moving closer. Lizzie

spotted her son's bandaged hand and became alarmed. She'd forgotten to tell Zack about Jonas's accident during the short time he'd been back. Had Zack noticed? "I didn't get to go last time."

"Then you should come," Zack said. He spied Jonas's bandage and frowned. "Jonas, what happened to your hand?"

Lizzie felt sick to her stomach as she waited for her son's answer.

Jonas stood taller and said, "I had an accident. It's better now. *Mam* took me to the doctor, and I got quilted." He raised his bandaged hand to better show it off.

Despite his initial concern, Zack looked amused. "Quilted?"

"Stitches," Hannah said before Lizzie could explain.

Jonas tugged on the gauze. "*Nay*, Jonas," Lizzie said quickly. "You mustn't take off the wrapping. You can show your stitches to *Onkel* Zack later."

"I won't be able to play baseball until my hand gets better," the boy said. "But we can play then, *ja*?"

The creases across Zack's forehead deepened. "*Ja*, we can play then."

He met Lizzie's gaze and raised his eyebrows questioningly. Lizzie silently mouthed, "I'll explain later."

The children's prattle kept their aunt and uncle entertained for the rest of the afternoon and during supper. They ate fried chicken, mashed potatoes and the green beans that Lizzie had put up fresh that summer. They shared apple pie and upside-down chocolate cake— Lizzie's favorite—afterward. As the day waned and the sky darkened, Esther and Zack stood.

"Time to head home," Zack said. "It's been a long day. A *goot* day, but a tiring one."

"*Ja*," Esther agreed. "We will see *ya* tomorrow and

then we can spend more time together." The children were clearly happy to have them back.

Lizzie walked them to the door. *"Guten nacht."*

"Guten nacht, Lizzie," Esther said as she headed toward the cottage.

Zack lingered outside the farmhouse, leaving the two of them alone. There was a long moment of silence while he gazed out over the yard. Finally he turned toward Lizzie and startled her when he said, "You look pale."

Zack studied Lizzie, noting the changes in her since he'd left. She looked tired and ill. Was she in pain? "Is your hip bothering you?"

She jerked with surprise. "I'm fine." She stepped off the porch and into the yard. The evening had turned cool. The scent of autumn filled the clean crisp air, dried leaves, the lingering aroma of baked goods, the bread and pies that Lizzie had made earlier in the day. As if feeling the chill, Lizzie hugged herself with her arms.

I'm worried about her! Zack felt unsettled. This concern for Lizzie was a new feeling for him, and he didn't know whether or not he liked it. He couldn't take his eyes off her. His gaze caressed her lovely features, her vivid green eyes and dark auburn hair.

"Zack—"

"Lizzie—" They had spoken simultaneously.

Lizzie chuckled. "You go first," she said.

He hesitated and then said, "I'm sorry we had to leave the way we did."

She seemed surprised by his apology. "Your *mam* hurt herself. Your *schweschter* called you home. I understood."

But Zack felt she deserved an explanation. "We've had cause to worry about her," he admitted. "Four years

ago, *Mam* found a lump—it was cancer. She had chemotherapy at a medical center near Millersburg. That's
why we moved from Walnut Creek. At the time, we decided the best thing for us to do was to move closer to the
treatment center and the doctors who were helping her."

"I'm sorry," Lizzie said, sounding sincere. Her lovely
green eyes regarded him with compassion. He studied
her smooth skin, pert nose and pink lips and found that
he liked her…a lot.

He acknowledged her compassion with a nod. *"Danki."*
He gestured toward the porch steps in a silent request for
them to sit, and they sat down, next to each other on the
second step. *"Mam* has moved in with Miriam. We didn't
want her to be alone while we were gone." Zack detected
the light scent of soap and a fragrance that was hers alone.
Lizzie seemed vulnerable and delicate beside him, but he
knew—had seen it for himself—that she was stronger
than she looked. He'd never known another woman with
her physical limitations who could do what she did day
in and day out for her children, the house and the farm
without complaint. *And she's managing well*, he thought.

It was hard to picture Abraham's first wife, Ruth, as a
mother to seven children. She'd been helpless, delicate,
unwilling to do much without Abraham's help. He'd understood the enormity of his brother's love for his young
wife—recognized everything Abraham had to do in order
to keep the woman he adored happy. Had his brother
cared about Lizzie in the same way?

Lizzie. He barely noticed her limp anymore. The only
time he saw it was when it became more pronounced
after she did too much around the farm and her hip gave
her great pain. Not that she said a word. She continued on
as if she hadn't done the work of three women in one day.

Zack admired her strength, her determination and the

love she bore for his nieces and nephews. *And she quilts and makes crafts, too, bringing money into the household for any items the children need.* She continued to amaze him.

"Zack?" She eyed him with concern, and he realized that he'd been silent as he took his time studying her, thinking about her. "About Jonas?"

He sensed that she'd grown uncomfortable. *"Ja?"*

"I should have told you. Jonas's accident was my fault."

"Yours?" He arched an eyebrow. "How so?"

"He and Zeke got into the barn, where they didn't belong. Jonas found Abraham's old sickle. It happened so fast. One minute Jonas and Ezekiel were playing outside the kitchen window where I could see them, and in the next I heard a sharp cry." She stood and began to pace, clearly upset by what had happened. "I hurried outside to see what was wrong and I saw Zeke as he ran from inside the barn. He was crying that Jonas had hurt himself."

"And that makes the accident your fault?" he asked.

She nodded. "I let the boys out of my sight. If I'd been more vigilant—"

Zack regarded her with fond amusement. "They are boys being boys, Lizzie. When I was their age, my *mam* fretted that I was always into trouble and getting hurt. You have seven children. Do you honestly believe that you can keep track of all of them every minute of every day?"

She seemed shocked by his reaction. He became startled to see her eyes fill with tears. Had she been that worried about his reaction? She who looked vulnerable but was in actuality strong?

"You don't blame me for Jonas's injury?" she rasped in a shocked whisper.

"*Nay*, I don't blame you. Why should I? Should I blame myself because I wasn't in Honeysuckle to prevent it from happening?"

"*Nay*, but—"

"But you were on the farm," he said, anticipating her next words. "Lizzie, you are a *goot mudder* to my *brooder*'s children. Never let anyone say anything differently about you."

He was pleased to see that she was humbled by his praise.

She stared at him, clearly fighting tears until she smiled and sat down, and his day suddenly brightened. "I'm glad you're back," she admitted softly.

He returned her grin. "I'm glad you missed me," he said with a teasing twinkle. She rose to her feet, and Zack wanted to tell her to sit; he wasn't ready to leave her company, but he understood. She was a woman who had to care for children and a busy household. *I'm going to make things easier for her*, he thought.

She seemed as if she wanted to go, but she still lingered a moment longer. "Zack?"

"*Ja?*"

"May I ask what kind of cancer your *mam* had?" Her green eyes were kind and sympathetic.

"Breast cancer." The memory of his mother's suffering still bothered him. *Mam* had gone through so much, yet she had finished the treatments with no sign of her earlier malignancy. *Thanks be to* Gott. "She is well now. The treatments were difficult but successful."

She looked relieved. "I'm happy that your *mudder* is all right."

He caressed her with his eyes; he couldn't help himself. He scolded himself when she suddenly looked uneasy. She averted her glance. He had frightened her with his attention, he realized, and knew enough to be careful in the future if he didn't want to scare her away.

"I am, too," he admitted and smiled warmly at her. He stood, straightened a black suspender and set his hat on his head. "I'll be in the *dawdi haus* if you need me. See you tomorrow."

"Tomorrow," she murmured with a nod.

As he left to cross the yard, Zack thought about Lizzie. He'd been gone only two days, but it felt as though he had been away too long.

She is Abraham's wife. He felt as if he was betraying his brother with his growing feelings for Lizzie, but he couldn't stop himself from caring about her.

Chapter Eleven

It felt good to have Zack and Esther back. Lizzie knew that she was being foolish since there was still a chance that he wanted to take over the farm, but she liked him. How could she not? He was charming, kind and he'd understood about her son's injury. *Zack doesn't blame me for Jonas's accident.* She'd experienced tremendous relief.

Saturday during those few moments alone with him, she should have brought up the farm, but it hadn't seemed right. She had told Zack about Jonas and that had seemed like more than enough for one day. Then yesterday there had been no opportunity for discussion, as they'd spent the day at Rachel and Peter's farm. *A wonderful-goot visiting Sunday and I didn't want to ruin it.*

This morning as she worked to rid her vegetable garden of the finished plants, she glanced toward Zack, who examined the animals out in the pasture. He reached up to stroke the mare's nose then hunkered down to check her hooves. He picked up something from the ground. As he rose to his full height, he caught sight of her and waved.

A sudden warmth filling her chest, she watched him

head in her direction. Zack carried his straw hat and a slight breeze tousled his dark hair, making him appear more attractive and approachable. He wore a royal blue shirt and black suspenders with his navy triblend pants. He had black work boots on his feet, and he carried a horse-feed bucket in his opposite hand.

"Hallo," he said with a smile. "Hard at work, I see." He set the bucket on the ground and the hat on his head.

Lizzie returned his smile. "I decided to clean up the garden before winter. The boys started the work, but—" she gestured toward a basket "—not everything is done. I just picked the last of the turnips." She leaned against the handle of her garden hoe, enjoying the cool breeze. "I like to work up the soil before the ground gets too hard." In the spring the weeds would cover the soil before she found the time to plant her early cool-weather crops.

Zack eyed what was left of her prized garden. "Do you need help?"

She wasn't offended, for she knew his offer was genuine and came from a good place. But she was almost done. *"Nay,* but I appreciate the thought. I'm about finished for today. I'm thinking of putting in more turnips."

"Couldn't hurt. You can pick them until late in the season."

"Ja." She hesitated and asked, "Do you like turnips?"

The smile transforming his face made her breath catch. "I've been known to take a second helping," he admitted.

"I'll plant more, then," she said. Lizzie tried not to notice how handsome he was.

They stood together for a moment in silence. She felt comfortable in the quiet, a fact that surprised her after recalling how awkward she'd felt in his presence previously.

"Rosebud is doing much better with her new shoe," she said of the mare.

"Ja," he said. "Mark Hostetler did a fine job of replacing it." A few minutes passed, yet he seemed reluctant to leave.

Lizzie was delighted. "Do you have enough bread?" she asked. "I've got some in the house and I'll be happy to make more."

Zack's dark gaze twinkled. "You provided us with enough bread in the cottage freezer to feed the entire congregation," he teased.

She blushed. "I wanted to make sure you had enough." She paused. "It's not that you're not welcome to eat with us." Jonas and Ezekiel ran out of the house and headed in their direction. "Will you take supper with us?" she asked before the boys descended upon their uncle.

"Ja." He grinned at the boys as they reached his side. "We'd like that."

"Onkel Zack?" Jonas asked. "Can I come help you today?"

"You mustn't get in your *onkel*'s way," Lizzie warned.

Zack reached out to ruffle the boy's hair. "You can help, but only if you do what I say and stay close. *Ja?*"

Jonas bobbed his head in agreement and grinned.

"Can I come, too?" Zeke asked, looking as if he was afraid he'd be forced to stay home with his *mam.*

"You can come, too," Zack assured him with a smile. He lifted his youngest nephew's hat and then set it back on his head at a different angle. "Where's your hat, Jonas?"

The boy shifted from one foot to the other as if he had energy to burn. "In my room."

Zack gestured toward the house. "You'd best get it.

It's going to be a sunny day. A man needs his hat to keep the sun from his eyes."

He waited while Jonas ran into the house and returned with his straw hat moments later. "I'm going to wear my hat like a man," the boy said.

Zack nodded. He glanced toward the barn. "Time for chores," he told his nephews. "Ready?" He smiled at the boys as they bobbed their heads. He redirected his smile toward Lizzie. "I'll see you at supper."

The warmth in his expression made her tingle. "Zack!" she cried out impulsively as he and the boys headed toward the barn. *Ask him about the farm*, her inner voice prompted. *Tell him you need to talk with him later.*

Zack stopped and faced her, and she tensed inside. She knew she should ask him, but she didn't want to spoil the moment. *Tonight.* She'd ask him tonight.

"I appreciate your help around the farm," she said. "And for including the boys."

He grinned. "'Tis my pleasure, Lizzie." Then he continued toward the barn with her young sons running to keep up with his long strides.

"We'll see you for supper, *Mam*," Jonas called over his shoulder as they reached the barn.

"What about lunch?" she asked loudly. She watched as Zack leaned close to whisper to the two boys.

"We're going to eat with *Onkel* Zack in the *dawdi haus*," Jonas said. She saw Zack lean to tell the boy something more. "That's all right, *ja*?"

She could feel the intensity of Zack's gaze across the distance. "That's fine, Jonas. Be *goot* boys and listen to your uncle."

"Ja!" her sons cried, and she caught Zack's answering grin. *That such a simple thing could make the boys and this man happy...*

Lizzie returned to work, feeling lighthearted. When Zack had first come, she'd had no idea that she'd be glad to have him on the farm. *He's* goot *for the children—and me.* The thought frightened her as much as it gave her pleasure. After supper, she would ask him about his intentions regarding the property, and everything would be fine.

Movement near the cottage caught her eye as Esther exited the house.

"*Goot* morning, Esther!" Lizzie cried.

"Lizzie!" Smiling, Esther headed in her direction. "Clearing the garden for the spring?"

"Ja." She set down her garden rake and reached for the garden hoe. "But I was thinking about putting in another planting of turnips."

"Sounds *goot*," Esther said with a grin. "We love turnips."

"You'll be coming to supper, *ja*? Zack said he thought you wouldn't mind."

"I never mind spending time with you and the children." Esther picked up a rake and began to work up a section of ground that had been previously dug up by Lizzie's children. "I'd like to contribute. How about a pie? Or some biscuits?"

Lizzie understood Esther's desire to contribute to the meal. When she and Abraham had been asked to the neighbors' for supper, Lizzie had insisted on bringing a side dish or dessert. The two women discussed what Lizzie planned for supper, and it was decided that Esther would bake apple muffins and cook the turnips that Lizzie had picked earlier that morning.

Lizzie handed Esther the turnip basket. "I'll see you later," she said. "You're more than welcome to join me for lunch."

Esther shook her head. "I'll eat something at the cottage."

"Zack plans to feed the boys there."

"We have plenty of *goot* food, thanks to you." Esther set down the rake. "I'll see you at supper. If you need me, come get me. I'll be in the *dawdi haus*. I'll be happy to help."

Lizzie regarded the woman fondly. "You're always nice to me."

"And why wouldn't I be? We're family," Esther said.

Her throat tightened with emotion. "*Ja*, we are," she replied. As Esther left her to her work, Lizzie grinned. This was the first time she believed that her late husband's siblings regarded her as family. She felt hopeful.

Esther returned to the house and went to her room. It was good to be back in Honeysuckle. She dusted the furniture and swept the floor. When she was done, she headed toward the kitchen with a corn broom in hand. She heard a hard rap on the back door.

"*Hallo?* Is anyone home?" a deep familiar voice called out.

David? Esther froze. Why would he be visiting the cottage? She was suddenly nervous. Her dress was wrinkled from doing chores. She touched her hair, wondering if it was still neatly pinned into place.

It was still hard to realize that David had gone on with his life and wed, as if the two of them hadn't been sweethearts. She was still single, and it was embarrassing.

"Esther?"

Heart racing, her stomach fluttering, she answered the door. "David."

He smiled and her nape tingled. He was extremely handsome. "I thought I'd stop in to say hello. I thought it was you at last Sunday's service, but I couldn't stay afterward. I found out it was you after you'd gone back to Ohio." His eyes were warm as he studied her. "And now you're home again."

She nodded mutely, recalling how much she'd loved him when they were younger.

"May I come in?"

She gasped. Where were her manners? "*Ja*, of course." She opened the door and watched as he brushed by her as he entered her kitchen. She was aware of his familiar scent, and the memories came flooding back of the times they'd spent together. "Tea?" she offered.

He nodded and sat at her kitchen table. "How is your *mudder*?" he asked.

Her hands shook slightly as she put on the teakettle. She held them behind her as she faced him until she felt in control again. "*Mam* is well. Miriam sent word that she'd fallen, but she was unhurt. We all worry about her since her cancer diagnosis."

David looked concerned. "She has cancer? I didn't know."

"How could you?" she said. His kind eyes made her relax. Suddenly it was as if they were young again and she felt at ease in his presence. He was married. She had nothing to fear. David had been an honorable boy, and she knew he wouldn't have changed. He was still honorable as a man.

The kettle whistled and she turned back to take it off the burner. She poured two cups of tea and sat down across from him. He'd moved on with his life and it bothered her that he'd found someone else to love and marry, although she had no right to be upset. He wasn't the one who'd left Honeysuckle. She wanted to ask him about his wife, but she didn't dare.

Thirteen years later and life had changed for each of them. David, at twenty-eight, had married and become a preacher. At twenty-seven, she'd spent her life taking care of her mother after her surgery and throughout her cancer treatments.

She realized that he was watching her, and she blushed. "*Mam* had breast cancer. Her chemotherapy treatments were successful. It was rough for a while, but she has been cancer-free for years now."

He looked relieved. "I'm glad to hear it. I shall keep her in my prayers."

"*Danki,*" she whispered. She took a sip of tea and set her cup into its saucer. "Would you like a cookie? I have some gingersnaps in the pantry." She started to rise.

"*Nay,* Esther. I can't stay long. I left my youngest son with Lizzie. He wanted to play with Jonas and Ezekiel, but they're out doing chores with Zack." He gave her a crooked smile. "I'm sure she's had enough of him by now."

"*Nay.* Lizzie loves children." She paused as her curiosity got the better of her. "You have a son?"

"I have two—Jacob and Jed. Jacob is five and Jed a year older."

Esther smiled, picturing the two young boys as younger versions of their father. "You've been blessed."

He nodded. David took one last swallow of tea and then rose. "It's *goot* to see you again, Esther. I'm glad you are home." The sudden intensity of his look made her face heat and her belly burn. "How long will you be staying?"

She shrugged. "I'm not sure. Zack asked me to come. He hasn't made any plans to leave just yet." She managed a smile. "We'll be here for a while anyway."

David grinned. "*Goot.* Then I shall see you again. Say *hallo* to Zack. Tell him that I was asking after him."

She followed him to the door. "I will."

"*Willkomm* home, Esther." He smiled at her and left.

She watched as he crossed the yard toward the main farmhouse. It was wonderful to see him again, but she shouldn't think anything of it. He didn't ask if she'd married. Perhaps because he knew that she was still a spinster? *Why did he come?*

David was the preacher and he simply wanted to welcome her back into the community. She stood at the door a long time, hoping for a glimpse of David's son, but gave up when there was no sign of them several minutes later. Seeing him again after all these years rattled her. He had made a new life for himself and it was time she started thinking about doing the same thing.

The weather had turned cool, but it was near harvest time, so the colder temperatures were to be expected. As she hung up the laundry to dry, Lizzie smiled at the sweet melodic chirping of birds raised in song. She realized with sudden sadness that winter would soon chase most of the birds away. *Will I have to leave, too?* There had been no time alone to talk with Zack last night. The children had kept him occupied with discussions about school and their Amish-community friends.

She pinned a pillowcase to the clothesline and then paused a moment to rub her hands together quickly to warm them. The older children were in school. Jonas and Ezekiel were with Zack in the back acreage, where he was instructing the boys about the importance of their farm crops and what it took to run a property of this size. She didn't know whether or not her sons understood Zack, but what she did know was that the boys loved spending time with their uncle.

She pinned a dress on the clothesline, then bent for another wet garment. A sudden breeze stirred the air, giving her a chill. She contemplated running inside for a heavy coat, but then the wind stopped, and the sun warmed her. Lizzie loved this time of year. The leaves on the trees splashed the landscape with color in bright and varying shades of gold, orange and red. The air was crisp and invigorating, especially during early-morning and late-evening hours before and after the sun made its appearance in the autumn sky.

Her hip tended to bother her more at this time of year, but she wasn't concerned. She was often too busy to pay much attention to the pain. This was the season for family and friends to get in their harvest before winter descended and snow carpeted the countryside. By early November, the crops would be in, the work done, and then it would be time for weddings within the community.

Until then, there was much to be done. At supper last night Zack had let her know that he'd be starting the harvest on Wednesday of next week. When Abraham was alive, he'd worked for days bringing in the crops and ensuring that the grain and hay were properly stored for future use. Her husband had never asked for, nor would he have accepted, help from his community.

Did Zack feel the same way? Bringing in the crops seemed like too much farmwork for one man. Matthew could help, but it would take five days, probably more, for the two of them to finish the job. And that was being generous in her assumption that the two of them alone could get the job done.

She wondered about Peter and Rachel. Would they

work with their neighbors to finish the harvest more quickly?

Lizzie secured her daughter's newly washed black *kapp* to the line. As soon as she was done, she would search for Zack, tell him that she had to talk with him. She could no longer put off talking about the farm, no matter the outcome of their discussion.

The low rumbling sound of tires crunching on dirt drew her attention. She moved closer for a better look as a dark automobile pulled down the driveway and parked near the farmhouse. The English driver got out of the vehicle and opened the rear door for the person in the backseat. An Amish woman stepped out.

Curious, Lizzie moved closer for a better look as the driver opened the trunk and pulled out a suitcase, which he set on the ground near the passenger. He then climbed back into his car and, with a wave, drove away.

"Mam!" Esther burst out of the *dawdi haus* and ran toward the woman in the yard, and Lizzie immediately knew the identity of their visitor.

As Esther reached her side, her mother smiled. Lizzie hung back, hesitant to intrude, anxious to meet her late husband's mother. And then she saw Zack crossing the pasture flanked by her two youngest sons.

Esther gestured toward the Fisher males and said something to her mother. The older woman nodded and waved at them.

Lizzie was unsure if she should come forward as Zack and his nephews slipped through an opening in the fence. Zack locked the gate behind them. She saw him speak briefly with the boys, who stared at their grandmother as they drew closer.

Esther spied her standing in the distance. "Lizzie," she called, "come and meet our *mudder*."

Their *mam* spun to face her, watched Lizzie's hesitant, uneven gait as she came forward. *I have nothing to be ashamed of*, she told herself, knowing that she'd done her best to take care of the children and the farm. As she studied her late husband's mother, she thought of Abraham. *Except for one thing.*

Her late husband's mother was of average size and wore a green dress, white cape and apron and a white *kapp* on her sandy-brown hair. Were her eyes brown like Esther's? Lizzie couldn't see from this distance. The woman's appearance on the farm made her nervous. What was she doing here?

Afraid and uneasy, Lizzie froze, unable to move on. She must pleasantly welcome her mother-in-law while putting her fears and misgivings aside.

Zack and the children reached the woman first, and for a moment, Zack's mother focused her attention on Lizzie's sons. It gave Lizzie a moment to observe the woman interacting with her two youngest.

"My, but you are big boys!" their grandmother exclaimed.

Jonas puffed up and nodded. "I'm Jonas. I'm four."

She smiled. "*Ja. Hallo*, Jonas." She turned to Zeke. "You must be Ezekiel. Your *endie* told me all about you."

Zeke widened his eyes as he peeked at Zack for guidance. Zack grinned as he placed a hand on the boy's shoulder.

"*Mam!*" Zeke exclaimed suddenly when he saw Lizzie. Conscious of her limp, she tried to walk so it wouldn't be as noticeable. "*Grossmama*'s come for a visit!"

Lizzie regarded Zeke with affection as she reached them. "*Ja.* Isn't it nice that she's here to see us?" Zeke bobbed his head. She turned to Zack's mother. "*Hallo*, I'm—"

"Elizabeth King Fisher," the woman finished with a smile. "You're my eldest son's widow."

The smile left her face. Lizzie nodded solemnly as she was hit hard by the painful memory of Abraham's death. His mother had suffered the loss, too, and she'd learned of her son's death only recently. "He was a *goot* man," she said. "I'm sorry."

"The loss is also yours." Zack's mother's gaze warmed in shared sympathy. "I'm Sarah Fisher." She paused. "And you are my daughter."

Sarah's words touched her deeply. "It's nice to meet you," Lizzie greeted. *Her eyes are the same color as Esther's and the same shape as Zack's.* She also saw her late husband's features in his mother's face.

"*Mam,*" Zack asked with concern, "what are you doing here?"

Lizzie felt a little better knowing that Zack hadn't asked his mother to come. She had visions of Zack declaring the farm his and them all moving into the farmhouse. Where would that leave her?

Zack's mother raised her eyebrows as she gazed at her son. "I've come to see my son and *dochter.* And I've come to meet Lizzie and my *kins kinner.*"

"But we only just left. I would have stayed and accompanied you if I'd known."

Sarah shrugged. "Ted Harris brought me. When I heard he was coming through Lancaster on his way to visit his daughter in New Jersey, I was happy to ride with him."

"Ted is a neighbor," Zack explained to Lizzie. He looked relieved that his mother had come with someone they apparently knew well. He lifted his mother's suitcase. "You must be tired. I'll show you to your room so that you can unpack and rest."

"*Nay*, Zack," Sarah said as he started toward the cottage. "I'll stay in the farmhouse with Lizzie." She sought Lizzie's gaze for approval. "Do you have room for me?"

Heart racing and a little bit afraid, Lizzie nodded. "*Ja.*" She managed a smile. "We have plenty of room." She made a quick decision about where she would move the two younger girls. Rebecca could sleep with Hannah and Mary Ruth. And Anne could move into her bedroom. That would leave Sarah a double bed in a fair-sized, comfortable room.

"*Goot!*" Sarah appeared satisfied. "You and I can become acquainted, and I can get to know my *kins kinner.*"

Zack seemed surprised. "*Mam*, are you sure you want to stay in the big *haus*? *Dat*—"

"Your *vadder* passed on years ago," Sarah said. "Since then, I've lived a lifetime."

Zack narrowed his eyes as if gauging his mother's reaction. He smiled, apparently pleased with what he saw. He captured Lizzie's gaze as if trying to read her reaction to his *mam*'s presence.

Seeing his concern, Lizzie smiled at him reassuringly. She could do this—be gracious and kind to her late husband's mother, the woman who had given birth to two caring sons and a wonderful daughter.

"Come inside, and we'll have tea," she invited. "Zack, I'll show you where to put your *mudder*'s suitcase."

Chapter Twelve

Zack followed Lizzie, his mother and his sister into the farmhouse. If Lizzie had reservations about her uninvited guest, she hid them well.

He had to respect the way she was handling his *mam*'s surprise visit. He himself had been stunned to see his mother. He and Esther had rushed home only days earlier, because she had suffered a terrible fall. But when they'd reached Walnut Creek, where his mother had moved in with his older sister, his only living parent had looked shockingly well, and his eldest sister, Miriam, had appeared sheepish.

Mam had been delighted to see him and Esther, although they hadn't been gone from home long. You would have thought by the way she'd acted that *Mam* hadn't seen them in years.

Later, while his mother was busy visiting with Esther, he'd pulled Miriam aside and asked the real reason why they'd been summoned home.

"*Mam* fell and got hurt," his sister had said. "She didn't seem herself. I was frightened for her. Her behavior right before she fell alarmed me. She was acting strangely."

Strangely? He'd frowned. "She's all right now? She seems fine."

"*Ja.* Thanks be to *Gott.*" Miriam had looked relieved. "It's as if she didn't fall. Do *ya* think 'tis possible that she suffered some kind of episode?" His sister clearly had been concerned. "She had all those terrible cancer treatments."

Zack had studied his mother from across the room. He had to admit that the treatments had seemed harsh, even worse than the disease. But *Mam* had come out of her surgery and subsequent chemotherapy surprisingly well. In fact, she'd looked better than she had in a long time. "If she did have an episode, it's passed. Keep a close eye on her after we go back. If it happens again, let us know."

Something flickered in Miriam's expression. "You're going back?"

He nodded. "Lizzie will need help with the harvest. The children—" He smiled. "I enjoy spending time with them. I've barely gotten to know them, and I don't want us to be strangers."

"How does Abraham's widow feel about this?"

Zack had shrugged. "She has been kind and gracious to Esther and me. It's obvious how much she loves the children, although I suspect that some of them haven't made life easy for her. She is a little thing, but she is strong. She works hard and never complains—"

Miriam had studied him closely. Her voice became quiet as she asked, "Do you have feelings for this girl?"

He'd felt an odd pull in his gut. "She's our late brother's widow."

"I know that, and that's not what I asked." She'd paused. "We usually don't have a choice in matters of the heart," his sister said.

"She's only nineteen."

"And yet she married our brother, who was at least sixteen years older." She paused. "Why would she agree to marry *him*?"

"I think her mother might have had a hand in Lizzie's decision. And the children needed a mother. She has great compassion for people, and I suspect she wasn't able to deny her love and care to seven motherless children. Perhaps she agreed because of the children."

Zack stared off in the distance, not really seeing. "She has a bad leg—or hip—I'm not sure which. I only know that there are times when she must experience great pain."

"Do you know what happened to Ruth?" she asked. They didn't usually speak of the dead, but it was a question that must have been on his sibling's mind because Zack had wondered about it himself.

"You know how Ruth was," he said as if it were the only explanation.

Miriam had nodded sadly. "*Ja.* I know. And there is no doubt you are right. Ruth wasn't a strong woman physically or emotionally." She hesitated. "And what of Rosemary?"

He had stiffened. "Has she come by the house looking for me again?" Rosemary Yost was a young Amish woman who had decided that she wanted him as her husband. He'd told her that they were nothing more than friends, but she was relentless in her pursuit of him.

"*Nay*, but she asks about you whenever we meet. We last saw her at church service and she wondered how you've been faring in Honeysuckle."

Closing his eyes, Zack sighed. "I told her that we were friends only."

"She is a stubborn one, that girl," his sister had said, and he'd agreed.

Now, days later back in Honeysuckle, Zack saw his mother comfortably seated in the farmhouse's kitchen and then looked to Lizzie for guidance. "Which room?" He held up his mother's suitcase.

"Up the stairs, turn right, first door to the left," she instructed without hesitation.

He smiled. *My old bedroom.* As he turned and headed toward the stairs, Zack heard his mother murmur to Lizzie. He thought he heard something about "boys" and "room." She was probably telling her that the room used to belong to him and Abe.

He stopped as he thought about his older brother. A wave of loss and pain hit him hard. His death had come as a shock. He remembered Abraham as a man with boundless energy, a hard worker, someone who had loved life and his wife Ruth to distraction.

Zack frowned as he climbed the stairs. Abe must have been devastated when he'd lost Ruth. His brother had loved her with a passion that went beyond anything Zack had ever seen. What would it be like to know such love?

A sudden thought occurred to him. Abraham had married again only a few weeks after Ruth's death. It must have been hard for Lizzie to marry a grief-stricken, devastated widower and take on an entire household of grieving, motherless children. The notion bothered him. Lizzie hadn't suffered life easily, and he, his sister and mother were making things more difficult for her.

He reached the top landing, then headed down the hall to his old bedroom. When he entered, he was pleased to find that the room was plain but clearly feminine and would be much to his mother's liking. A lovely quilt in ivory, greens and blues covered the double bed. From the dresses hanging on a wall peg, he realized that two, if not all, of the girls slept here, which meant that Lizzie was making adjustments to the household in order to accommodate his mother. It was usual for women to allow for unexpected guests within the Amish community; a door was always open for family or friends to stay, but Lizzie had lost her husband recently after nearly two years of marriage.

Zack set the valise near the end of the double bed and then returned downstairs. He entered the kitchen to find Lizzie, Esther and his mother chatting and smiling over cups of tea.

A pound cake sat in the center of the table, cut into slices. Each woman had a plate with a piece and some-one—most probably Lizzie—had cut a slice for him and put it before an empty chair.

He sat down and smiled at Lizzie gratefully. He saw her blush and then look away, and he was charmed. She might have been his brother's wife, but she was on his mind a lot lately. At this moment, he was enjoying himself too much to be worried.

Lizzie sat with the Fisher family in the kitchen, wondering why she felt more comfortable in their presence than she did with her own family. She loved her parents and siblings; they all meant well, even if they did treat her differently. Her mother kept herself distant from her, as if she was afraid to face the fact that she'd given birth to a daughter who was less than perfect. She knew her mother loved her, in her own way, but she felt the love *Mam* gave to her brothers and sisters more. Only William treated her like everyone else, and she adored him for it.

"More cake?" she asked when everyone had consumed a helping.

"I've had enough." Sarah smiled her thanks.

"I'll have another," Zack said with a grin. He extended his plate toward her. "It's delicious."

Lizzie smiled, amused, as she cut him a huge chunk of butter pound cake and set it carefully on his plate.

He laughed, pulled the cake closer and then dived into eating it as if it was the best thing he'd ever tasted.

She watched with a strange surge of fondness until she realized that Esther was watching her and not her brother. Lizzie caught the speculative look in Esther's soft-brown eyes and looked away. Did Esther suspect that she liked Zack but was torn over her growing feelings? Did Zack's sister know something that she didn't? Something that made Esther feel sorry for her? Like Zack's plans for the farm? As her stomach burned, she swallowed against a suddenly tight throat. "More tea?" she asked her mother-in-law.

"*Ja.* It's delicious." Sarah accepted a second cup of tea. "What time do the children arrive home from *schule*?" she asked pleasantly as she set down her filled teacup.

"Soon. Usually right around two thirty," Lizzie said.

The woman glowed with pleasure. "I'm eager to see the rest of my *kins kinner*."

"They are wonderful children," Lizzie said, warming to her. "Do you have others?"

"Miriam has nine children," Sarah said. "Her eldest son, John, is married with two *kinner*—Jane and Jacob. Her daughter Mae, Miriam's oldest, has four and is expecting a fifth. I have sixteen grandchildren and six and soon-to-be seven great-grandchildren."

"You are truly blessed to have such a large family and so many *kins kinner*," Lizzie said.

"*Ja*, I feel blessed. I thank the Lord every day that I am here to enjoy each and every one of them."

Lizzie recalled Sarah's fight against cancer. "I can understand why." She felt a sharp jolt of pain as she thought of the child she had wanted desperately but lost. She blinked back tears as she stood quickly, and with head bowed, she began to gather up the dirty dishes. She went to the sink and filled a basin with water.

"Lizzie?" Zack whispered, leaning close. He had come up from behind her where she stood at the kitchen sink. "Are you well? Is your hip hurting?"

She felt the impact of his nearness. The rumble of his deep voice shivered against her skin. Shaking her head no, she reached to wipe the corner of her eye with the edge of a dish towel, then turned to smile at him reassuringly. "I'm fine, Zack."

He considered her a long moment until the heat rose in her face. He didn't move, and Lizzie was stunned to realize that she liked having him close. Shaken, she hid her trembling hands in the water as she went back to doing dishes.

"What are you two whispering about?" Sarah asked.

Lizzie knew some measure of relief when he stepped back. She sensed rather than saw Zack shrug as if they had spoken of nothing much. "I know we just enjoyed Lizzie's delicious pound cake," he said, "but when is supper?"

His mother and sister laughed. Amused, despite herself, Lizzie relaxed, her anxiety easing. "You're hungry still?" she asked him, capturing his gaze.

His expression cleared as if he were relieved to see her smile. "I like food."

"You like cake," Esther interjected with a laugh.

"I'll bake another," Lizzie suggested. "What kind?"

"Apple, chocolate." At that moment, he looked boyishly appealing, and she could see him as an eleven-year-old boy at the time of his father's death. She blinked, trying to banish the mental image. She didn't need to be thinking of Zack as anything but her late husband's brother.

"Apple chocolate?" She furrowed her brow as she thought. "I haven't heard of that recipe."

"Both," his mother explained.

Before Lizzie could question her, Esther spoke up. "He wants both apple *and* chocolate cake. He's telling you that he likes both kinds."

Lizzie examined the man next to her, enjoying the sight of his stunning good looks. "I can make both." And his handsome face brightened as his lips curved upward. She felt something akin to happiness flush her with warmth.

He leaned across the sink as he reached for a cup and placed it in the dish basin. *"Danki,"* he leaned close to whisper before he shifted back.

The warmth of his breath brushed her neck, her ear, and then was gone, leaving her reeling from feelings she had no right to experience—or want.

Chapter Thirteen

The supper table was filled with noisy laughter and conversation. Lizzie watched with pleasure the way the children interacted with their grandmother. They were clearly overjoyed to see her. Her daughter Anne grinned happily at Lizzie, obviously relieved and glad that her *grossmama* was so nice.

Zack sat at the other end of the table, teasing Matthew, who seemed to blossom under his uncle's attention.

"*Onkel* Zack, it's nearly harvest time, isn't it?"

"*Ja*, Matt. It is." Zack addressed her. "I spoke with Peter Zook. He is going to help bring in the harvest. Afterward, we'll go to his place and do the same."

Lizzie was pleased at the news. "Peter's wife, Rachel, is my oldest and dearest friend," she explained for Sarah's benefit. "She will be coming, too?" she asked Zack.

"*Ja*. And why would she not? She offered to bring her specialty dish. She said you would know what that is."

Lizzie laughed. "*Ja*. I know."

Zack stared at her. "And you'll not tell us?"

"*Nay*," she said. "I'll let it be her surprise."

"*Mam*, may I help with the food?" Mary Ruth asked. Lizzie, stunned by her eldest daughter calling her *Mam*, realized that she was staring. She grinned. "I wouldn't have it any other way."

"We can all help," Esther said. "We can work together here—if that is all right, Lizzie."

Lizzie inclined her head with a small smile curving her lips. "I'll enjoy that."

Suddenly, there was excitement among the Fisher females about what to cook and bake for the harvest meal and who would make which dish. The eagerness of her daughters to assist thrilled Lizzie as did Esther's and Sarah's delight in participating and being here, on the farm, for the event.

After the main meal, Zack came up to her with dishes in his hands and a soft smile on his attractive face. Lizzie looked at him in disbelief. "You're helping in the kitchen?" she said. "That's women's work. My father and brothers would never— Zack, you don't have to do that. With all the girls in this house, we have plenty of help."

"I know it's not usual for most men, but I honestly don't mind. I did chores for my *mudder* while she was ill. I just got into the habit of helping, I guess."

Lizzie took the plates from him and put them in the dishwater. "Well, it's not necessary, though it is appreciated." She picked up a bowl of mashed potatoes and tried to brush past him to get to the refrigerator to put them away. But Zack didn't move to allow her to pass. In fact, he shifted to block her exit.

Overwhelmed by intense feelings for him, she experienced alarm. "Zack—"

He placed a hand on her arm. With the weather cooler, she had taken to wearing her long-sleeved green dress. Still, despite the cotton fabric between his fingers and her, she felt the warmth of his touch as if his hand had encircled her bare skin.

"Lizzie," he asked softly, "are you happy here on the farm?"

She shot him a startled gaze. "Happy? *Ja.* Of course I'm happy. Why would you ask?"

There was warmth in his dark, nearly black eyes. "You do so much for everyone. I've realized how much you've sacrificed to be here for the children—and my *brooder.*" His mention of his brother was said in an agonized whisper, but she didn't glimpse anything in his expression but caring and concern for her.

She thought of her hurried wedding and her and Abraham's subsequent life together afterward. It had been rough going at first, but then it had quickly become rewarding because of Annie, Jonas and little Zeke, who had needed her desperately. Annie had been three, Jonas two, while Ezekiel, the baby, had been barely a year old.

"Don't imagine me as anything more than I am. A simple, plain woman who has done her best for her husband and children," Lizzie warned him, though she was pleased by his words.

"*Ja,* but they weren't your children."

She gasped and felt the blood leave her face. "They are my children—the children of my heart. I love them and you can't say otherwise."

Zack furrowed his brow. "Lizzie—"

Lizzie blinked back tears. "Excuse me a moment." She left the kitchen and hurried up the stairs to her bedroom. Once inside her room, she shut the door and leaned against it. *I was wrong. He doesn't regard me as family. He doesn't understand how I feel about the children.*

She breathed deeply, trying to calm herself. Closing her eyes, she replayed in her mind her conversation with Zack. She straightened and moved toward the bed, where she sat down. The mattress gave under her weight and she bent over, cradling her head in her hands.

Zack didn't mean to hurt me, she thought. He had been so nice to her at times that she'd believed she'd weep happy tears, having never experienced his level of kind concern.

She was angry with herself for caring what Zack thought, for caring about him. Given her marriage to his older brother and her current circumstances, she should be keeping herself emotionally distant from him.

She lost her battle with tears as she cried for her dead husband and for the children and the painful loss they'd suffered. She wept for the loss of her baby before the child had a chance to live. And for being afraid of losing everything—everyone—she'd ever cherished. While she may be falling in love with Zack, she knew for certain that they'd have no future together. How could they? He wanted the farm, not her. She could feel it in her heart.

A knock on her bedroom door made her spring to her feet. *"Ja?"* she asked.

"Lizzie?" It was Sarah. "Are you all right? Zack thought you weren't feeling well, and he's worried."

Lizzie wiped her eyes with both hands. "I'm fine. I'll be right down."

There was a long moment of silence, and then Zack's mother said, "If there is anything I can do, please let me know."

Her words made Lizzie smile. She went to the door, opened it. *"Danki."*

"I endured many such moments after Zack's father passed away." Sarah's answering smile was gentle.

Lizzie could only nod. If it were only the loss of her dead husband bothering her, then she would be happy to talk things through with her mother-in-law, a woman who had suffered greatly but come out the better for her losses. "I appreciate your kindness."

"Things will get better in time," Sarah said. "I never thought I'd be able to enter this *haus* again without seeing my husband, Daniel, without hurting." She placed an arm around Lizzie's shoulders and Lizzie resisted the temptation to lean into her.

"You seem to be doing well here," she said.

"Ja." Her mother-in-law looked past Lizzie into the room that she and her husband must have shared at one time. "I see him everywhere still, but it's now a *goot* feeling. I miss him, but I am happy again."

The two women made their way toward the stairs as they talked.

"You know about my cancer?" Sarah asked, meeting her glance.

Lizzie nodded. "Zack mentioned you were ill."

"Ja. It was terrible. I never expected it. I rarely get sick, and then to learn I had cancer and could die... Believe it or not, it wasn't the worst thing I'd ever lived through. That moment came when my husband died. He was gone and I was left with only the memory of his loving eyes and boyish smile. The cancer was awful, but when I was undergoing treatments, I'd lie in bed at night and think of my Daniel, and I knew he was there with me, encouraging me to fight this disease. He was telling me that there were family who still needed me and wanted me to live." Her eyes twinkled. "We Amish are pacifists, but battling cancer isn't a fight we should avoid."

"There is nothing in the *Ordnung* about turning the other cheek to cancer," Lizzie agreed, referring to the book of their faith and rules of Amish life. There was such emotion in Sarah's voice that Lizzie felt the urge to cry again.

Sarah's eyes filled with moisture. She laughed as she

blinked them away. "Enough tears, *ja*?" She reached for Lizzie's hand. "There are children downstairs who need you. And my son—he is sick over something he might have said to upset you." She seemed to be posing a question that Lizzie was unwilling to answer.

Lizzie squeezed gently, then released the woman's hand. "Then I guess we should finish the dishes so that we can enjoy dessert."

Sarah's lips twitched. "The dishes have been washed, dried and put away."

Lizzie laughed. "And the children are all waiting at the table for cake and ice cream."

"*Ja*, I'm afraid so."

Lizzie preceded Sarah through the house and into the kitchen. As Sarah had mentioned, the children—and Zack and Esther—were seated at the table, waiting for her return—and for dessert.

"Everyone ready for cake and ice cream?" she asked as she approached the table.

"*Ja!*" the children and Esther chorused together.

Zack, Lizzie saw, regarded her silently with worry in his expression. She knew then that he hadn't meant to hurt her. He probably still didn't know what he'd said wrong.

She had to pass him to get to the pantry, where she'd put the cakes—two of them—one chocolate and one apple. She grabbed both of them carefully and then reached over Zack's shoulder to set them on the table directly in front of him. She became instantly aware of his scent and his warmth as she rose hurriedly and moved to get the ice cream from the gas freezer in the back room.

She raised the lid to the chest freezer and leaned in to take hold of a tub of ice cream, one of the several she'd made earlier in the season while the little ones had napped and the older children had been in school. Abraham had been alive then, working on something out in the barn.

Lizzie spun around and nearly bumped into Zack, who had come silently into the room. She started to stumble, and he gently grabbed hold of her shoulders to steady her. "Zack!"

"Lizzie," he murmured. "I didn't mean to upset you." She saw his throat bob as he swallowed hard. "I'm sorry if I hurt you. You are a *goot* mother. I know you love the children as your own—and they *are* yours. Everyone can see it. I…" He hesitated, as if unsure how to best word what he wanted to say. "I'm only concerned with your happiness."

Lizzie looked at him in stunned amazement. "My happiness?"

He ran a hand across the back of his neck. "You work hard. You never complain. I know your leg—your hip— hurts you something awful at times, but you never let on that you're in pain." He stared at her with concerned obsidian eyes. "I'm worried about you."

"Zack, I'm well—"

"You may say so, but I think not. I worry. I can't help it. You need to take time for yourself, especially when you are hurting. Take a bath or a hot shower—"

She blushed and his eyes twinkled. "Why?" she teased. "Am I in need of washing?"

His gleaming gaze ran down the length of her, respectful but assessing and no less impactful to her state of mind. "You're in need of tender, loving care, Elizabeth King Fisher."

He took the ice cream bucket out of her hand and left the back room. Lizzie stayed behind for a moment, trying to still her rapidly beating heart and to come to grips with what he'd just said. *He cares for me.* Could it be that she was mistaken? Or was he simply a concerned brother-in-law looking out for his brother's widow? It was nice to have someone—Zack—care enough to be concerned.

Tucking a few stray strands of auburn hair beneath her prayer *kapp*, Lizzie drew herself upright, and ignoring her aching hip, she returned to the kitchen to happily join the others for dessert.

Chapter Fourteen

The week flew by despite the fact that Lizzie's world had shifted. Having another woman—her mother-in-law—in the house made her feel slightly on edge. It wasn't that Sarah Fisher wasn't kind and considerate. On the contrary, she was kindness to a fault. Lizzie realized that it was her own inadequacies that bothered her. Because of her bad hip, she was frequently afraid of falling. And she feared that she would say something unintentionally that would alert her husband's family to her responsibility in Abraham's death.

It was Friday, and this Sunday was church day. Lizzie had found out only that morning that services were being held at their farm. She had no idea why the location had changed unexpectedly. Her church community hadn't expected her to host services so soon after Abraham's death. Why had things suddenly changed? Was it because Abraham's family had moved onto the property?

"How did this happen?" she asked Zack as she met him that morning while crossing the yard toward the chicken coop. He was handsome as always in his work clothes as he was doing farm chores.

He raised a questioning eyebrow. "How did what happen?"

"Church services. I thought the Samuel Yoders were hosting this week."

Zack appeared surprised by her concern. "Their son James is ill. I thought we could fill in for them." As he looked at her, his dark eyes seemed to delve into her soul. His tone was soft as he continued, "It's been over two months since A—your husband died, Lizzie. Don't *ya* think it's time to return to the living?"

"By hosting service?" She scowled at him. "I live every day, Zack. I live for the children—and for the farm."

"When was the last time church service was held here?" he asked.

"The day before Abraham's death," she said, her eyes filling with tears. Annoyed with herself, she turned away.

"Lizzie—" he entreated, his deep voice causing a tingle to run down her spine. He sounded contrite. She paused and turned back. "I didn't know." His expression was kind and nearly her undoing.

She closed her eyes to shut out his attraction and to get herself under control. "I know you didn't." She lifted a hand to her forehead, where a sudden headache had arisen since learning that she'd be hosting services. She knew it was an honor, but on top of everything else, it seemed too much too soon.

"You're hurting," he said after a thorough examination of her face. "Hip?"

She shook her head, then promptly grimaced as the shooting pain intensified.

"Headache," he guessed, his voice—and his gaze—gentle. He approached her, and she briefly closed her eyes. This caring side of him was hard to resist and made her believe in things that couldn't be.

He shifted to stand behind her, settled his hands on her shoulders. She jerked. "Close your eyes again," he whispered. She obeyed. "Breathe deep. Don't think about what's bothering you. We are all here to help."

He began to knead her shoulders and the muscles above her shoulder blades. His touch was soothing, and she should object. It wasn't proper for him to touch her, but the pain, the worry, was slowly easing, all because of his simple touch. His fingers slipped to her neck, gently squeezed and massaged away the soreness. Then he raised his hands to her temples and began to ease away her pain with the circular movements of his fingertips.

Her headache slowly eased. She breathed deeply, liking Zack's touch. The thought that what she was allowing was wrong filtered through the enjoyment. She stiffened.

"Danki," she gasped and pulled away. "It's better."

She put a few feet between them. He didn't say anything, but she could sense that he studied her, probably wondering what she was thinking and feeling.

She drew herself up and faced him. "There is a lot to do before Sunday services."

He smiled. "That's why Rachel, *Mam* and Esther are planning to clean the *haus* and get everything ready."

She gazed at him, wishing for things she couldn't have. "Rachel's coming?"

Zack nodded.

She shifted uneasily. "I should feed the chickens," she said.

He shook his head. "Mary Ruth fed them earlier."

Lizzie gaped at him. "She did?"

"Ja." He frowned. "Has she never done so before?"

"Ja, she has," she admitted, but she didn't tell him that it wasn't without an argument. Arguing wasn't the way

of the Lord, so she had stopped trying to rush her eldest daughter past her grief.

Zack seemed satisfied with her answer. *"Goot."* He glanced toward the barn. "Services in the *haus* or the barn?"

"The *haus*," she said, resigned to the fact church services would be held on the farm on Sunday. "The barn is too drafty and there is too much to do to clear things away."

"I made a start on that," he said. "I cleaned up the clutter, and now everything is in its place." He seemed proud of his accomplishments.

She wasn't sure how she felt about his clearing the barn without telling her. She didn't want to think too closely about why he'd felt that it was his right to do so without asking.

"I'll go up to the *haus*, then," she said. He looked mildly disappointed. "Do you know when Rachel plans to come?"

The sudden clip-clop of a horse's hooves on the dirt driveway drew her gaze just after Zack, having noticed first, grinned and gestured toward the buggy that was making its way closer to the farmhouse and yard.

"It seems she's here," he said.

Lizzie was overjoyed to see her friend. She needed Rachel, who never judged, to help her sort out her feelings. But would she have time alone with Rachel? *Nay,* not likely. She would have to wait for another time to talk with her closest friend.

"Rachel!" she cried as the young woman steered the buggy into the barnyard, parked the vehicle and waved.

Rachel climbed out and went to secure the horse, but Zack was there to take care of it for her. She thanked him with a respectful nod, then approached her. "Lizzie." She smiled warmly. "I'm longing for a cup of tea. Shall we?"

Lizzie grinned. "With cake?"

"Ja," Rachel agreed, and the women moved toward the farmhouse. "So tell me—how are things going on the Fisher farm?"

Lizzie opened her mouth to tell her, then stifled the words she wanted to say.

Rachel slid her a sideways glance. *"Ach,* as bad as that?" Her eyes filled with concern.

"Nay. Everyone has been kind and wonderful."

"But—"

"I'm not accustomed to it."

Rachel laughed. "Get used to it, Lizzie. It is called family."

"Ja, but—"

Rachel placed a hand on Lizzie's shoulder. "For whatever reason, your family—your parents and siblings—are different, but these people are your family now."

"Do you honestly believe that?" Lizzie was afraid that things would change or that she'd wake up from dreaming—the fact of Abraham's death and the loss of her child reminded her that life offered heartache in unexpected ways.

Rachel frowned. "What's wrong?"

Lizzie shook her head and looked toward the front porch. She wanted to confide in Rachel but now was not the time. She forced a smile. *"Hallo,* Sarah. I hope you slept well. I'd like you to meet my *goot* friend Rachel Zook." She turned to Rachel. "It's my pleasure for you to meet my mother-in-law, Sarah Fisher."

She watched Rachel and Sarah exchange greetings, and they all entered the farmhouse, where Lizzie put on the teakettle and pulled from the pantry the leftover apple cake that Zack hadn't consumed the day before.

Not long afterward, Naomi Beiler, Ellen Beachey and Dinah Plank arrived to help Lizzie clean and prepare for church services. Pleased, Lizzie flashed each woman a grateful smile.

"Ellen, what about the shop? Shouldn't you be there?"

Ellen shrugged. "*Dat* wanted to work, and he brought *Mam* with him."

Lizzie understood. Ellen's mother's mind wasn't what it once was. She got lost in the past, often forgetting things. "It's wonderful to see you. I've started Mrs. Emory's quilt."

"I'm glad to hear it. Those aprons you brought already sold. I'll drop the money by on Monday."

"No need. You have enough to do. I made a few more. I'll bring what I have Monday and we can square up then."

The women went to work. Sarah, Esther, Ellen and the girls tackled the upstairs rooms while Rachel, Naomi Beiler and Dinah Plank helped Lizzie clean and prepare the first level. "I didn't expect you," Lizzie said to Naomi as they worked side by side in the gathering room.

"Dinah and I wanted to help. I know this must be difficult for you, hosting services so soon…" She trailed off, unwilling to mention Abraham's death.

"I'll get through. And I appreciate the help. You're a kind woman."

"*Nay.* I simply believe in living the Lord's way," the woman replied. She peered through the side window glass. Jonas and Zeke were playing in the yard, and no doubt Naomi could see them. "How is Jonas's hand?"

"It's healing well." Lizzie ran a dust cloth across a window in the gathering room. "It was *goot* of you to watch the children while we were at the doctor's."

Naomi paused in sweeping the floor and made light of Lizzie's thanks with a wave of a hand. "They are *goot kinner*, and they enjoyed spending time with my Aaron and Michael."

Lizzie nodded. During the ride home, she'd heard all about Naomi's children and how much Matthew, Anne and Zeke had enjoyed playing outside with them. Naomi's daughter Emma was her eldest, and she often minded her brothers. Rebecca and Hannah had talked about Emma and how much they liked her.

"Lizzie?" Dinah said. "I swept the kitchen floor. What would you like me to do next?"

"Would you mind pulling out my baking ingredients?" Lizzie asked. "I left some recipe cards on the counter."

"I'll be happy to." Dinah returned to the kitchen.

"I finished in the bathroom," Rachel said as she entered the room. She held a bucket of soapy water and a towel draped over her right shoulder. "What's next?"

Surprised, Lizzie raised her eyebrows. "I believe we've finished downstairs. I'll check with Sarah—"

"The upstairs is done," Sarah announced as she swept into the room with Ellen, Esther and Lizzie's daughters.

"Then all that's left is the baking."

Lizzie turned to Naomi. "Tea or coffee? I'm hungry. How about lunch first?"

Naomi smiled but shook her head. "I should get home. I don't dare leave my oldest in charge for too long."

"I should get back to the store," Ellen said. "*Dat* might be ready to head home."

Dinah approached from the kitchen. "I'd like to stay if I can get a ride home."

"I'll take you home, Dinah," Rachel called from the kitchen. Dinah returned to help Rachel.

"I appreciate all the help," Lizzie told the two women

who were ready to leave. "I don't know why I was so worried about getting the house ready for services. You've all been wonderful." It was the greatest thing about being Amish. The community was always ready to lend a helping hand.

"We're glad to help," Naomi said. "You know we're always here for you."

"Danki," Lizzie said. It had been Naomi and Dinah who had helped on the day of Abraham's funeral. She blinked back a tear at the memory and smiled at the women, deeply touched by their friendship. She walked outside with Ellen and Naomi to their vehicles, which were parked side by side. "I don't have much time for meetings, Naomi," she said, "but if there is any way I can help…"

The widow smiled. "You helped with the haystack supper and we loved having you. I know you are busy raising the children on your own. Take care of yourself and your family—that's the most important thing." Naomi climbed into her vehicle. "I will see you at service," she promised. Then with a wave of her hand, the woman left.

"Ellen." Lizzie regarded her friend, who'd been a godsend since her husband's passing. "You're always there for me. First selling my quilts and crafts and now this— cleaning my *haus* on a day your shop is open."

Ellen shook her head. "Having your craft items in the shop is *wunderbor* for business. As for helping you—" She smiled. "We're friends and I'm glad. I only hope I can be as *goot* a *mudder* as you if Neziah and I are blessed with a child."

"But Neziah has two sons, and they adore you," Lizzie said. "You are already a *mudder*."

She brightened. "I love Asa and Joel as my own."

"That's all you have to do," Lizzie said. "Love them and with the Lord's help all will be well. Neziah and his boys have taken to you like ducks to water."

Ellen laughed, but it was clear that she was happy with her choice of sweetheart and his two sons. "I'll see you on Sunday."

"I'll look forward to it." Despite her initial reservations and fear about hosting church, Lizzie was now eager to host church service for her community. She watched and waved as Ellen steered her horse-drawn buggy toward the main road. Then she reentered the house to find that Sarah and Esther, with Dinah's help, were preparing lunch. Rachel had gathered the children and pulled chairs from the other room to accommodate everyone.

"Where are Zack and Matt?" Lizzie asked.

"They went to see Peter at the *haus*," Rachel said. "Something about discussing the harvest."

Lizzie quickly pitched in to help and soon there was enough food on the table to feed everyone. Esther had brought bread and macaroni salad from the *dawdi haus*; she had made both the evening before in anticipation of feeding the helpers.

"This is a feast!" Dinah exclaimed as she took a seat at the kitchen table.

Lizzie laughed. "My children are healthy eaters."

Lunch was a fun affair. They ate sandwiches with Esther's bread and the roast beef that Lizzie had cooked earlier in the week. Jonas and Zeke exclaimed exuberantly over the wonderful taste of their aunt's macaroni salad, which made all the women, especially Lizzie, eye them with amused smiles playing about their lips.

When they were done, the women cleaned up quickly. "Are you sure you don't need us to stay and help?" Rachel asked after Lizzie insisted that Rachel and Dinah had enough work of their own to do at home.

"*Nay*, I have plenty of help with my daughters."

Rachel and Dinah left minutes later, heading in the direction of Dinah's apartment over Beachey's Craft Shop.

Lizzie returned inside after seeing the women off. Then with Sarah and Esther's help, she began to prepare food for the shared midday meal after Sunday church service.

Esther was excited yet nervous. It was church Sunday, and David Hostetler would be officiating services. She hadn't seen him since his visit on Monday. Dressed in Sunday best, she followed Zack across the yard to the farmhouse. Her blue dress was freshly laundered, her black apron and *kapp* newly made. This morning she had combed and rolled her brown hair with more care. She didn't want a hair out of place when she met David's wife for the first time. *Vanity is a sin*, she reminded herself. She hoped the Lord would forgive her and understand that she simply wanted to make a good impression. She entered the house to see Lizzie rushing about frantically trying to get the children ready for church.

"Esther!" she cried gratefully when she saw her. "Would you check in the gathering room, make sure all of the benches are in place?"

"*Ja*, of course, Lizzie." Esther was sure that the room was ready but she understood Lizzie's anxiety.

After lingering outside for a few moments, Zack entered behind her. He apparently heard Lizzie's concern. "Everything is ready," he said to reassure her. "We set up the benches at first light. Don't worry." Lizzie looked relieved by Zack's assurance.

Families within the community began to arrive in their buggies. Esther saw the David Hostetlers arrive, and she felt her anxiety level kick up a notch. To her surprise, she saw that he came alone, except for his children. She was puzzled yet relieved.

Where was David's wife? Esther frowned. Was she ill? She hoped not. She wasn't sure how she'd feel while meeting the woman who had won David's heart, but apparently the moment wouldn't be today.

She hung back in the kitchen, watching through the window as buggies and wagons wheeled down the dirt lane and parked in a row in the yard near the barn. Ellen Beachey arrived with her parents and Dinah Plank. In a separate vehicle, Neziah, Ellen's sweetheart, drove his father, Simeon; his younger brother Micah; and Neziah's two sons, Asa and Joel.

"Esther!" her mother called from the other room. "It's nearly time for service."

"Coming." She felt her stomach churn as she left the kitchen for the gathering area. The room was crowded with all the benches in place, but no one seemed to mind. She approached the women-and-children's area of the room and sat on a bench near her mother. Heart beating wildly, Esther stared at the area reserved for the preacher and waited for David to appear.

She didn't have long to wait. Once everyone was seated, Preacher David Hostetler stepped into place and greeted everyone with a nod. After he gave a short but inspiring introductory sermon, the congregation opened the *Ausbund*, the Amish book of hymns, and began to sing the first of several chosen songs for today's service. They sang several stanzas but not the entire hymn, which would take too long if sung in its entirety. As it was, the chosen stanzas of the first hymn, led by Deacon John, took over a half hour to sing. Esther enjoyed singing, but she couldn't keep her eyes from David as he waited for his part of the service to continue.

Esther took note of two other church elders in the room—another preacher and Bishop Andy. She'd met the deacon at the last service she'd attended in Honeysuckle, and she'd found John Mast and his large family pleasant and likable.

The song ended, and David began to preach. He spoke of the Lord and of the teachings of the *Ordnung*. He was a wonderful, eloquent speaker, and she hung on his every word.

They sang the *Loblied* next, the hymn that was always sung second during church. Esther sang louder than she usually did, caught up in the word of the Lord, inspired by Preacher David during his sermon.

Hours went by with the deacon reading passages from the Bible interspersed with song and moments of prayer. Then church service ended. Esther stood and began to slide down the row of seats to get out so that she could assist with the food. As she headed toward the kitchen, she experienced a funny feeling in the pit of her stomach.

"Esther," her mother whispered as she made her way down the row behind her. "The preacher—isn't that David Hostetler? If I remember correctly, you used to think highly of him." She was silent and Esther could guess the next direction of her thoughts.

Esther glanced back. "*Ja*, 'tis David. He's married now."

"He was a nice boy."

Esther swallowed hard, remembering how much she'd cared for him. "I'm sure he's a nice man, as well. He is a preacher." She forced a grin.

"He's not married," Lizzie said, jumping into their conversation. "David's wife died two years ago. He is raising his two sons on his own."

Esther stopped to glance in the man's direction. David was talking with Bishop Andy. Two young boys approached him, and he smiled and placed a loving hand on each boy's shoulder. As if sensing her regard, he suddenly looked in her direction. Their gazes locked, and Esther felt her heart flutter. Embarrassed, she looked away. "We need to take out the food," she quickly said to her sister-in-law, and Lizzie agreed.

Esther didn't make eye contact with her mother, but she could feel *Mam* studying her closely.

"Mam," Mary Ruth said as she came up to Lizzie. "I'll get the drinks. Shall I ask *Onkel* Zack and Matt to set up a food table on that side of the room?" She gestured toward her selected spot.

"Ja, that looks like a *goot* place," Lizzie said.

The men, Esther saw, were moving benches to create eating areas for the church members.

Esther refused to look again in David's direction, for she knew she'd been staring. She moved toward the kitchen, eager to get out of the room before she made a fool of herself. She had nearly escaped when she heard his voice, a sound as familiar to her as her own breathing.

"Esther, it's *goot* to see you again."

She tensed, drew a deep calming breath and then faced him. The boys were no longer with him. It was David alone, looking handsome and tall. No other man had ever made her feel so small and feminine as he did. She held her hands tight to her sides to still the trembling and smiled. *"Hallo,* David."

He appeared happy to see her; she could see it reflected in his blue eyes and his masculine grin. She gazed at his handsome face and knew that she'd never stopped loving him.

Chapter Fifteen

"I didn't know if you'd stay," David said.

"I'm still here."

The preacher nodded his head, his blue eyes warm, kind. "*Goot.* I don't know if I told you, Esther, but you look lovely. You haven't changed." He studied her with an intensity that gave her goose bumps. "You're still the young girl I knew and loved."

She blushed, unsure how to answer. She remained silent, but she felt secretly pleased.

He looked around the room. "The other day I never asked if your husband was joining you in Honeysuckle."

She opened her mouth to answer. "I—"

"She isn't married," her mother said, coming from behind her. Horrified, Esther turned a darker shade of red.

David smiled, his gaze settling on *Mam.* "Sarah. 'Tis *goot* to see you. It's been many years."

"David." She greeted him with a nod. "I see you've grown up nicely."

"*Mam!*" Esther exclaimed. She flashed her mother a beseeching glance that silently said, "Please don't embarrass me."

Mam took the hint. "I should go. Lizzie will need help in the kitchen."

David looked concerned. The mention of Lizzie, Esther realized, must have reminded him that she and *Mam* had suffered from Abraham's death, too. "I'm sorry for your loss." He hesitated, holding her mother's gaze before focusing his blue eyes on Esther. "He was a fine man and a wonderful *vadder*."

Sarah nodded, clearly appreciating his words. "*Ja*, he was a *goot* son." She addressed Esther. "I'll be in the kitchen," she said, and then she nodded toward the preacher and left.

"I should go, too," Esther began and turned as if to leave.

"We'll talk again later?" he asked.

She was startled yet secretly pleased by his question. She gave a demure nod.

"*Dat!*" An adorable young boy of about five years old rushed up to David and tugged on the bottom edge of his Sunday-best black vest.

David gave the child a tender smile. "*Ja?* What is it, Jacob?"

"Will we have time to play with Jonas and Zeke?"

Esther could see that Jacob was a miniature version of his handsome father. They wore clothing identical to that of all the men and boys within their Amish community— white shirt, black vest and pants. Like the other men, they had removed their black felt hats and hung them on wall pegs when they entered the house. She enjoyed watching father and son.

"After midday meal," David told the boy gently. "Where did your *brooder* run off to?"

"He went with Jonas to the kitchen to see if they can have a cookie."

David sighed good-naturedly and shook his head. "Tell Jed that he shouldn't be bothering the women in the kitchen. He'll have plenty of food to eat soon enough."

Despite herself, Esther watched the exchange with amusement. She knew she should leave, but she couldn't just walk away. Watching David as a father was wonderful and sweet, and she felt that little heartbreak that reminded her that she might have married him if she hadn't moved to Ohio with her mother, if she had stayed with Abraham and Ruth in Honeysuckle. Sometimes things weren't meant to be.

David shook his head with a loving look toward his son, who scampered off in search of his brother. "I apologize. That's Jacob. He's five." He frowned. "I should have introduced you."

"You have been blessed," she said with a glance over her shoulder in time to see David's son run out of the room.

The men were shifting benches. The two of them were obstacles in their path, and Esther knew it. "I'm in the way."

"You could never be in the way," he said, and her eyes widened as she looked at him. He wore the calm, contented look of a man of *Gott*. But then, David as a young man had been calm and accepting with a deep love for *Gott* and his family. And perhaps her, she thought with sadness for what she had lost.

"It was nice to see you again, David," she said, determined to leave.

"So you don't have a husband?"

She blushed. *"Nay."*

He appeared pleased. "Then you won't mind me visiting on occasion?"

"Ja." She stiffened. She liked the thought of seeing

him again, but what would the community think? "I must go."

He furrowed his brow. "*Ja*, I can visit or, *ja*, you mind?" he asked.

She gazed into his eyes, wanting him to visit more than anything. She whispered, "*Ja*, you can visit."

His lips curved in a beautiful smile that stole her breath. "I will see you again soon, then, Esther." He paused. "At your *dawdi haus*."

She didn't disagree. Her mind reeled with thoughts of him courting her. She hurried away, escaping to the kitchen and the sanctuary of the women's company with the mental image of David Hostetler on her doorstep. She gasped. *Stop*, she scolded herself. *You are being fanciful. He is an old friend who wants to talk with you. Nothing more!* As she entered the room, she saw her mother and Lizzie chatting as they worked. There were several women cramped into the room and no one seemed to mind the close proximity as they unwrapped previously prepared food and set dishes on every available space on the counter and kitchen table.

Esther went to work. She wouldn't mind seeing David at the cottage. She wouldn't mind at all. But the proper thing would be to have Zack or someone nearby to chaperone them.

"Esther?" Her mother saw her as she approached.

"Ja?" Could her mother read her thoughts?

"We have two little boys who would like a cookie." *Mam* gestured toward the corner of the room.

Esther relaxed. "Chocolate chip or gingerbread?" she asked, eyeing the eager boys with a growing smile.

"Chocolate chip," her nephew said, and his friend Jed, David's eldest son, agreed.

She pulled two cookies out of Lizzie's cookie jar and

handed one to each boy. "Go and eat your cookie, but no more treats until you eat a proper meal first. *Ja?*"

"*Ja!*" the boys echoed each other.

Stifling a grin, Esther shooed them out of the kitchen. "You may play outside until I call you when it's your turn to eat."

"They seem in a hurry," Ellen said, coming up from behind.

"*Ja*, they are eager to run and play."

"I did the same thing with Neziah's two a few minutes ago. They love their cookies."

Esther smiled. "Don't we all?"

Zack sat at the table with the men of their Amish church community. His nephew Matt had chosen to sit beside him. As he ate, Zack enjoyed watching Lizzie as she moved about the room serving the churchmen. Today, he couldn't detect her limp.

She looked calm and unhurried. She had managed fine during her first church service on the farm since Abraham's death. He saw her set down a bowl of potato salad and then pour some iced tea for Preacher David.

Zack caught her eye and signaled for her to come. "May I have some potato salad?" he asked.

She smiled and gave him a helping.

A little imp inside him had him waving her over again once she got to the other side of the room.

Once again, she came, and he asked for something else, and she brought it to him.

She went back to serving at another table, and he bent and whispered in Matt's ear. Matt grinned, caught Lizzie's eye and signed for her to come.

"May I please have some iced tea?" the boy asked with a straight face as he held out his cup.

Lizzie smiled but her eyes narrowed. She poured her son's tea and then asked Zack, "Would you like some tea?"

He shook his head. "But I appreciate the thought."

He waited until she reached the other side of the room again. There were other women who were closer, but he wanted Lizzie. He again caught her attention and gestured for her to come.

She smiled, but the good humor didn't reach her green eyes. *"Ja?"*

"Sweet-and-vinegar green beans?" he asked.

She turned to get them, her stance stiff. He had irritated her, and when she turned back, he couldn't stifle a grin.

Her eyes widened. "You are a tease, Zack Fisher," she accused.

"Ja." He regarded her warmly. "I couldn't resist. You are handling everything so well today. I felt the urge to give you a hard time." He grinned. "I wanted to make your day."

He saw her visibly relax. "You had best watch yourself, Zack."

Amused, he arched an eyebrow. "Or what?" he challenged.

She narrowed her green eyes. She looked flushed, her cheeks a pretty pink from rushing to serve the men, but mostly him and Matt. A sheen of moisture glistened across her forehead and a hint of teasing retribution entered her expression as she stared at him.

She glanced toward her son. "Matthew Fisher, you had best be done with your meal."

But Matt, he saw, just raised his chin, unafraid, as he continued to play his part. "May I have some more iced tea?"

And she laughed, a tinkling sound that shivered pleasurably along Zack's spine.

"That's enough, Matthew," he warned.

The boy sighed. "But we were having fun."

Lizzie glared at both of them with mock anger. "I'll show you how to have fun doing some extra chores tomorrow, young man."

But Matt could tell that she wasn't serious, so he simply grinned at her and said, "Aw, *Mam*."

Lizzie's face brightened and her eyes filled. It was clear that Matt had never called her *mam* before, and she was more than pleased that he just had.

Lizzie woke up Monday morning, feeling good that church services had gone so well. She had thought it would be hard, seeing everyone back on the farm when Abraham was absent, but Zack, Esther, Sarah and the children had made the day easier for her. They were her family. As long as they continued to accept her, she would be content.

She recalled Zack and Matt's teasing during yesterday's postservice meal. She'd felt annoyed when Zack—and then Matt—had called her over to ask for one thing or another. She'd been on the far side of the room when they'd gestured for her to approach. At first she hadn't understood why they simply hadn't asked one of the other churchwomen serving those seated near them. Later, when she saw Zack's dark eyes full of laughter, she understood. Zack Fisher had been teasing her with Matthew's help!

She went downstairs to prepare breakfast. She put on the coffeepot and took out eggs, bacon, green peppers, onions and potatoes. She decided to make omelets with home fries. As she chopped up the onion and green pepper, she found her thoughts returning to Zack and his playful side. She liked it. That he had enlisted Matthew's help in his teasing made her chuckle. Matt's expression when she'd pretended to be stern with him made her laugh out loud. As if thinking of the man had made him materialize, Zack entered the kitchen from outside. Her amusement faded and embarrassment took its place.

"Zack," she greeted. She was surprised to see him. She thought he'd been in the barn, tending to the animals.

"You the only one awake?" he asked as he reached for the coffeepot she'd prepared on the stove.

"For the moment."

"So we're alone," he said.

Her gaze shot to his face. "*Ja*, I guess so."

His expression was sober. "There is something we should discuss."

"*Ja?*" Her heart began to beat double-time as fear gripped her hard. "Is it about the farm?" Zack nodded. "You came to Honeysuckle to claim your inheritance." She waited several seconds while tension filled the air, making it difficult for her to breathe.

She sensed him stiffen. "Who told you?"

Fired up by the truth, she faced him defiantly. "No one. I just knew." She set down her kitchen tools and crossed her arms. "And you didn't think to tell me that you are going to take away my home?"

His dark eyes flashed. "Did I tell you that I was taking your home?"

"*Nay*, but…" She felt her anger dissipate. "But you don't deny that your father intended you to have the farm and the property."

Zack shook his head. "No, I can't deny it."

Lizzie felt as if the life had suddenly been sucked

out of her. "I sec." She picked up a fork and began to beat eggs.

"Do you?" he said, his voice unusually harsh.

She looked at him and received the impression that he was disappointed in her. "I—ah—I don't understand."

He softened his expression. "Exactly."

She realized that she'd made a dreadful mistake. "You didn't come to talk about the farm, did you?"

Zack shook his head. "*Nay.* I wanted to ask you about the corn wagon. One of the wheels is bad, and I wanted to get it fixed and make sure you didn't mind."

Mortified that she'd jumped to conclusions, Lizzie felt the sting of tears. "Not if you think it needs fixing."

IIc nodded as he set his unfinished cup of coffee on the kitchen table then left. Lizzie stared as the door closed behind Zack's retreating back. Her tears spilled over, and she swiped at them with the backs of her hands as she returned to making breakfast. She had handled that badly, but learning the truth, that Zack was indeed the heir to the farm, had hurt more because he'd never told her.

She realized that she'd had a vision in her head of how their discussion about the farm would go. She'd ask him about his intentions, and he'd tell her that she was worried about nothing. If he had wanted the farm, he would have told her, wouldn't he?

But the conversation hadn't gone that way at all. Zack had admitted that the farm was rightfully his, but he hadn't given her any insight into his thoughts or his future plans.

Then why did she feel as if she had somehow disappointed him? Because she'd been angry—a sin in the Lord's eyes—and defiant that she wasn't happy to learn the truth?

Lizzie realized that confronting Zack had only made things worse. They'd laughed and enjoyed a good working relationship. Now the farm stood between them.

Dear Lord, what am I going to do? There was only one thing she could do: pray and dry her tears before the children and Zack's mother came downstairs.

Zack stomped toward the barn, aware that he'd been remiss in discussing the farm with Lizzie. Yes, he had come to Honeysuckle to claim the farm, but after getting to know Lizzie, he'd begun to rethink the situation.

She was upset that he hadn't spoken with her about it. He had meant to, but it never seemed the right moment. They had gotten along so well that he'd decided that there was no reason to discuss his inheritance. Why should they when he'd already made up his mind that the farm was hers as long as she wanted it?

He admitted to himself that he was disappointed. She seemed to challenge him, make him feel as if he were guilty of a sin by not talking about the farm sooner. He should have told her calmly that she had nothing to fear, but he'd been too hurt to respond. Despite the right and wrong of it, he was in love with his sister-in-law. Every day he fought his feelings, but even the thought that he was betraying his brother couldn't stop his growing love.

He should go to her and explain that he wouldn't take her home away, but he didn't think she would listen. Despite their growing friendship, she had made up her mind not to trust him in this matter and there was nothing he could do.

Her behavior convinced him that she didn't share his

feelings. She couldn't care for him if she didn't trust him. Was there something he could do to win her trust?

He'd done all he could, he realized. And that made him sad, not angry.

Chapter Sixteen

Lizzie went about her early-morning chores, cleaning up after yesterday's church services. She entered the kitchen and stared at the counter. Several community women had left behind food. There were muffins and a pie, cakes and cookies. She'd put the vegetables and apple salad in the refrigerator Sunday afternoon. So much food, she thought. The community women had left enough to feed a huge crowd. It was thoughtful of them and it was nice to know that they cared about her.

"Lizzie, I stripped the beds for you, and I'm going to put them in the wash," her mother-in-law said as she entered the kitchen, carrying a basket of sheets and other linens.

"You didn't have to do all that work," Lizzie said quietly. Her confrontation with Zack hadn't gone well and she hid the fact that things had gone wrong between them. "I would have done it."

"Nonsense," Sarah said with a smile. "It's my pleasure to be able to help. I'm not one to sit idle."

Lizzie saw Zack's smile on his mother's lips, and she couldn't help responding in kind, although inside she was feeling anything but happy. She hadn't seen Zack since their discussion about the farm and the wagon wheel. In a way, she was glad because she wasn't ready to face him yet, to be reminded that her life on the farm was still in jeopardy since he hadn't assured her otherwise.

"What else can I do?" the woman asked, drawing Lizzie from her thoughts. "Surely there is more I can do to help."

"*Nay*, you've done a lot—too much. 'Tis been a *goot* workday, don't you agree?" Lizzie looked about the kitchen, pleased that everything was back in order.

"*Ja*. And services went well yesterday," Sarah commented, and Lizzie, despite her initial fears about hosting services, had to agree.

As Lizzie moved about the house, checking to see that all was in place, something occurred to her that made her begin to wonder about Sarah's insistence in helping with all of the housework. *It's not that I don't appreciate her help.* Did Sarah think that because of her bad hip she couldn't handle the work? She was certainly capable of house- and farmwork. Hadn't she been doing it alone since Abraham's death?

Lizzie drew in a calming breath and silently scolded herself. Her mother-in-law was a kind woman, who only wanted to contribute. It wasn't because Sarah thought her incapable of doing chores.

She caught Sarah's unfathomable expression before the woman headed to the washing machine in the back room. The memory of it made Lizzie self-conscious. *Stop it*, she admonished. Sarah was a kind woman, and they'd gotten on well. *Stop worrying. It's nothing! She knows that I can do my chores.*

She heard the closing clink of the gas-powered washing machine lid as Sarah put on a load of laundry. In less than a minute, the woman returned to the kitchen, and Lizzie offered her breakfast.

"Are the children awake?" Sarah asked. Her appearance was as neat as a pin despite having carried laundry down from upstairs.

Lizzie nodded. "Up, had breakfast and left for school." She knew she must look a sight. She had spilled milk on her skirt when she'd poured Anne a glass of it earlier and Zeke had accidentally bumped her arm. Normally, a stained dress wouldn't have bothered her, but it did this morning.

"They're gone to *schule* already?" Sarah widened her eyes. "Did I oversleep?"

Lizzie pulled dishes from the cabinet. "*Nay.* They got up early. While I made their lunches, Mary Ruth poured each of them a bowlful of cereal."

Sarah was thoughtful as she met Lizzie's glance. "Did you eat?"

"*Nay,*" Lizzie answered. "I thought to wait for you, Esther and Zack, if he's hungry." Since their mother had arrived, Esther and Zack had been eating regularly with them at the farmhouse. Would that change after her and Zack's discussion? "Tea?" she asked Sarah as she pulled out a tin of loose tea.

"*Ja,*" her mother-in-law said. She moved toward the window, peered out. "Zack is readying the buggy. Is he going somewhere?"

Lizzie shrugged. He hadn't told her of his plans, not after the way she'd jumped to conclusions. "To the Zooks', most likely," she guessed. "He must have eaten one of the muffins from the plate I sent over yesterday." She would miss him at breakfast. She still cared about him despite the knowledge that he could forever change her life. "Has Esther eaten?"

"I'll check." Sarah immediately headed for the door. "I won't be long."

Lizzie had gathered eggs earlier. She grabbed several from her basket and cracked them open, watching as the yolks and whites slipped into her bowl. She then whisked them with a wire whisk, added seasoning and milk, then set the bowl aside.

Her hip hurt this morning. She'd been on her feet a great deal the past two days, much more than usual. On impulse, she took a bottle each of cider vinegar and honey out of the pantry. As she put on the teakettle to heat, she added vinegar and honey to a mug. After the water boiled, she added the hot liquid to the sweet and bitter mixture. The brew was an Amish cure for pain. She took a sip of the familiar tea, grimaced and added a bit more honey. She would try this remedy first. If her pain didn't ease, she would swallow some aspirin or ibuprofen. Whenever the pain became agonizing, she had something stronger to take that the doctor had given her. She rarely used the English doctor's pills. She didn't like how they made her feel, and if she felt forced to seek one for relief, she usually took it before bedtime or during the night if the throbbing pain kept her from sleeping.

Sarah returned within minutes. "Esther will be over soon. She said that she gave Zack bread and jam, but she didn't eat yet."

"I'm glad. Eggs? Ham? Potatoes and toast?" Lizzie asked.

"Sounds *goot*." Sarah reached for a cooking apron and tied it about her waist.

Lizzie sipped from her brew and then went to work. She took potatoes from the pantry and then scrubbed and peeled them.

"Would you like me to cut them?" Sarah asked.

Lizzie smiled. "*Ja*, I'd appreciate the help."

Sarah cut up potatoes and then suggested she chop up onions to mix in. While her mother-in-law handled that, Lizzie sliced a loaf of bread and then set out some of the muffins that Katie Yoder had brought the previous day.

She had noticed her mother-in-law staring at her as Lizzie cooked the potatoes with onions while frying the eggs. Zack hadn't been to the house, so his mother wouldn't know that they had exchanged words.

She slid the cooked eggs into a stainless-steel bowl, placed a plate over top to keep them warm. "Is something wrong?" she asked, catching the speculative look on Sarah's face.

Sarah stared at her a long moment and then commented, "You're not like my son's first wife, Ruth."

Lizzie felt her happiness wither and die. "I—I suppose not." She finished cooking the potatoes, dumped them onto a plate and then excused herself to get Jonas and Zeke. She ran up the stairs, fighting tears, refusing to cry, refusing to allow Sarah's words to hurt, but as in the past when she'd been called Limping Lizzie by some of the children, words still had the power to hurt her.

"Jonas? Zeke?" She entered the boy's room to find them seated on the floor, playing Dutch Blitz, a game played with four decks of colored cards. "Breakfast is ready," she told them, forcing a smile.

"Coming," Jonas said without looking up.

Zeke caught her eye and stood. Her little one appeared concerned as he approached her and slipped his little arms around her waist. *"Mam,"* he said. *"Mam."* He patted her back as if he saw that something had upset her. And just like that, she felt better. A child's comforting touch was all she needed to pull herself together.

Her thoughts chased one after the other as she waited

for the boys to precede her down the stairs. She knew she wasn't like Ruth. Abraham had mourned his first wife so deeply that she'd wondered if he'd ever get over his grief. The older children had missed their mother with a depth that was difficult to see. Ruth had been special. She was simply Lizzie, the young woman with a limp. She worked hard, loved her new family and did what she could to help ease their pain. The little ones didn't remember their mother. The memories of her youngest daughter, Anne, included those of an unhappy woman who'd had problems after the birth of Ezekiel.

She was sure that Sarah didn't mean to be hurtful. They had gotten along well, hadn't they? After a short period of adjustment during which she had come to know Sarah Fisher, she had enjoyed having Zack's mother in the house.

Lizzie followed her sons into the kitchen. Esther had arrived, and the boys greeted their aunt and their grandmother Sarah as if they hadn't seen them in weeks instead of only hours.

"Everything smells *goot*!" Jonas said with a grin.

"I'm hungry." Zeke sat in a chair and waited as the women put the food on the table.

"I wish *Onkel* Zack could have eaten with us," Jonas said.

There was a flurry of sound from the back of the house. The door opened and Zack walked in.

"*Onkel* Zack!" the boys exclaimed.

"Is it time for breakfast yet?" He grinned, and her heart started to pound as she studied him. He didn't appear to be angry with her; it was as if their earlier discussion had never happened.

"I thought you were going to the Zooks'," Esther said.

"I will, but I've time. Didn't want to miss out on breakfast with my family."

Lizzie blushed as he looked in her direction. His wink startled her. "Do I smell eggs and potatoes?"

"With onions!" Jonas told him.

"Sounds *goot*!" He pulled out a chair and sat down, and Lizzie asked if he'd like coffee. "*Ja*, and some of the delicious-smelling food."

Zack's presence made breakfast enjoyable. Something about him made her feel better now that he'd come. Had she misunderstood his intentions? Jumped to the wrong conclusions? She knew it wasn't wise to think too much about her late husband's brother, but she cared for him, was unable to get him out of her mind.

Later that afternoon, Esther sat at the kitchen table, mending one of her brother's shirts. "*Endie* Esther, do you want to play Dutch Blitz?"

She smiled at Abraham's two youngest sons. "I must finish the mending." She had a dress seam to fix and a small pile of the children's clothes. "Let me sew Uncle Zack's shirt and my dress. Then we'll see."

She had offered to watch the boys for her sister-in-law this morning. She could tell Lizzie was in pain after the busy day of church services with a meal afterward, and cleaning the house the following day. Although Lizzie never complained, Esther had seen it in her eyes. Her mother had gone with Zack to the Zooks', and they planned to stop to visit a woman she'd known years before. Preacher David had mentioned that Alta Miller was feeling poorly, and Sarah had been concerned.

Thoughts of this past Sunday brought on her musings about David. It had been good to see and talk with him after all these years. She'd felt like a young girl again in his presence, until she reminded herself that she was not only older but still unmarried.

David is a widower, she thought. *What was his wife like? Was she comely like Rachel Zook? Or plain and big like me?*

It wasn't that she was fat. She wasn't overweight, but then, neither was she thin or small. She was a tall, big-boned woman who had never found a husband. She had given her teenage heart to David Hostetler years ago and had never gotten it back.

She plied sewing needle into cloth in neat, even stitches, mending a torn seam on Zack's shirt before fixing the hem. The image of David and how he'd looked when they'd last spoken had stayed with her long after he'd left the farm. She loved everything about him: his bright blue eyes, the warmth of his smile, the way his expression grew loving whenever he looked at his sons. She still couldn't get over the fact that he was a preacher. His sermon, eloquently given and appreciated by all, had convinced her that the congregation had chosen well in making him a church elder.

It was a warm October day, and Esther had opened the interior doors and windows to allow the fresh autumn air to filter throughout the cottage.

"Hallo!" a deep voice called from in the yard. "Anyone home?"

Esther recognized David immediately. She pushed back her chair and stood. David was at her back door with his face pressed against the screen.

"Hallo," a smaller, young voice said, and Esther saw David's son Jacob at his father's side, his face pressed against the screen and peering inside in an identical fashion.

"David, Jacob," she greeted, opening the door. With

a hand gesture, she invited them into her kitchen. Esther felt herself blush and hoped David didn't notice. She stood at the door, staring out into the yard, as she took a moment to gather her composure.

"I don't see your buggy," she said calmly, although she felt anything but calm inside. The man's slow grin did odd things to her insides. Her stomach felt jittery and hot.

"Jacob and I walked over. It's a nice day for a stroll." He smiled down at his son. "Jacob was hoping to spend some time with your nephews."

"Jonas and Zeke?" she asked. Jacob bobbed his head up and down. Esther noticed that her nephews had disappeared. "They can't be far. Jonas! Zeke!" she called. "You have company."

The boys ran out from a back room. Zeke held a fistful of Dutch Blitz cards, and several of them threatened to escape from his clenched fingers.

"Jacob!" Jonas cried. "*Ya* want to play Dutch Blitz with us?"

Jacob looked up, sought his father's guidance. David's gaze was warm as he met Esther's. "*Ja*, you can play for a while," he told his son.

Stunned by her reaction to him, Esther could only stare.

"Esther?" he asked with concern.

She shook herself out of a trancelike state. "It's nice that you brought Jacob to play." She found herself fumbling nervously with her apron hem. Seeing her mess, she hurriedly picked up needle and thread and the pile of clothes, then stashed them in her mending basket.

"Would you like tea?" she asked, playing the perfect hostess. "Or *coffe*?"

David studied her, his blue eyes assessing. "Tea, please."

She sensed him watching her as she put on the tea-kettle, took out two cups and two plates for the cake she'd quickly decided to serve. She felt herself tremble and paused, closed her eyes and garnered control of herself again.

"I only have tea bags," she apologized as she placed one in each cup.

"I know," he said with a small smile, and she recalled that she'd made him a cup of tea during his first visit. "I use tea bags."

"I've got cinnamon *coffe* cake. I didn't bake it," she spoke quickly. "Rachel Zook did. It's very *goot*, though. 'Tis her specialty." She reached to the far edge of the counter for the cake plate. She grabbed a knife and raised it to cut, then stopped, breathed deeply and faced him. "Do you want *coffe* cake? If not, I think there are brownies left. I'll check the pantry." She moved to brush by him on her way to the cottage pantry.

David reached out, his hand encircling her arm, making the air rush out of her lungs. "Rachel's *coffe* cake is fine, Esther. Then come and sit down. Enjoy cake and tea with me."

He had captured her attention; she was reluctant to look away. She was afraid that she was mistaken in what she thought she saw—good humor and a keen interest in her as a woman.

"David—"

"Esther, make your tea and get your cake and then sit," he urged as he released her arm.

"All right," she whispered. She blushed, and she knew her face had turned an unbecoming shade of red. She avoided his regard as she fixed two cups of tea and cut two pieces of coffee cake. After she put tea and cake before him, Esther hesitated until David raised an eyebrow.

She made a move to sit on the other side of the table, but he rose and reached for her hand, stopping her.

"Here," he said with a tender smile. "I don't bite." He pulled out the chair next to his.

She saw his gentle expression and felt herself relax as they took their seats.

"Tell me more about your life since you left Honeysuckle," he encouraged. "I want to know everything." He took a tentative sip from his cup. Something flickered in his expression. "You remembered how I like my tea?"

Esther nodded. "It was just the other day," she began, but she had in fact remembered from their early days together and she suspected that he knew that.

"So you didn't remember from when we were sweethearts?" His blue gaze seemed to caress her features.

"Not exactly sweethearts," she said, not agreeing or denying it. She was stunned how he could affect her still with only a simple look. "We were just—"

"Friends," he said as he broke off a piece of cinnamon coffee cake and lifted it to his lips. "*Nay*, we were more than friends—and you know it. If you had stayed in Honeysuckle, we would have been more to each other— much more."

Esther felt a rush of tears, which she blinked back. "I should check on the boys." She stood, fleeing to hide her reaction to his words. Had he missed her as she had him? She had loved him with the passion of a young girl's heart.

"Don't go. They're fine. I can see them from here. You're not running away from me, are you?" He took a bite of cake. He watched her as he chewed with obvious enjoyment. "I told you I'd come to visit."

"I know," she whispered. She felt twisted up in knots. This was David and he was a preacher. Why was she suddenly afraid to be in the same room? *Because you still care for him*, an inner voice whispered. *And you don't want him to know or feel sorry for you.* The last thing she needed was to have David Hostetler pity her.

Chapter Seventeen

David noticed the blush rising in Esther's face and was intrigued. He had never expected to see her again, especially when she didn't return for her eldest brother's funeral.

She wasn't married. He wanted to know everything about her—what she'd done after she'd left Honeysuckle, how she'd fared over the years. He couldn't stop looking at her; it was so good to see her again. He felt the years disappear as if she'd never left Honeysuckle. He had always been comfortable in her presence, but there was something more. Being with her made him feel alive in ways he'd forgotten. Till now.

She didn't say a word as he took a second sip of the tea she'd made for him, just the way he liked it. He was still stunned that she'd remembered.

"Tell me about Ohio," he urged. He waited patiently for her answer.

She had been staring into her cup and now she met his glance. "What would *ya* like to know?"

"Where you lived. It must have been hard after you lost your *dat*."

She nodded. "*Mam* was so unhappy. She said she

couldn't remain in Honeysuckle on the farm. We moved to live near my sister Miriam."

David furrowed his brow thoughtfully. "I don't remember meeting her."

"I think you did. She is much older than us. She married when I was very young. She came home once or twice to visit but not for a long time before my *vadder*—" She broke off. Cradling her teacup, she stared into the steaming brew.

"I was sorry for your loss." David studied her bent head, liking what he saw. From the first moment of their meeting, he'd appreciated her features. She had smooth skin and a pretty profile. He had never forgotten the warm brown color of her eyes or the warmth of her smile.

She was quiet for too long.

"Esther?"

She drew a deep shuddering breath. "I didn't want to leave. I wanted to stay in Honeysuckle with Abraham and Ruth. *Mam* convinced me that it wouldn't be fair to them if I did. They were newly married and needed their time alone."

Her hand shook as she lifted the teacup. Afraid that she would spill her tea and burn herself, he reached out to cradle the cup and her hand.

"And so you were a *goot dochter*," he murmured.

She shot him a look, shrugged. "I had no choice." Sorrow settled in her expression. "I didn't want to go. I didn't want to obey my *mudder*."

"But you did."

She sighed. "*Ja*, I did." He felt the impact of her warm brown gaze. "You married."

David inclined his head. He had married at age twenty-one and had spent five years with his wife. "I did. Margaret was a fine woman. And a *goot* wife."

"Margaret?" she asked quietly.

"Margaret Yoder. She was a year older than me. We had Jed during the first year of our marriage. Jacob came twelve months later."

He saw compassion in Esther's gaze. "And you loved her?"

He looked away. "I cared for her. She was a *goot* mother for the short time she was here after the boys were born."

"I'm sorry," she breathed, warming his heart.

He rewarded her with a smile. "The Lord has plans for us that we don't always see or recognize." He watched her eat a piece of cake, continuing to study her as she finished the bite.

He wanted to spend time with her. There was something about her that made him feel at home in her presence. He longed to tell her that he needed to see her again.

"Esther—"

"*Endie* Esther!" a girl's voice called. Suddenly the back kitchen door opened and five of Abraham Fisher's children entered the room.

Mary Ruth halted when she realized that Esther had company. He saw the girl recognize him and relax. "Preacher David. I didn't expect to find you here."

Jonas and Jacob ran into the kitchen, asking for a snack. Jonas saw his sisters and brother and stopped abruptly. "I'm hungry," he told Mary Ruth as if defending his request for food.

David watched Lizzie's eldest daughter nod in understanding.

Esther rose from the table. "You all must be hungry. Sit down and I'll give you cake or brownies, whichever you prefer." She looked almost relieved as she sprang into action, getting cups and filling them with milk or lemonade and then cutting cake and brownies.

As he watched her, David realized that the time for wooing had passed…for now.

He realized that he and Jacob needed to get home. Jed would be back from school soon, and he didn't want his son returning to an empty house. As he stood and told her he had to leave, he saw a myriad of expressions cross Esther's lovely face. Relief. Disappointment. Shyness.

And he knew that they would meet and talk again, for he wanted to get to know the woman Esther had become. This time he would court and win her, for he had a feeling he was going to love her even more than the young fourteen-year-old girl he'd loved many years ago.

"So how was she?" Zack asked his mother about her ill friend. He had left her with Alta Miller and run some errands before returning to bring *Mam* home.

"She's doing well," his mother said with relief. "It was bad for a while, she told me, but she's finally recovering."

Eyes on the road, Zack steered the horse left onto a paved country road, handling the leathers with ease. "What was wrong?"

"She has been suffering from depression. She went to an English doctor. He identified the problem and treated her with medication."

Zack heard his mother sigh and he flashed her a concerned look. "Are you all right?"

"*Ja.* Just remembering how it was. If it wasn't for Dr. Rosemont, I might not be here today."

"You had a skilled doctor, and while the treatments were—" He searched for the right words but nothing strong enough came to mind. "—hard on you, you survived," he finished. "But you would tell me if you weren't feeling well, *ja*?"

She smiled at him. "I'm not *goot* at hiding how I feel. Esther and you can tell when I have the slightest irritation."

He regarded her with loving warmth. "We love you, *Mam*. We want you with us a long time."

She sniffed. "Apparently, I'm meant to be here on this earth longer than my eldest son—"

He squeezed her arm gently. "*Gott* loves us. If He felt it was Abraham's time, then He must have had a reason."

His mother was quiet for several moments. The only sound was the clip-clip of their horse's hooves on macadam and the squeak of the buggy springs and turn of its wheels.

"I'm glad Lizzie came into Abe's life after Ruth passed on," *Mam* said.

Zack had thought the same thing more than once. Lizzie was a lovely woman with compassion and the ability to love his brother's children as if she'd given birth to them. He realized the reason their conversation about the farm had gone wrong was because he'd been taken by surprise—and was hurt that, after getting to know him, she would think him capable of forcing her from her home.

"She's stronger. Better for Abraham than Ruth was." *Mam* bit her lip as if she'd confessed something she shouldn't have. "I told her so."

Zack raised his eyebrows. "You told Lizzie that she was stronger than Ruth?"

His mother frowned. "I told her that she is different than Ruth."

"And?" he asked.

"That's all I said." Concern filled his mother's gaze. "She—" *Mam* stopped, looked horrified.

"*Mam*," he said, "how did she react?"

"I don't know. At least I didn't think anything of it, but now I recall that after I mentioned it she ran out of the room to find the children."

Zack felt an ache settle within his chest. "Lizzie married my *brooder* only three weeks after his wife's death. I'm sure it wasn't easy for her. He would have been grieving, his children devastated. Seeing their grief, she must have wondered if she'd ever win a place in their hearts and in their life."

He heard his mother groan. "Because of me, she thinks she doesn't measure up."

"*Ja,*" Zack said worriedly. That plus the fact that he hadn't assured her that her life on the farm was safe had to be weighing heavily on Lizzie's mind.

"I'll talk with her. Lizzie is stronger. She was better for your *brooder*. Had he lived, Abraham would have found joy in having a life partner who worked by his side rather than a weak girl who needed to be coddled."

Zack silently agreed. He had come to Honeysuckle expecting one thing and found something greater, more wonderful, instead. Now the girl who had stepped in to fill a loved one's position in the house was in pain. If his mother couldn't convince her, then he would. The last thing he wanted was to see Lizzie hurt. She had brought warmth and joy into the Fisher family and she needed to be cherished, not condemned, for marrying his older brother. Could he convince her that, despite her fears, he had her best interests at heart?

Lizzie lay in bed, staring at the ceiling. She didn't remember the last time she'd been able to lie down in the afternoon. Esther had Jonas and Ezekiel over at the cottage. With the rest of the children at school and Zack and

Sarah away for the day, the house was quiet, eerily so. While she appreciated the time to rest, she also felt lonely, as if she weren't needed here. It was an odd feeling since she'd been busy to the point of barely being able to take a breath since she married Abraham.

Tears filled her eyes as she thought of her dead husband. Had he felt her lacking? Sarah had. She had made it clear that she was different than the woman Abraham had first married.

Her hip still ached but it was easing as much as it could, considering her condition. She had resorted to taking two ibuprofen tablets and wondered if she should have taken four.

She sat up and had a good cry; there was no one there to hear. She wept until she was spent and could garner the strength to carry on. She would accept whatever the Lord had planned for her. She prayed for guidance and became determined to put her sorrow behind her. The children needed her, even if no one else did.

As she lay down again, she thought of Zack and enjoyed the comfort of knowing he was near. She cared for him a great deal, more than she should. *Have I ruined our friendship, Zack?*

He hadn't said anything more about the farm. He'd come for lunch at the house with Esther. His good humor warmed the room and proved infectious to his mother, sister and the children. Would he change his mind about the property? And what if he didn't? Could she fault him for wanting what was rightfully his?

The thought of leaving her home brought on a fresh onslaught of tears. She mentally berated herself. *You are a member of the Fisher family,* an inner voice said. *You married Abraham, took his name, cared for his children.*

Zack seemed to have forgiven her their argument. Perhaps their friendship would mend—it already seemed as if it had. Things would be fine as long as he didn't discover that she was the one who had urged Abraham into the barn loft from which he'd fallen to his death.

A soft knock on her bedroom door startled her. *"Ja?* Who is it?"

"Lizzie? It's Sarah. May I speak with you a minute?"

Lizzie sprang out of bed and hurriedly wiped her eyes. It was at times like this one that she understood why the English had mirrors while the Amish didn't.

She straightened her prayer *kapp* and attempted to brush the wrinkles from her dress. Knowing that there wasn't anything else she could do to hide the fact that she'd been crying, Lizzie opened the door.

Sarah stood there, looking concerned as she tentatively entered the room. She walked a few feet, stopped and turned to face Lizzie, who hoped that it wasn't too obvious that she'd cried. "Lizzie," she began, and Lizzie was surprised by the woman's look of uncertainty.

Her strength and her desire to help others kicked in, and Lizzie became concerned. "Sarah, what's wrong? Your friend—Alta—is she all right?"

Sarah nodded. "It's not Alta I'm worried about. It's you."

Surprised, Lizzie raised her eyebrows. "Me?"

"Ja." Sarah studied her intently and Lizzie felt herself blush. "Lizzie," she said, "I believe you misunderstood me this morning, and I feel terrible about it."

Lizzie didn't know what to say, so she waited for Sarah to continue.

"When I told you that you were different than my son's first wife, I meant that as a compliment, not a complaint. It wasn't until Zack and I were coming home from

Alta's that I realized that you may have taken my words the wrong way."

Hope rose within Lizzie and the ache in her heart started to ease.

Sarah looked about the room, her gaze settling on her rumpled bed. "You were lying down," she said and Lizzie gave a nod. "Is your hip hurting you?"

Lizzie debated whether or not to tell her. Finally, she sighed and said, "*Ja*, but it's not as bad as it was earlier. I took ibuprofen," she admitted.

"*Goot.*" Sarah lifted a hand to rub the back of her neck. Lizzie waited for her to finish what she had to say.

"You and Ruth are so different," her mother-in-law began. "We loved Ruth—we did. We knew her all of her life. When her parents decided to move from Honeysuckle, Abraham asked her to marry him, and she agreed. She loved him—I don't question that. But was she *goot* for him? He loved her, as well, but as a wife, Ruth wasn't a strong woman, while you—Lizzie—I don't doubt for one moment that you were the woman he needed. You married my son while he was grieving, took care of his children and made him a home, and coming to know you like I do, you did it with compassion and love. You are a woman that any *mudder* would be proud to have as her son's wife."

As she listened, Lizzie felt a fresh rush of tears, but she blinked to control them. Sarah smiled as she approached and placed a hand on Lizzie's shoulder.

"*Danki.*" Lizzie laughed and wiped her face when she saw that Sarah had become emotional and was brushing away her own tears.

Sarah gazed at her a moment and then she put her arms around a stunned Lizzie. "Never doubt that I'm pleased that you married Abraham." Sarah released her and they smiled.

"Mam!" Anne's loud voice traveled up from downstairs.

Lizzie grinned. Her mother-in-law accepted her. Perhaps Zack and Esther accepted her as family, too.

"The harvest is the day after tomorrow. The Zooks will be coming. We have food to fix." Lizzie went to the bed, smoothed the bed quilt into place. Sarah moved to the other side and helped her.

They could hear running footsteps on the stairs.

"Mam?" Anne, the first child to enter the room, saw Lizzie and her grandmother. *"Hallo, Grossmama."* Rebecca and Matthew followed her in.

"Mam, may we have a snack?" Matt said.

"Mam, Nancy wants you to look at our papers." Nancy Miller was the children's teacher. She was young, unmarried and lived near the one-room schoolhouse in Honeysuckle.

Sarah met Lizzie's gaze with laughter in her eyes. "It sounds like everyone is home and life is about to get busy again."

"Thanks be to *Gott,*" Lizzie said as she urged the children from the room.

Chapter Eighteen

On Tuesday, Lizzie, Sarah and Esther worked to get ready for the harvest. Although only the Zooks would be coming to help, Lizzie felt that it was always wise to fix enough food for a large gathering.

The children were home from school. The teacher had postponed class for all students until after harvest time, as the children would be expected to help.

Zack entered the house, his hands dirty and with a streak of soil across one cheek. "Food?" he asked with a grin.

Lizzie handed him a bar of soap and a towel. "You've been digging in the dirt, Zack?" she asked, knowing that he'd been working in the barn.

He regarded her with good humor. "*Ya* want me to wash first?"

She nodded. "Where is Matt?"

He looked out the window. "He'll be here. He's cleaning up at the pump." He slipped outside again and joined his nephew, where he proceeded to wash his hands and share the soap and towel with Matthew.

"All clean," Zack pronounced as he and Matthew entered the house.

"Goot," Sarah said. "Fried chicken?"

He nodded, and Lizzie felt his eyes on her. She loved this playful side of him. She removed the frying pan from the stove and forked up pieces of fried chicken and set them to drain on paper towels layered on a plate. She took a pan of cooked corn off the burner and dumped it into a serving bowl. Sarah had made mashed potatoes, and she set a bowlful in the middle of the table.

The children were chatty as they ate their meal while the adults listened. Lizzie continually felt Zack's eyes on her, and she frequently looked his way to see if there was a problem.

"Do you need anything?" she asked him.

He smiled warmly, his eyes crinkling at the corners, lighting up his face. *"Nay,* just appreciating this *goot* food." Lizzie inhaled sharply, aware of how handsome he looked. Zack was the first man she'd ever been attracted to, and the knowledge frightened her. It was wrong to feel this way about a man with her husband gone only a little over two months—and because Zack was Abraham's younger brother. Zack was friendly and helpful, and she was grateful their friendship was still intact. He seemed to appreciate her efforts in everything she did for the farm and the family.

"What time will the Zooks be here tomorrow?" she asked, hoping that talk of the next day's harvest would help her get herself under control again.

"They'll be here before sunrise," he said, and Lizzie expected no less.

"Onkel Zack, can we help, too?" Jonas asked.

"Ja, Jonas, you and Zeke can help, but it may not be in the fields." He took a bite of fried chicken, chewed and swallowed. "Whatever job you have, it will be no less important."

Jonas and Zeke looked pleased.

Lizzie frowned. What possible job could a four-year-old and a three-year-old do? She would talk with Zack about the matter later.

Soon, they were done with lunch, and Zack and Matthew went back to the barn. "To check on the machinery," Matthew explained before they departed.

"Matthew has enjoyed spending time with Zack," Sarah said.

Lizzie agreed. "Having his *onkel* here has been *goot* for him. Matt took his *vadder*'s death hard. All of the children did."

"And you," Sarah said softly.

"Ja," she said truthfully for different reasons. "I can't say it hasn't been difficult, but we've managed."

Her mother-in-law handed her a clean, wet dish to dry. "You have more than managed. You've done a fine job, *dochter.*"

Lizzie swallowed hard. *"Danki,"* she whispered.

"Mam." Esther returned from showing her nieces what to do in the house. "Would you like your sheets washed?"

"Nay," Sarah said. "Just did them yesterday."

Esther left quickly and Lizzie heard her call up the stairs, "None of the beds, girls! Just dust and sweep and make sure all is tidy."

"Ja, Endie Esther," answered a voice that Lizzie recognized as belonging to Mary Ruth. The girls had been helpful all day and Lizzie felt pleased as Esther reentered the kitchen. The females in the house spent the afternoon wrapping the baked goods they'd made earlier that day.

That night Lizzie fell into bed, feeling as if she'd accomplished a lot. Her hip ached as usual but not as bad as it had in the past. Having Sarah and Esther's help as well as the girls at home had made chores easier for her. It was nice to work together. Lizzie felt happy in their company, and she looked forward to seeing Rachel and Peter.

The next morning, just before dawn, Lizzie climbed out of bed, careful not to wake Anne, who slept soundly beside her. She dressed quickly and without a sound. Years of experience had her able to roll and pin her hair in the dark. She slipped socks on her bare feet and then carried her shoes out into the hall, before closing the bedroom door silently behind her.

No one stirred as Lizzie crept down the stairs to the first floor and headed for the kitchen. She lit a candle from the stove and then set it into a stand on the countertop. Then she went to work by candlelight, filling a stovetop percolator with water and then the basket with ground coffee. She placed the coffeepot on the burner to brew, then pulled out dishes and breakfast items for her family and the Zooks, who would be arriving soon.

Lizzie paused a moment to enjoy the quiet and peer out the back window. There was a beam of light moving across the yard. Zack with a flashlight, she thought with a smile. She met him at the back door, held it open until he slipped inside past her.

"*Goot* morning," he murmured, his eyes kind and his smile infectious.

She answered him in kind. "Are you ready for a busy harvest day?"

He nodded. "Busy but exciting," he said as if he anticipated the harvest. "Is that *coffe* I smell?"

"*Ja*. Want a cup?" She saw his answer in his smile and took a mug down from the cabinet. She poured him coffee, added two spoons of sugar with a splash of milk and handed it to him. He accepted the mug and took a sip.

He gazed at her warmly. "You remember how I like my *coffe*."

"It's not hard." She reached for the plate of muffins and extended it to him. "To hold you over until we can serve you a proper breakfast."

Sarah came downstairs, followed by the children. They were all dressed and ready for the day's work.

"*Onkel* Zack, we're going to help," Jonas said.

"Would you like to be our water boys?" he said. "We get awful thirsty in the fields. If you can bring us water whenever we come back for a drink, that would be help-ful. It's hard work but I think you both are up for the task."

Lizzie smiled approvingly at Zack over the boys' heads. Jonas and Zeke seemed eager to help. He had chosen the perfect job for them.

There was just a hint of light in the morning sky when a buggy pulled into the barnyard. "The Zooks are here," Lizzie said.

Suddenly, four vehicles followed the Zooks' buggy. Sev-eral more arrived and parked in a row in the barnyard. She recognized the Shetler brothers with Neziah's two sons. She waved to Bishop Andy and his family and several other members of their close-knit Amish community. Anne Stoltzfus arrived with fresh pumpkin pie and a smile. Lizzie raised a hand in greeting.

Surprised by the number of helpers, Lizzie followed Zack into the yard and caught sight of her friend Rachel, a basket in one hand and a plate in the other.

"What's all this?" Lizzie asked her friend, gesturing toward all the folks who had arrived behind the Zooks. "I didn't expect everyone." She was touched that the com-munity had taken time from their own harvests to as-sist them.

"This is called help, and you'll have a lot of it today," Rachel said. She held up the basket. "I brought biscuits and pancakes. Both are still warm."

Lizzie widened her eyes. "How early did you get up to cook these?"

Rachel shrugged as if it were nothing.

"No earlier than all the other women here." Women and children had come with the men, each bringing their share of food. Ellen had driven over with Dinah Plank, ready to help Lizzie feed the workers.

"Lizzie?"

Lizzie turned, surprised to see her mother, father and two brothers.

"Mam! Dat!" She was glad that they had come.

William and Luke waved as they joined Zack; Neziah; Micah; and Rachel's husband, Peter, along with a man she didn't immediately recognize in the dark. Lizzie saw that he was Joseph Lapp when he stepped into the house and set down a pail of goat's milk. Joseph made his living as a dairy goat farmer.

"Danki, Joseph," she said. "It's kind of you to bring this." She saw his face turn red as he nodded, then went outside. It was rare to see the man out and about. He came to church, then went home immediately afterward. But he never ignored someone in need. She wondered how Anne Stoltzfus was faring with the man's goats always venturing into her vegetable garden.

Lizzie's mother brought fresh eggs and bacon that was already cooked.

"Mam, it's so nice that you came all this way to help."

"You're my *dochter"* was all her mother said.

"How did you know we were harvesting today?" she asked, pleased that her family had come.

"I told her," Sarah admitted, coming up from behind.

"Your *mudder* and I stopped to chat in McCann's Grocery the other day."

Lizzie widened her eyes. "You know my *mam*?"

"*Ja*," her mother-in-law said, "but it's been a long time."

Lizzie watched as her mother grinned at Sarah. She hadn't known the two knew each other, although she should have guessed. *Mam* had been the one to encourage her to accept Abe's offer of marriage, an offer that most likely had been her mother's idea from the start. *She knew that Abraham was a widower in need of a wife.*

The men had gone into the fields and begun work. Some of the workers used corn binders while others cut corn by hand. Zack had replaced the broken wheel on the corn wagon, and she watched as he hitched up their black Belgian and steered the horse toward the closest cornfield.

Beyond the corn crop, workers began to cut and roll hay into large round rolls, which they left in various locations in the hayfield. The weather was good for harvesting, sunny and cool with barely a breeze to stir up the corn and hay dust.

The women set out food for breakfast and served the workers who came in from the fields to eat. They didn't stay long, as they were eager to get the job done. Lizzie watched with delighted affection as Jonas and Zeke ran to Zack and the other men with a pitcher of cold water and plastic cups. Zack pushed back his hat when he saw their eager approach. He grinned widely as he accepted their drink offering, and then he took a sip before tapping the brim of each boy's straw hat playfully.

The boys love Zack, Lizzie thought. He was better with them than their father had been. After Ruth's death, Abraham had grieved too deeply to pay much attention to his children. *And now all the children call me Mam.* She had a feeling that Zack, Esther and now Sarah's presence on the farm had something to do with the older ones' change of heart.

Zack. She loved him. She stiffened, startled by the realization that her feelings for him were more than friendship, stronger than anything she'd ever felt or known. She knew that she was attracted to him, but this was more. She was afraid to hope, to long for something that she might never experience…a relationship with a man who loved her as much as she loved him. She loved him, which meant that she trusted him. He wasn't going to take over the farm, not without considering her wish to stay.

The men were back at work. The harvest was coming along nicely. The morning flew by and suddenly it was time for the midday meal.

The women set out the food on tables in the yard, and the men came in to eat in shifts. Lizzie served the men while keeping an eye on her children, especially her youngest three. Jonas, along with Asa and Joel Shetler, ran to bring water and cold drinks to the workers whenever they needed them. Lizzie smiled as she kept a fond eye on them until she realized that someone was missing— Ezekiel. She searched for her three-year-old, but she didn't see him anywhere. Her heart started to pound hard in fear as she recalled the last time one of her children had slipped from her sight. Jonas's injury had been serious enough for a trip to the medical clinic.

"Have you seen your *brooder* Zeke?" she asked Rebecca.

"Last time I saw him he was over there." Her daughter gestured toward the end of the yard where several children played running games.

Lizzie hurried in their direction, but she didn't see Ezekiel in the group. And then she heard his young voice.

"Hallo!" he called, drawing her attention to the barn-loft window. Terror-struck, she ran into the barn, her stomach churning with fear.

"Zeke!" she cried at the base of the ladder to the loft. "Come away from the window." Images of Abraham's body on the concrete floor near the ladder haunted her as she began the climb up the ladder rungs toward the hayloft and her three-year-old son.

"Zeke, stay where you are. I'm coming!" Lizzie placed one foot on the next rung followed by the other. Each step higher hurt her hip, but she thought only of Zeke and getting him safely down without incident. "Stay away from the window. Not too close to the edge," she warned. "How did you get up there?" She spoke calmly, but inside she felt a mess of fear.

Her foot took a sudden misstep and Lizzie slid down the ladder, scraping and slamming her fingers on the rungs as she slipped. She jarred her legs and her bad hip painfully as she fell and hit the concrete. She cried out and lay there, gasping, her hands and hip hurting. She tried to get up, but the pain in her hip was too severe.

"Mam!" Zeke cried. *"Mam!"*

Lizzie looked up to see Zeke moving toward the ladder as if he planned to climb down. *"Nay*, Ezekiel. Stay!" she managed to gasp out. "Don't move!"

"Jonas!" Zeke screamed, and Lizzie looked over to see her four-year-old son enter the barn. He caught sight of her lying near the base of the ladder and hurried to her side.

"Mam!" He looked frightened.

Lizzie attempted a smile to reassure him, but she must

have failed miserably because Jonas wasn't to be consoled.

"Jonas, run for help. Find *Onkel* Zack," she urged. "That's a *goot* boy," she whispered as he ran out of the barn, calling loudly for help.

After what seemed like long minutes but must have been only seconds, Zack entered the barn and ran to her.

"Zack, Ezekiel's in the loft." She pointed toward the hayloft. "Please get him down." Her gaze begged him to take care of her son first. She was relieved when he understood.

Zack climbed up the ladder as Neziah and Micah Shetler came to stand near the barn entrance, ready to lend a hand. "Zeke, come here," he urged. The boy obeyed and Zack grabbed hold of him with one arm and then climbed down to set Zeke safely on the ground. Lizzie sighed with relief and closed her eyes.

"Mam," Zeke sobbed, running toward her.

"I'll take care of her, Ezekiel," Zack promised. "You and Jonas, go outside with Neziah and Micah." Jonas and Ezekiel obeyed, and Neziah placed a hand on each boy's shoulder as he and Micah led them out of the barn.

Zack hunkered down beside her. "Lizzie," he whispered, "you're hurt." She felt his hand brush along her cheek, her forehead. "Let me help you."

He lifted her easily and carried her out of the barn, across the yard and into the house. Lizzie felt embarrassed as she caught Bishop Andy's disapproving look. She turned away, deciding that she didn't care. Being carried by Zack was a new and thrilling experience for her, and so she focused on the joy of his rescue. Surely, the elders couldn't find fault in a man assisting his injured sister-in-law.

She met Zack's gaze, saw concern in his dark eyes.

She blushed, aware that she looked disheveled. She felt her breath quicken as she closed her eyes. Why did she have to go and fall in love with him?

"You all right?" he asked softly.

"Ja." She bit her lip. She should tell him to put her down so she could walk on her own, but the pain in her hip reminded her that if he set her down she wouldn't be able to stand. So she accepted his help, hoping that by doing so she hadn't ruined her reputation and his.

His breath stirred the tendrils at her forehead that had escaped from her head covering. She swallowed hard and wondered what she was going to do about her growing love for him. Zack entered the house through the back door, then walked through the kitchen to the gathering room, where he placed her gently onto a chair.

"Lizzie—" he began, his expression earnest. Whatever he had to say was lost when her mother hurried to her side after learning of her mishap.

"Lizzie!" her mother exclaimed. "Are you all right?"

"I'm fine, *Mam.*"

Her mother shot Zack a grateful look. "Zack, *danki*!" She began to fuss over Lizzie as she asked Zack to get someone to bring her a bag of ice.

Zack left and brought back a bag of ice a minute later. Her mother, who always seemed unflappable, began to cry as she accepted the ice from him. "You could have been seriously hurt or killed," *Mam* sobbed, "and it's my fault!"

Lizzie stared at her mother in startled silence. She exchanged confused glances with Zack, who seemed to realize that mother and daughter needed to be alone. Lizzie heard him as he urged the curious newcomers who suddenly appeared in the doorway to leave the room. He then gave her a look that said he'd be near if she needed him, and he left her alone with her mother.

"I'm sorry," her mother cried.

"*Mam*, I'm fine. It's all right. I'm not seriously hurt."

"*But you could have been*," Lydia sobbed, "and 'tis my fault!"

"*Mam*, how could it be your fault? I'm the one who climbed the ladder."

To her shock, her mother began to sob in earnest, and Lizzie could only stare at her in shock and discomfort. Finally, she reached out to touch her mother's shoulder. "*Mam*, sit down. Let's get you some water. Or would you like something else? I'll just ask Rachel to—"

"*Nay!*" her mother said, clearly still upset, although her tears had stopped. "I'm fine," she said more calmly.

"Sit, *Mam*," she urged softly, with compassion. Her mother's tears had surprised and moved her.

Mam pulled a chair closer and sat down. She reached for Lizzie's hand. "Lizzie, I know you think that I didn't love you like your *brooders* and sisters. But it's not true. There is something I should have told you years ago." Her voice was calm and even, but her eyes said differently.

Lizzie frowned. *"Mam?"*

"You don't have congenital hip dysplasia," her mother confessed. "You were injured in an accident when you were a toddler. It's my fault that you have that limp."

Chapter Nineteen

Lizzie stared at her mother as the truth began to dawn on her. *Is Mam responsible for my limp?* "What happened?" she asked gently.

Her *mam* sat straighter in the chair and Lizzie saw that she fought tears. "You and your *brooders* were playing in the yard. I was on the front porch keeping an eye on you while I did some mending. You were two. William was seven, Luke six. Susan wasn't home. The boys were playing ball, and you were toddling about the grass." She suddenly smiled. "You loved to pick wildflowers."

Mam drew a sharp breath. "I snipped myself with my sewing scissors. Foolishly, I got up and ran inside to grab a dish towel. I was gone less than a minute. When I ran back to the porch, you were gone and I couldn't find you. I asked the boys where you were, but they didn't know. They'd been too busy playing. And then suddenly I heard you crying, and it was an awful, frightening sound. You had climbed onto the other end of the porch and fallen off the edge. You landed awkwardly, and I knew by your cries that you were hurt. I ran and picked you up, and you screamed louder. Your leg hung at an odd angle, and I knew you were seriously injured, and it was my fault."

"*Mam*, it wasn't your fault."

"*Ja*, it was. I never should have gone into the house, not even for a few seconds." Her mother lost the battle with tears. "I took you to the doctor. He said that you'd sprained your leg and that you would heal. But you didn't. You started to limp but I gave it some time. I took you back to the doctor, but he said there was nothing he could do. You had damaged your hip. He said that we could take you to a specialist in Philadelphia, but he said it wouldn't matter, because he didn't believe that there was anything that could be done."

Her mother got out of her chair, knelt before her and took hold of her hands. "I watched you struggle for years. And I was the one responsible. I had hurt you and there was nothing I could do. I knew life would be tougher for you than my other children and so I became determined to make you strong."

Tears filled her eyes in sympathy for her mother. Lizzie understood about feeling responsible. Hadn't she felt responsible for Jonas's injured hand? What if his hand had been hurt so badly that he'd never have the full function of his fingers? She knew exactly how her mother must have felt. She'd been in her shoes but had come out on the better end. *That's why* Mam *treated me differently*.

"*Mam*." Lizzie studied her mother with compassion. "You're not responsible for what happened. It was *Gottes Wille*. I've managed to live a *goot* life, haven't I? And I *am* stronger because of my limp."

Her mother stood. "I urged you to marry Abraham."

"*Ja*, and because of you, I have a home of my own and a family. I love the children and I enjoy living on the farm. No regrets," she murmured.

Lydia looked at her. "*Nay?*"

Lizzie smiled. "*Nay.* I am happy here."

Mam's sigh was released with a shudder. "I love you, Lizzie. I always have. When I heard that you'd fallen, I panicked and thought the worst. I'm sorry I didn't tell you long ago." She examined Lizzie with a concerned eye. "You're in pain. Can I get you anything? More ice? Something to drink? Something to ease the hurt?"

Lizzie managed a smile for her mother. "Upstairs in my bedroom is a bottle of aspirin. Would you send one of the children for it? Ask Anne. She knows where I keep it."

"Lizzie," her *mam* said as she turned away.

Lizzie clasped her hand. "'Tis all right, *Mam*, honestly."

For the first time, she understood her mother and the knowledge gave her peace. Despite what Lydia had told her, she didn't hold her mother responsible.

However, she *was* responsible for what had happened to Abraham. She never should have urged him to go up into the barn loft. *Abraham's family doesn't know.* What would they say when she finally confessed the truth?

Esther was surprised when David Hostetler arrived to help with the harvest. He'd come with his two young sons earlier that morning.

"Esther," he'd greeted.

"Can we stay and play with Jonas and Ezekiel?" Jed asked.

Esther couldn't help smiling at both boys; they were small replicas of their father.

"*Ja*, you can play with my nephews." She looked at David. "I didn't expect to see you today," she admitted.

"Are you glad or sad to see me?" he asked, his bright blue eyes studying her intently. He was dressed for field work in a dark blue shirt and triblend denim pants. His straw hat was pushed back slightly, allowing her a good view of his features.

"David—"

"Glad or sad?"

She blushed. "Glad," she whispered.

He grinned. "*Goot*, because you will be seeing a lot of me in the coming weeks."

"I will?"

He patted his boys' backs, urging them to find Jonas and Zeke, before he returned his attention to her. "*Ja*, Esther Fisher, because I intend to win your affection."

Her heart skipped a beat. "*Ya* do?"

He nodded, his features softening as he studied her with a smile. "It's been years since you've been in Honeysuckle. I intend to convince you to remain here…with me."

She inhaled sharply. "You are sure of yourself," she challenged, upset by his confidence.

"*Nay.*" His large hand settled on her shoulder, making the skin beneath her dress tingle and feel warm. "I trust in the Lord. I've learned to follow whatever He tells me."

Her insides melted. "And you think He wants you and me to spend time together?"

"*Nay*, I believe that He wants you and me to live a lifetime together."

"Why do you say that?" she'd whispered, feeling a little thrill.

"Because I've been praying to see you again since you left Honeysuckle when you were fourteen." He left her with that startling claim as he joined the group of workers in the barnyard.

Lizzie and her mother had had more than enough time to talk alone, Zack thought as he stood at the kitchen window and gazed out into the busy yard. The workers had gone back to work. The children were running about the yard, laughing and chasing each other. Zeke and Jonas, he was glad to see, had suffered no lasting effects from their mother's fall. He was eager to see her again, to see for himself that she was all right.

The knowledge that Zeke had climbed the ladder to the loft turned his insides cold. Abraham had fallen from the loft. Seeing Zeke up there must have terrified Lizzie.

"Lizzie," he murmured beneath his breath. A sweet woman who must have captured his brother's heart easily if Abraham had felt anything close to what he himself felt.

Emotion slammed into him hard, and he swallowed against a lump. She was his sister-in-law—his older brother's widow, and he liked her. Too much. It was wrong.

He knew that he should keep his distance. It was the right thing to do—but how could he? He was drawn to her. Seeing her, spending time with her, made him happy. *I love her.* He moved away from the window as Lizzie's mother entered the room. "Is she well?" he asked her.

Lydia King nodded, her eyes shimmering. "She is a *goot dochter*," she said. "Always has been."

"Is she alone?" he asked. Lydia nodded. "I'm going to speak with her." He hurried toward the gathering room.

Seeing her in the same chair he'd placed her in, he went to her side. Lizzie had her injured leg propped up by a wooden footstool with a fresh ice pack on top of her apron in the area of her hip.

He approached and saw her through the eyes of a man who realized that he was in love and that, wrong or not, he wanted her in his life.

"Zack." She met his gaze, stark joy evident in her

green eyes. Tendrils of dark auburn hair had escaped from beneath her prayer *kapp*, and he felt the strongest urge to tuck those red strands gently back beneath her head covering and around her ear.

He examined her face for any sign of pain. She seemed relaxed and happy. He felt a tremor of relief. "Are you all right?"

"*Ja.* I'm fine...thanks to you."

He frowned. "Me?" And she inclined her head. He had carried her inside, but that didn't make him a hero. He shifted uncomfortably. "Did your *mudder* and you have a nice talk?" he asked.

"*Ja,*" she murmured as she gestured for him to take a seat in the next chair. "She told me something I never knew."

When he raised an eyebrow in question, she said, "I wasn't born with congenital hip dysplasia. I fell off our front porch when I was two and hurt my hip." She blinked as if fighting tears of emotion. "*Mam* felt responsible. I always thought she treated me differently because she was ashamed, but it wasn't that at all. It wasn't because she loved me less than my *brooders* and sisters that she held herself back from me. Knowing what I'd have to face as I grew older, she wanted to make me strong."

"You thought she didn't love you because you were less than perfect in her eyes," he said, understanding. He hurt for the little girl she'd been and the pain she suffered as a young woman.

Lizzie looked down as she fingered the edge of her apron. She suddenly seemed too shy to meet his gaze. "*Ja,*" she whispered.

"Lizzie." He studied her with a surge of overwhelming tenderness. "You are an amazing woman."

He saw her surprise as she locked gazes with him.

"I'm just a woman," she said. She appeared uncomfortable with his praise.

"*Nay*. You're a loving young woman who cared for a grief-stricken man and his motherless children. I look around this house and see all the changes you made here since you came—wonderful changes." He recognized doubt in her eyes and sought to reassure her. "You wonder why I'm amazed? Because you made life better for my *brooder* and the children and because, had she lived, Ruth wouldn't have been as *goot* a mother and wife as you."

He saw pain cross her expression. He immediately rose. "What can I get you? Do you need me to carry you upstairs? Would you like to lie down?" She quickly shook her head. "More ice?" he asked as he watched her shift the bag of ice as if seeking more relief from the cold.

"I am fine, Zack," she said softly. She moved as if to rise, but then grimaced and sat down again.

He hunkered down beside her, captured her hand and looked up into her eyes. "*Danki*," he said.

"What for? It is I who am thankful. If you hadn't come to help Zeke…" She bit her lip, an action he'd seen her do whenever she felt uncomfortable. Did he make her uncomfortable? he wondered as he rose to his feet. He hoped not.

"Zeke and Jonas?" she asked. "Are they all right?"

"*Ja*. They're outside playing. I had a talk with both of them. Neither one will be climbing into the loft without adult supervision."

Her brow cleared and she seemed relieved.

"Lizzie?" Her brother entered the room. He barely gave Zack a glance as he hurried to his sister.

Lizzie beamed at her brother. "William."

"William," Zack murmured with a nod. "*Mam*, Esther and I will keep an eye on the children while you talk with your *brooder*."

"*Danki*, Zack," she said, turning her attention to her brother. Zack left quietly, not wanting to intrude on them. But he would return to check on her later. He wouldn't be able to stay away.

Chapter Twenty

Lizzie met her brother's questioning gaze and arched an eyebrow. "What?"

"You care for him," William said.

She paled. "I—" She didn't like the topic of conversation. "I don't feel well." Her feelings for Zack Fisher were her own and she had no intention of sharing them with anyone, not even with her brother.

William was immediately concerned. "Shall I carry you upstairs?"

"*Ja*, I'd like to lie down for a little while." Zack had offered to take her to her room, but she knew that if he did, she might end up making her feelings for him known.

William swung her easily into his arms, then carried her toward the steps. "Do you need more ice?"

She shook her head, and he continued up the stairs to her bedroom. Being carried by her brother was a different experience than being carried by Zack. William set her on the bed, and she smiled at him. "Close the door on your way out, please," she said. "I'll be down again soon."

"Not without someone's help," her brother insisted.

She conceded his point. "Would you send Matt up in a half hour or so?"

He agreed. After he'd closed the door, Lizzie lay on her bed and stared up at the ceiling. She recalled the strength and warmth of Zack's arms as he'd carried her into the farmhouse. She'd liked the feeling. She liked everything about Zack, from the top of his dark-haired head to the soles of his black work shoes.

She closed her eyes and envisioned how it might have been if she and Zack had met under other circumstances and her childhood accident had never happened. Would he have paid her any notice if circumstances had been different and he'd stayed in Honeysuckle after his father's death? Would he have shown enough interest to talk with her, spend time with her?

Her thoughts followed that direction as her hip pain eased and she slowly drifted off to sleep.

Lizzie woke up abruptly when someone knocked on the door and she recalled why she was in her room.

"Come in," she called out as she struggled to rise.

The door opened as she swung her legs off the side of the bed and tried to push to her feet.

"Lizzie, sit down," a familiar voice scolded, and she realized that Zack had come to help her, not Matthew.

"I— What are you doing here?" she asked nervously. He shouldn't be in her bedroom. Naomi Beiler and Bishop Andy would certainly disapprove.

He approached with a small smile hovering about his lips while his dark gaze held concern for her.

"I can carry you more easily than Matt can."

She blushed with embarrassment. "How long have I been asleep?"

"Two hours."

She widened her eyes. "The harvest," she wailed.

"Done. Everyone has gone home, including your *brooders*. You'll have to accept me as your helpmate."

She was relieved that no one but the family knew that Zack was here to help. "No need. I can walk on my own." She pushed herself off the bed. As her feet touched the floor, she couldn't control a grimace.

Zack made a *tsk* sound. Then he picked her up and carried her downstairs. "Lizzie, you can be stubborn," he said softly.

She closed her eyes, leaned her head against his shoulder, unwilling for him to see how much she liked being in his arms. He carried her easily down the hallway and stairs. She could hear the thrumming of his heartbeat in her ear, smell his clean scent, feel the soft feathering of his breath against the top of her head. He took her into the kitchen, and she lifted her head away from his chest. She didn't want anyone to guess how she was feeling.

Zack's mother stood at the stove, cooking dinner. Someone had set the table, most probably the girls. Esther came out from the back room and was the first to see them.

"*Goot!* You're up. Zack, put her in this chair." Sarah didn't seem concerned that Zack had gone upstairs alone to get her.

Lizzie waved her arm. "I should help with dinner."

Sarah turned as Zack placed her in a chair. "*Nay, dochter*, you shouldn't. You fell and hurt yourself." She eyed her with concern. "How are you feeling?"

"Better." Her hip pain had eased, but her fingers ached. She flexed her hand and realized that Zack was watching her.

"You hurt your fingers," he said, as if becoming aware of it for the first time.

She avoided his glance. "I'm fine."

"Lizzie," he said strongly. She looked up, saw the look in his eyes and felt herself tremble. There was caring and concern, and something else she couldn't identify. "Let me see."

She reluctantly held out her hands. "See? I'm fine. No bruises. Just a bit sore from when I slipped."

"Let me see you move them."

She wiggled her fingers. He seemed satisfied with what he saw—or didn't see. *"Goot."*

Sarah called her grandchildren in for supper. Soon the room filled with Lizzie's seven children. Each one came in, their gaze immediately settling on Lizzie. She smiled reassuringly. "I'm fine," she said.

Mary Ruth and her sisters grinned. Matthew looked more cautious and sought guidance from his uncle, who nodded. Her eldest son looked relieved.

Jonas and Zeke weren't as easy to convince. Zeke looked as if he would cry, and Jonas eyed her with a worried expression.

"Come here," she urged with a smile.

They obeyed silently, and she grabbed each of their hands. "I'm fine. Don't worry. Zeke, next time, don't climb up into the loft, *ja*?"

He nodded. *"Ja, Mam."*

"Jonas?" The boy looked at her. *"Danki* for getting help." She managed to smile at everyone except Zack, whom she was afraid to look at, for she feared her heart would be on display for him.

"Let's see. Your *grossmama* and *Endie* Esther made a nice meal for us, and I'm hungry. I slept through the midday meal."

Everyone sat down, and Lizzie was pleased to watch as her family relaxed, ate and laughed as they talked about the harvest and seeing their community friends.

Lizzie's gaze went from one child to another and from Sarah to Esther…and then to Zack. Zack locked gazes with her, and she managed a smile that she wasn't sure was convincing. Something about his expression promised that he planned to have a word with her in the near future. She turned away, wondering what he'd hoped to say and fearing her reply. His behavior today both pleased and worried her. He was her brother-in-law. If only she could forget that.

In the days that followed, Lizzie and Zack worked side by side on the farm in easy camaraderie. Now that the harvest was in, Zack helped her with the animals. In the afternoons, he concentrated on making any needed repairs before winter set in.

"Lizzie, do *ya* have a hammer?" he asked one morning.

Lizzie looked at him. "A hammer?" She shrugged. "In the barn?" she guessed.

He suddenly grinned at her. *"Ja."*

She stared at him. "If you know where one is, why did you ask?"

Zack chuckled. "To see if you knew."

She laughed. He was irresistible when he teased her, which he seemed to do more often of late. It was as if the topic of the farm had never been discussed between them. Not discussed, she thought. She had done the talking; he hadn't given her an answer as to his intentions.

Her smile vanished. "Where are Jonas and Zeke?" she asked.

"Safe. They are with Esther in the *dawdi haus.*"

She released a heartfelt sigh. Zack placed a hand on her arm. "Lizzie, they are fine. They both know to stay out of the barn."

His touch burned through her dress sleeve. "You talked with them." She casually pulled away.

"*Ja.* They understand."

She blinked back tears. "*Nay.* They weren't there the day their father fell out of the barn loft."

He reached for her hand, laced his fingers through hers. "That's a *goot* thing. It must have been hard for you to find him."

"*Ja.*" She blushed when she realized that she was squeezing his hand. "I'm sorry." She attempted to withdraw, but he held on. She was dismayed how much she liked the warmth of his hand against hers.

"I guess I should get back to work," she said.

"Me, too." He gave her hand a gentle squeeze and then released it.

"Will you be back for lunch?" She still felt the warmth of his fingers as she self-consciously straightened her *kapp.*

He nodded. Lizzie stood a moment as she watched him walk away. The friendly familiarity between them, their teasing banter, she could handle. But as soon as she felt in need of his comfort, she was afraid. She had no right to rely on Abraham's brother, no right to love him as anything more than a brother-in-law. Yet she loved him still. He was kind and funny toward her, and she knew that no matter what happened between them in the future, he would always hold a special place in her heart.

The following Monday, Lizzie noticed that Sarah had become quiet. "Is something wrong?" she asked.

Sarah regarded her with affection. "I miss my other daughters—Miriam and Sadie."

Lizzie had not met Sarah's other children. "You want to go home," she said quietly.

Sarah nodded. "I've enjoyed being here, but it's time for me to leave."

"You will come back and visit?" Lizzie had become fond of Sarah and hated the thought of her going.

"*Ja*, and perhaps Miriam and Sadie will come with me. I think you would enjoy meeting Miriam most particularly."

"Your eldest daughter?"

Sarah nodded. "We are close, but it was not always so. At first, my relationship with her was the way yours was with Mary Ruth."

Lizzie was confused. "Why didn't you get along?"

"My husband was a widower when I married him. Miriam was ten. He and his first wife had no other children. Miriam was my child in my heart, and I had to wait patiently for her to understand. Fortunately, she realized how much I loved her before Sadie was born."

"You moved to be near Miriam after your husband's passing," Lizzie said, realizing how much Sarah's situation had been similar to hers.

"*Ja.*"

"And you are as close as any *mudder* and *dochter* even though you are her stepmother."

"More so because of what we've been through together."

"Do you think Mary Ruth will come to accept me in the same way?"

Sarah tied an apron around her waist. "She already has."

"But if you leave—"

"That won't change, Lizzie. Mary Ruth finally understands that you are there for her no matter what and that you will love her always."

"I'm glad you came." Lizzie took out flour, sugar, eggs and milk in preparation for baking.

"I am, too. You are nothing like I thought you would be. You are more than I ever could have wished for my son."

Lizzie had never told Sarah about her role in Abraham's accident. Should she tell her? What if Sarah didn't understand? What if Zack found out and resented her for it? She couldn't tell, at least not yet.

Tuesday afternoon Zack sought out her company. "Lizzie."

"*Hallo*, Zack." Lizzie examined his grim expression and experienced a sudden chill. "What's wrong?"

He shook his head. "There is nothing wrong, but my *mudder* wants to go home. And I'll be going with her."

Lizzie was surprised. "*Ja*, she said she was ready to leave," she said. But would he come back or stay in Ohio?

"The harvest is in, and the repairs have been made for the winter."

"*Danki*," she whispered. She wouldn't look at him; she wouldn't cry. "When will you go?"

"The day after tomorrow," he said. "I already called for a car."

She nodded but didn't meet his gaze; she didn't want to look foolish. She had no right to ask for anything else from him. He had come, she had thought, to take over the farm, but he'd stayed instead to help her with all the things that Abraham would have done if he'd been alive.

"And Esther?" Lizzie dared to ask. "Is she going, too?"

"*Nay*, she has decided to stay."

"I see." Lizzie had noticed the way Preacher David followed her sister-in-law with his eyes. Was there a relationship brewing there? She was pleased that Esther would remain. "It has been nice having you here," she admitted.

Something flashed briefly in his dark eyes. "You, Lizzie Fisher, were a nice surprise. My *brooder* was lucky to have married you. You are *goot* for the children."

Lizzie felt warmth curl in her belly. She couldn't quite process the fact that he was leaving. She had to step away now or else break down in front of him.

"I should get back to work," she said.

"I have a few more things to fix before I go." Zack's gaze seemed to focus beyond the barn.

"Will you be in for lunch?" They were talking pleasantries when they should be talking about Zack's future plans for the farm.

He nodded. "I will see you at lunch, then."

As he walked away, she could no longer hold back the tears. The wetness ran down her cheeks, and she wiped the tears away with trembling fingers.

Back to work, she thought, pulling herself together. She must go on as she had before she'd ever met Zack Fisher. It wouldn't be easy, but she would do it.

Chapter Twenty-One

"Did you tell her?" Esther asked her brother as Zack entered the kitchen.

"*Ja*. I'll take *Mam* home, and it will give me time to think about what I want to do."

Esther cut him a slice of apple pie and pushed it in his direction. "But you will return."

"I have to." Zack gratefully accepted it and forked up a taste.

"Because you love her."

His shocked look confirmed her suspicion. "It's that obvious?"

She shook her head. "Only to me. I know you too well not to see how you feel about her." She paused. "You should have talked with her about the farm."

Zack was silent for a long moment. "She brought it up. I was hurt that she didn't trust me enough, so I didn't tell her that the farm was hers for as long as she wanted it."

"You should have told her," Esther insisted. How could a man as intelligent as her brother be so dotty headed with the woman he loved?

Lizzie approached the *dawdi haus*. She had come to see Zack and Esther. She'd wanted to ask a favor of Zack and to invite Esther to move from the *dawdi haus* into the farmhouse after Zack and Sarah left.

Zack was coming out of the cottage as she neared the door. His appearance startled her and she tripped and fell.

"Lizzie!" Zack crouched beside her and helped her to her feet. "Are you all right?" His fingers remained firm but gentle after he'd set her on her feet.

She nodded. He stared at her a long moment. "Did you need something?"

"I thought to ask if you'd allow Matthew to help you finish the repairs before you leave."

Zack's dark eyes filled with warmth. "*Ja.* He is learning fast and will someday make a fine farmer."

"*Goot, goot,*" she murmured. "I should get back to the *haus*." She started to leave and felt his hand on her arm stopping her.

"What's wrong?" he asked. There was concern, kindness and warmth in his expression.

Lizzie blinked rapidly against tears. "You're leaving and we never finished our discussion."

"About the farm." His expression became unreadable. "*Ja.*"

"I don't have time to discuss this right now."

"Will you ever have time to talk about this?" she asked stiffly. "*Nay.*" She held up her hand when he opened his mouth to reply. She could see the answer in his beautiful dark eyes, and it stung. "I will see you later." Then she hurried off, not once looking back to gauge Zack's reaction as she limped quickly away.

Lizzie stood on the covered front porch of the farmhouse, watched as a large black car drew into the yard and Zack, with Esther, exited the *dawdi haus*.

"I loved staying here with you," Sarah said from behind her.

Lizzie smiled at her with warmth. "I'm so glad you came. I appreciated your help, and the children loved getting to know you." She saw that Sarah had carried her valise out onto the porch. "Here," she said, reaching for the bag, "let me help you."

Sarah shook her head. "Zack can get it."

Lizzie smiled weakly and turned back to watch as Zack put his suitcase into the trunk of the vehicle. "I'm sorry you have to go."

Esther spoke with her brother then approached the farmhouse. "*Mam*, you're ready."

"*Ja.*" Sarah smiled warmly at her daughter. "You're staying here." Esther inclined her head. "Does it have something to do with the preacher?"

Her daughter's blush gave her answer. "I like it here in Honeysuckle."

"You didn't want to move when you were younger," her mother said. "I should have allowed you to stay."

"*Nay, Mam.* You were right. It wouldn't have been fair to Abraham and Ruth. I'm glad I went. It was important for me to be with you when you were sick."

"I'm well now." Sarah placed a hand on Esther's arm. "Stay and live your life."

Esther grinned. She turned toward Lizzie. "You don't mind if I stay?"

"I'm pleased that you are," Lizzie said. In fact, she'd been overjoyed when she learned that Esther would remain in Honeysuckle. "You've all given so much to me and the children." Her heart fluttered as she looked past Esther to watch Zack's approach.

"Zack—" Esther began.

"I'm here," he said from behind his sister. "It's time," he said to his mother. Sarah handed him her valise.

"You will let us know that you arrived safely?" Lizzie asked.

Zack held her gaze as he agreed. He addressed his mother. "All set?"

"I'll be right there," his mother said. As Zack headed toward the car, Sarah turned to Lizzie. "You're a fine young woman, Lizzie Fisher."

Lizzie blinked back moisture. *"Danki,"* she whispered, trying not to cry. "I hope that we will see each other again."

"We will," Sarah promised and then she asked her daughter, "You will write?" Esther nodded.

Sarah joined Zack near the vehicle. Esther trailed her mother but Lizzie remained on the porch. There was a huge lump in her throat, and she didn't want them to see her tears. She didn't want Zack to go, but at the same time she was afraid what would happen if he stayed. She didn't understand. Why was he unwilling to discuss the farm?

Zack assisted his mother into the car. While his sister talked with Sarah through the open window, he returned to the porch. Lizzie held her breath as he drew closer.

"You've done well here," he said with a look that melted her heart. She managed to return his smile. "I'll be back," he promised, giving her hope for the first time. He continued to study her with intense dark eyes. "And then we will have that discussion."

"We will?" she whispered.

He cupped her face, and she blinked up at him, aware of his touch. "I have to go, but when I return…" His voice trailed off. "We'll talk about the future."

Heart racing, Lizzie stepped away. "Have a safe trip, Zack." Whose future was he talking about—his or hers?

"Take care, Lizzie." Zack left her where she stood and climbed into the front passenger seat of the vehicle.

Lizzie waved from the porch as the car drove away with Zack and his mother.

Esther climbed the porch steps, her gaze compassionate. "You will miss him," she said.

Lizzie nodded; she couldn't deny it.

"He will be back."

"But will I be able to stay?" Lizzie murmured beneath her breath. Esther looked at her with concern until Lizzie smiled at her reassuringly. "Would you like to move into the farm *haus*? We would love to have you live with us."

"*Nay.* I'm happy in the *dawdi haus*. I'll stay where I am, if you have no objection."

Lizzie assured her that she didn't. "I'm glad you're here."

A buggy entered their dirt lane and pulled into the yard, drawing their attention. Lizzie recognized Preacher David Hostetler. Her quick glance toward Esther noted the revealing pink in the woman's cheeks.

"I have work to do," Lizzie said, excusing herself. "I'll leave you to visit with David."

Esther flashed her a look of surprise, and Lizzie grinned at her knowingly before she opened the door to enter the house. She couldn't keep her lips from curving upward as she overheard David greet Esther warmly and her sister-in-law's shy, telling reply. Once inside, Lizzie moved to the window to watch Esther and David as they walked together toward the cottage with David's youngest son, Jacob, running ahead of them.

She loved Zack. She had prayed to the Lord about her feelings, and she had the sudden thought that He approved. She loved her first husband, Abraham—it was a quiet love that had blossomed from friendship and the shared task of raising the children and working the farm. But her love for Zack was different. It was warmth and racing hearts and the wild excitement she felt just being in his presence. She loved Zack as a woman loved a man. She'd loved Abraham as a young girl cared for her mentor.

Lizzie felt a burning in her belly. She wasn't betraying Abraham with her love for Zack. But Zack might feel differently. She sensed that he cared for her, was attracted to her, but could he get past the fact that she was his brother's widow?

Chapter Twenty-Two

"I thought you'd left," David said as he walked with her toward the *dawdi haus*.

"*Nay*, I decided to stay." Esther was pleasantly aware of every little thing about him—the way he moved, the warmth in his smile, the tenderness in his azure eyes. "I like it here in Honeysuckle."

"*Goot.*" His pleased voice made her look at him. "I'd like you to stay," he said softly. "I'd like to court you."

Esther felt her face redden. "You would?" she whispered.

He grinned, and she caught her breath. Age had made him even more handsome than when he was a teenager. "*Ja.* You're the woman for me. I felt it when we were young, and I believe that God brought you back to me for a second chance."

She didn't know how to respond. Joy filled her heart but she was afraid to trust it. "I—"

"I want to marry you, Esther Fisher, and I'm not patient enough to wait too long." His blue eyes regarded her with love.

Her heart tripped for joy. He wanted to marry her—November was the month for weddings and that was only a short week away. She lifted her hand to touch her *kapp* self-consciously. "David—"

"*Ja*, Esther?" He stopped near her door and faced her, and she felt the impact of his regard all the way down to her toes.

"Why?" she asked breathlessly. "Why do you want to marry me?" No one had shown an interest in her since she was younger.

He furrowed his brow as he studied her. "Why wouldn't I want to marry you? You're a kind and compassionate woman. You were lovely as a girl and you're even more so now. I look into your eyes and see the truth of you. I love you. Never doubt my affection for you. We were made to be man and wife."

Joy flushed her with warmth. "I—I love you, too."

Her words made him grin and his blue eyes darkened to navy blue.

"The boys?" she asked. "Will they object? They must miss their *mam*."

"*Nay*, they barely remember her. They've spent time with you and your nephews." His expression softened as he glanced toward his youngest son, who had stopped ahead to watch a squirrel run across the lawn and climb a tree. "I can tell that they already love you." He faced her. "My sons need a *mudder*. They need *you*. Are you ready to be their *mam*?"

Esther thought of his young sons. They were adorable and sweet, and while she didn't expect them to behave always, she knew that she wanted to be their mother. "Your sons are precious," she said with a smile. "I'd like nothing better than being their *mudder*."

"Nothing?" he teased with a gleam in his eyes.

Face turning red, Esther laughed. "Except to have you

as my husband." David grinned, and Esther knew that she would marry this man this moment if given the chance.

His voice dropped. "As I wish you to be my bride."

Tears filled her eyes as she gazed up at him. "After we left Honeysuckle, I never thought I'd have you again in my life."

"If you'd stayed, I would have asked to court you once we were older, and we would have married. But then you were gone, and so years later I married Margaret. We had a *goot* life together and when she died..." He trailed off, and she could feel the pain he must have suffered after the death of his wife. "I never forgot about you. *Never.* But I can't say that I didn't love Margaret, because I did."

Esther remained silent. He had loved another woman, but why shouldn't he have? Neither one of them knew that she'd return to Honeysuckle, and they'd been so young. Loving Margaret, being a good husband to her, was so like David. She would have been disappointed to know that he'd married without love. His successful marriage to Margaret boded a happy future for her and David.

David stood watching his son Jacob, who had gone on to discover Lizzie's freshly tilled vegetable garden. The boy glanced toward his father.

"*Dat*, can we have a garden someday?"

He blinked and smiled at his son. "It takes hard work to have a *goot* garden." He met Esther's gaze. "I admit I've been buying produce from Anne Stoltzfus, the local midwife. She's an avid gardener with the best vegetables for purchase in the area."

Esther could tell that he was concerned with her lack of response. "You said that you never forgot me," she said, bringing the subject back to the past. "I never forgot you, either." She blinked back happy tears. "Years ago, when *Mam* moved us to Walnut Creek, I wanted to stay in Honeysuckle to be near you." She sniffed and then tried to laugh but failed. "I wasn't allowed."

David tenderly wiped away her tears. "Your *mam* needed you," he said with understanding.

"*Ja.* Although I didn't realize it back then. I believe *Gott* has a plan for each of us. I realized after my *mudder* became ill that He wanted me with her to help."

He nodded. "And now He brought you back to me."

She beamed at him. "*Ja*, so it would seem."

David reached for her hand, clasped it within his warm fingers. "I want to be your husband."

The heat of his touch made her feel alive. "And I want to be your wife," she admitted huskily.

David appeared overjoyed. "Let's have a cup of tea and talk about our life together." He kept hold of her hand as they continued toward the cottage. "We can ask Jacob how he feels about having you come to live with us."

"All right."

They followed young Jacob into the house and sat, enjoying tea, while Jacob drank milk and ate cookies. His father addressed him. "Jacob, how would you feel about Esther coming to live on the farm?" He paused and Esther waited expectantly. "As my wife and your new *mudder*."

"Can Jonas and Zeke come sometimes to spend the night?"

Esther chuckled. How like children to look at life so differently than adults. With a glance, she sought David's approval and then said, "*Ja*, they're my nephews and I love them. They can come visit and spend the night."

Jacob bobbed his head as if satisfied. "I like Esther and I think she should marry us."

Esther and David exchanged happy looks. "Sounds like a *goot* idea to me," his father said.

"You're quiet," Zack's mother said as their hired driver drove his car away from the farm and turned onto the paved main road.

Zack looked at her, managed a small smile. "Just thinking."

Mam regarded him with understanding. "You didn't want to leave."

He released a sharp breath. *"Nay."*

"But you'll go back."

He certainly hoped so. He nodded.

"You needed time to think," his mother said, surprising him as she often did.

"Ja."

"You love her —Lizzie," *Mam* said, shocking him with her knowledge of his feelings and thoughts.

"She was my *brooder*'s wife." Despite his feelings for Lizzie, he still struggled with the thought that his love for Lizzie was a betrayal to Abraham.

"She is your *brooder*'s widow," his mother pointed out gently. "He is no longer with us." She paused, placed a hand on his arm. "He is with his beloved Ruth now. Why shouldn't you be with the woman you love?"

Zack felt his throat tighten with emotion. "You don't think me wrong for feeling the way I do?"

"I told Lizzie and I'm going to tell you. She is a woman I'd be happy to have as my son's wife." She smiled. "You are my son, *ja*?"

Despite himself, he chuckled. *"Ja.* There is no doubt about that. *Dat* always said that I take after you in stubbornness and determination."

"That you do, Zack." Her smile widened. "Since we

are so alike, I suggest you think about what I would do if I were you." She squeezed his arm gently before releasing it. "If I were a man who loved a woman as much as you obviously love Lizzie, I'd take my mother home and head back as quickly as possible to Pennsylvania. Then I'd do everything I could to win her heart so that she'll marry me and spend the rest of her life with me... but that's only what I'd do if I were you."

A gust of wind blew through the open car window, and his mother reached up to hold her head covering in place. Their driver apologized and rolled up the glass.

"That sounds like you," he said with a grin.

"And you," she pointed out. "There is something else you need to think about," she continued. "If Lizzie hadn't married your *brooder*, then you and she never would have met. What if Lizzie was meant to marry Abraham because the Lord's plan was for her to be with you?"

"I never thought of it that way." Zack leaned in to kiss her cheek. He felt a lightening in spirit; he was pleased that his mother saw things differently. "I love you, *Mam*," he said softly. "You are a smart woman."

Sarah lifted her chin as she straightened her *kapp*. "*Mudder* always knows best, son. Never forget that."

"Abraham!" Lizzie screamed as she jerked awake. As she sat up in bed, she realized that she'd been trapped in her recurring nightmare. It had been weeks since she'd had the dream, but apparently it was back to haunt her sleep and her waking hours. In the nightmare, she relived the day of her husband's death, when she'd gone into the barn and found Abraham's broken and bleeding body lying on the hard concrete floor. He had taken a tumble from the loft after climbing up to remove a nest of kittens. Lizzie had asked him to bring them down because she'd feared the children would be unable to resist the climb to visit with them and then fall.

I'm responsible, she thought. If only she'd blocked off the base of the ladder instead of asking him to take down the kittens.

Her heart beat rapidly as she sat up in bed, shuddering, hugging herself with her arms. It was afternoon. The older children were still in school, the younger ones with Esther at the *dawdi haus*. She had decided to try to nap because sleep had eluded her since Zack's departure. *And now I'm dreaming of Abraham's death while napping.* Would she ever be free of the nightmare?

Tears rolled down her cheeks as she pressed a hand over her thundering heart. "I'm sorry, Abraham," she sobbed softly. "You were a *goot* man and husband."

She longed for Zack. She missed having him near. He said that they would talk when he came back, but would he return or would he change his mind?

And if he doesn't come back, what then? Lizzie gasped a sob of pain. She brushed her tears away but she couldn't stop crying.

I love him.

But does he have feelings for me?

She climbed off the bed and moved to the adjoining sewing room, the place where she'd slept alone during the first year of her marriage. She took up a needle and worked on Mrs. Emory's daughter's wedding quilt, which was coming along nicely. She concentrated on the task of making neat, even stitches in her attempt to block out the horrible images in her nightmare.

Quilting and other crafts continued to be her solace when she couldn't sleep. The work was also her joy during the happy occasions in her life. Quilting was the

Lord's gift to her, and she was grateful for the talent He gave her.

As she fingered the quilt's edge, Lizzie closed her eyes and prayed. *Please, Lord, help me to accept whatever happens. Give me the strength to endure and the knowledge of Your will.*

Lizzie sighed as she left the sewing room. She needed to bathe. Her body ached all over, especially her hip. The hot water would help ease the soreness, and then afterward she'd fix herself a vinegar-and-honey tea.

She filled up the tub after carrying clean clothes into the bathroom. She felt her eyes tear as she turned the tap and adjusted the water temperature. "Come back, Zack," she whispered. She prayed for him to return. No matter what they might discuss during their talk, she knew one thing.

She loved him with all her heart.

Chapter Twenty-Three

Lizzie kneaded fresh bread dough at the kitchen work-table. She planned to make several loaves today for her, the children and for Esther to keep in the cottage freezer. She smiled as she thought of her sister-in-law. She and the good preacher were spending a lot of time together. Late yesterday afternoon, Esther had confided in Lizzie about David's marriage proposal. Lizzie had been happy and excited for her.

"Am I foolish for agreeing to wed him?" she'd asked. "I'm not a young girl."

"He loves you. You love him." They'd been sharing a pot of tea, and Lizzie had set her teacup back onto its saucer. "You'll be foolish if you don't marry him."

Esther had eyed her curiously. "It wasn't the same for you when you married my *brooder,*" she said as if she'd just realized it.

"*Nay,* but I don't regret my choice. Your *brooder* had lost his beloved wife. I came into the household when he and the children were grieving. It was difficult at first, but things got better between him, the children and me."

"But you were not the *mudder* they'd lost." Esther reached for Lizzie's hand.

Lizzie had managed a smile, although remembering that time in her marriage was difficult for her. "*Nay*, I'll admit that life here wasn't easy at first. The older children resented me, but Anne, Jonas and Zeke accepted my love and loved me in return. That was all that I needed to keep me going."

Esther gave her fingers a squeeze and then withdrew. "I hope someday that you're as happy as I am."

"That's a lovely hope, Esther." But without Zack's love, she knew such happiness would be elusive.

Esther had hugged her, and Lizzie had returned the embrace with tears in her eyes.

Thinking back to their conversation, Lizzie felt glad for Esther. She would do everything she could to make sure that Esther and David's marriage ceremony would be a celebration to remember.

Zack will come, she thought with a tingle of anticipation. He wouldn't stay away from his sister's wedding. She had thought that Zack would have returned by now. He had promised to come back, but other than a call to Beachey's Craft Shop to say that he and Sarah had arrived in Walnut Creek safely, there had been no word or sign of him.

Lizzie froze while working the bread dough. She wiped her brow with the back of her hand. Closing her eyes a moment, she sought to regain her balance, and then she went back to working the bread. Lizzie focused all of her attention on the work so that she wouldn't think, wouldn't worry that her feelings for him were unreciprocated.

She pounded the dough with her fist, rolled it and then kneaded and pressed it. Lizzie was so involved in the work that she barely heard the door opening behind her. It was as the door shut with a click that she realized she was no longer alone.

"Mary Ruth?" Since it was late afternoon, she figured the children had returned from school. Her eldest daughter was usually the first to arrive, with the other children coming a few minutes afterward. She was deeply touched that all seven of them had continued to treat her with respect and love. Every time one of them called her *Mam*, her heart melted.

Mary Ruth hadn't said a word, so Lizzie said, "Not a *goot* day?"

"It's an extremely *goot* day," a deep masculine voice answered.

She gasped and faced him. "Zack," she breathed.

He looked wonderful. She studied his handsome face, noting the red in his cheeks from the cooling temperatures, the warm gleam in his dark eyes and the heart-stopping smile that curved up the corners of his attractive mouth.

"Lizzie," he said as he approached. She couldn't move as she stared at him. The last thing she'd expected was to see him again—so soon after his departure.

And while joy filled her at the sight of him, a niggle of fear filtered through the gladness, dimming the happiness as she wondered about the talk they were going to have.

"You—you're back. Did Sarah come with you?"

He shook his head. "*Nay*, *Mam* wanted to stay."

Her hands were covered with flour and she knew there were streaks of flour dust on her face. "I wondered if you'd changed your mind." The intensity of his gaze made her look away.

"Lizzie." His voice was soft, almost tender.

She was surprised to see a look in his eyes that she'd never expected to see. Affection. *Love.* She drew herself to her full five-foot height. *Nay*, he didn't love her. She was a fool for even entertaining the thought.

Zack studied her closely. A myriad of emotions passed through his expression. "Walk outside with me," he urged.

"I'm making bread," she hedged. What if she were wrong about the warmth in his dark eyes?

"The bread can wait." His presence frightened her, not because she was afraid of him, but because her love for him was so strong.

"Do I need a coat?" She covered the dough with a clean tea towel, then went to the sink to wash her hands. She tried brushing off her face to remove any flour dust and then gave up because he'd already seen her.

"Ja. It's chilly," he warned. Lizzie retrieved her winter coat from a wall hook and was startled when he took it from her hand and held it while she slipped her arms into its long sleeves. She felt the weight of his hands settle briefly on her shoulders before he released her and stepped back.

Lizzie couldn't contain a shiver as she stepped into the chilly outside air. She didn't feel the cold; she was too aware of Zack beside her. It was only as she began to fear their discussion, what he had to say about the farm, that she experienced a chill.

They walked past the barn and into an open field until they were out of view of the farmhouse and cottage. Zack stopped suddenly, placed his hands on her shoulders and turned her to face him.

"There is something I need to tell you."

Aware that he didn't remove his hands, Lizzie trembled, expecting the worst. *"Ja?"* She stared at him. "Is it time for our discussion?"

He furrowed his brow. "Discussion?"

"About the farm."

He nodded. "About the farm…and something else." He focused his dark eyes on her.

She closed her eyes. "Something else?" she echoed.

"Lizzie, look at me."

She reluctantly opened her eyes.

"I had time to think about the farm—and you—while I was away."

"You're going to move into the farm *haus*," she said. She hugged herself with her arms as she met his gaze. "Zack, I know the farm is rightfully yours. Abraham was only managing the farm until you were old enough."

"I admit that it was my first thought when I learned that you had married my *brooder*," he said, and Lizzie felt a shaft of pain. He reached for her hand, pressed it against his chest. "I didn't know you. How could I leave the farm to a woman I didn't know? How could I leave his children with a stranger?"

"I understand." He must have been shocked to learn that Abraham had remarried, especially given the knowledge that his brother had been deeply in love with his first wife.

"And then I met you. You were nothing like I expected." He gave her a crooked smile. "You were a slip of a girl, and I didn't know if or how you would manage. So I convinced Esther to move into the *dawdi haus* with me." He smiled and the warmth of it made her breath catch. "It didn't take long before I saw that you managed," he said, "well beyond my expectations."

"And you were torn," she offered, understanding how he must have felt. "You wanted the farm, but I was living in the farmhouse with the children."

He gave her a nod. "But then I saw how hard you worked and how much you loved the children. I saw your kindness and compassion and the way you gave of your-self to everyone and everything, and I—" Lizzie blinked up at him "—started to care for you."

She felt her heart leap in hope. "You did?" she said, unable to believe it was true.

Zack nodded. He lifted a hand to touch her cheek. The warmth of his fingers sent away the cold. He caught her other hand, placed it next to the one against his coat front. "I love you, Lizzie. I want to spend the rest of my life with you."

Lizzie stared at him in shock. *"You...love...me?"* She was afraid to hope, afraid to believe. She didn't know what to think. He couldn't possibly love her—it was all too good to be true. "You can have the farm," she said. "Just please let me keep the children. I don't know where we'll go, but we won't stay and be in your way."

He frowned. *"Nay*, you'll not be going anywhere. The farm is yours. I don't want it if you're not living here with me as my bride. I'm not asking to marry you so that I can have the farm. I want to wed you because I love you and want you to be my wife. The farm will always be your home, and if you don't love me as I do you, then I will leave and return to Ohio."

"You love me," she gasped, blinking against tears of joy. "You really love me as much as I love you?"

"You love me?" he said, his dark eyes brightening with joy. "Thanks be to *Gott*," he breathed. "Then it's set. We'll marry next month—"

Zack had yet to learn the truth of Abraham's death and her role in it. She retreated several steps back, her spirits plummeting. *"Nay,"* she said. "I can't. You won't want to, once you find out what I did."

Zack tried to pull her into his arms, but she resisted.

"Tell me what's so terrible that I won't want to marry you."

"I'm responsible for your *brooder*'s death."

"*Nay*, I don't believe it."

"It's true." She hid her trembling hands in the folds of her skirt. Lizzie released a sob. "That day…there were kittens in the hayloft. I was afraid that the children would try to climb up to see them. I didn't want them to fall and get hurt, and so I asked—*begged*—your *brooder* to go up and bring them down."

She hugged herself, lost in the awful memory of that terrible day. "I still don't know exactly how it happened, but when he didn't come back to the house, I went to check on him. I— I found him lying in a pool of blood on the cement floor. He had fallen from the loft and landed hard."

She realized she was crying openly and swiped a hand across her wet cheeks. "I could tell by the angle of his head that he had broken his neck and died instantly." The tears splashed onto her hand that held the collar of her coat closed. "The blood was from where he hit his head." She dashed a hand across her face.

He stared at her in silence. She spun as if to escape. "Lizzie—" His soft, even voice stopped her.

"I'm sorry," she whispered brokenly. "Your *brooder* was a *goot* man. He didn't deserve to die."

Zack pulled her into his arms, stroked her hair as she leaned into his strength. "You're not responsible for his death, Lizzie. It was his time. *Gott* called him home. It was *Gottes Wille*. You were thinking of the children's safety and that's a *goot* thing. Do you know how many times Abraham climbed into that loft?" he asked.

She shook her head as she met his gaze.

"Hundreds of times." He regarded her with tenderness. "You are *not* responsible for his death."

"I'm not?" Dare she believe him?

Zack shook his head. *"Nay."*

She began to tremble. She felt a burning in her gut that spread to her throat and her eyes. "I'm sorry," she gasped, turning to escape.

He caught her arm, drew her back into his embrace. "You've carried the weight of this on your shoulders," he said gently. His gaze filled with compassion and understanding. "You should have told me sooner. I would have comforted you if I'd known."

"You would have?" she ventured, afraid to hope. He didn't blame her for his brother's death. His concern was only for her. She recognized his love for her in his eyes. Lizzie caught her breath with joy.

Zack settled his head on hers. "Marry me."

"I'm a cripple," she gasped. "Why would you want to marry me?"

"You are not a cripple." He caressed her cheek, her shoulder. "You face life with spirit and everything you have to offer." He cradled her cheek and stroked her with his gaze. "I love you. Let me court you starting now, right from this moment. We can post the banns and marry next month."

Lizzie saw the further proof of his love in his smile. *He loves me!*

"I don't know if I can have children with this hip," she said sadly. She would tell him about her miscarriage later. That belonged to her marriage with Abraham, and her life with Zack was a fresh start, a new beginning.

"We have seven children. Why should we need more? The choice is the Lord's and not ours to make." He smiled as he touched her cheek. "You alone make me happy."

She ran trembling fingers along his jaw. "Then I will marry you, Zack Fisher. And I will love you forever and until the end of time."

Zack shook his head. "And I'll love you for as long as I live and beyond."

With a cry of happiness she hugged him, loving the feel of his strong arms around her. They held each other quietly for a time. Lizzie loved the rhythm of his steady heartbeat beneath her ear and his soft breaths against her neck and head.

"Mam?" she heard Mary Ruth call.

"The children!" Lizzie gasped. Would they be happy about their plans to marry?

"They love you as I do," Zack said, sensing her concern. "They'll be happy to share our lives as a family."

"Then we should tell them the news." He released her reluctantly, and Lizzie clasped his hand as they started back toward the farmhouse. Lizzie recalled the forgotten bread dough and understood why Mary Ruth sounded concerned.

The children were in the yard as they strolled hand in hand toward the farmhouse. Mary Ruth was the first to catch sight of their approach.

Mary Ruth grinned as she glanced down at their clasped hands. "Welcome back, *Onkel* Zack. *Mam*, I can tell you're glad to have him back." Her eyes twinkled. "So when are you getting married?"

Lizzie released a pent-up breath. Her daughter's simple words were enough to reassure her and Zack that all would be well in the Fisher household. *Thanks be to* Gott.

Epilogue

Lizzie and Zack decided to marry on the third Thursday of November. Esther and David decided to wed, as well, and share their special day. Their banns had been published in church right after the brides-to-be had accepted their sweethearts' wedding proposals. The November morning of their wedding day was chilly, but Lizzie and Esther were too excited to care about the cold weather. They had talked until late the previous evening before retiring to their rooms for a good night's sleep. Their only thoughts were of love and their spouses.

It was not yet dawn, and the farmhouse overflowed with family and friends. Fifteen married couples had come the previous day to prepare the wedding feast and set up the house for the bridal party and guests. Lizzie was in her upstairs bedroom donning her wedding gown with Mary Ruth's help. The plain dress of light green, according to her daughter, brightened her eyes and made her beautiful. Lizzie's mother and sisters were also in the room. They had come to help the bride and wish Lizzie happiness.

After Mary Ruth was called downstairs, *Mam* pinned Lizzie's dress closed and fixed her hair. Lizzie knew it gave her mother pleasure to see her happy and in love, so she regarded *Mam* with a tender smile as *Mam* stepped back and studied her with affection.

"Are you ready?" her sister Katherine had asked.

Lizzie smiled with pure joy. "*Ja*, Katie. I've never been more so."

It had been months since she'd seen either one of her sisters. Katherine had been too busy at home to visit, walking about with Mark Troyer, while her married sister, Susan, had been living in Indiana with Amos Mast, her husband of six years. All of her siblings had come for her wedding, and Lizzie was pleased and grateful to have them share in the day. Her relationship with her mother had improved since her mother had confessed that she felt responsible for Lizzie's limp. Lizzie finally felt her mother's love.

"You look…lovely," *Mam* said.

"*Danki,*" Lizzie whispered. She reached to capture her mother's hand and then turned toward her sisters with her other hand extended. "*Mam*, Katie, Susan—I'm so happy you're here."

The females in the King family blinked rapidly against tears of emotion. They formed a circle and briefly held hands. "We should head downstairs," her mother said briskly. "There's still much to do."

"Go. Zack and I will be leaving as soon as Esther and David are ready." Lizzie peered out her bedroom window toward the *dawdi haus* across the yard. Dawn was but a promise in a star-studded sky when the cottage door opened and Esther appeared, followed by her mother and her sisters, Miriam and Sadie. Sarah King held a lantern to light the way. As if drawn by sense, Esther glanced toward Lizzie's bedroom window. Lizzie, lit up by the burning oil lamp behind her, waved. With a huge grin, Zack's soon-to-be-married sister waved back. God chose that moment to make the sun rise. Lizzie felt as if the dawn brightening the dark sky was the Lord's silent message of His approval of her marriage to Zack.

William brought around the buggy that would take Lizzie and Zack with Esther and David to the wedding services at the Peter Zook farm. Zack waited downstairs as Lizzie descended the steps and saw him. He looked up, and their gazes locked with silent messages of love.

Zack held out his hand as Lizzie came abreast of him in the hall near the bottom landing. "Are you ready?" She nodded as she locked fingers with his. "Nervous?" he asked.

She smiled as she shook her head. *"Nay."*

He grinned, and his dark eyes brightened. "Then let's be on our way, shall we?"

Esther and David stood by the buggy. Lizzie gave them a grin, and then she and Zack waited while the preacher and Esther climbed into the backseat. Zack and Lizzie then climbed in to sit in the second row.

Lizzie's brother Luke sat beside her brother William as William drove from the Fisher farm toward the Zook property less than a mile down the road. Rachel and Peter were happy to host the wedding nuptials. With the opening of a pocket door between two rooms in their house, there was extra space for the large congregation of wedding guests who would arrive later that morning at nine o'clock.

Zack bent and whispered in her ear, "So, how do you feel about becoming Mrs. Fisher?"

Lizzie chuckled. "I'm already Mrs. Fisher."

He caressed her with his gaze. "Mrs. *Zachariah* Fisher."

Lizzie caught her breath. She was aware of his scent, his warmth, his closeness, and she had thanked the Lord over and over throughout the night that He'd given her this special man to marry.

"I'll love it," she murmured huskily, "as I love you."

He gently squeezed her hand. The vehicle shifted as William steered the horse onto the Zooks' dirt driveway. "We're here," her *brooder* announced.

"We're here," Lizzie called back to Esther. Esther and David were quiet. Lizzie glanced over her shoulder and saw that they were too busy gazing lovingly into each other's eyes to hear or notice anything going on around them.

Lizzie laughed and tapped David's knee. "Preacher?"

He seemed to realize that he'd been addressed. *"Ja?"*

"It's time," Zack said with a grin.

David laughed self-consciously while Esther beamed at her bridegroom and then transferred her glowing gaze to her brother and Lizzie.

Rachel and Peter were in the bridal party. Normally, each couple would have two couples standing with them, but since they were family and sharing their wedding day, they decided that they would share the same wedding party, as well.

"Are Susan and Amos here yet?" Lizzie asked. Her married sister and her brother-in-law would be the second bridal-party couple.

"They're in the buggy behind us."

Lizzie sighed. *"Goot."* She stifled the strongest urge to touch the face of her husband-to-be.

Zack's gaze flared, and she knew he understood what she was feeling.

When the weddings guests arrived, each bride and groom with their attendants were seated in the front row of church benches. After the house was full, the ministers went into the next room followed by the brides with their grooms while the congregation sang hymns from the *Ausbund*. The elders gave a brief instruction about the couples' marital duties before the couples returned to the main room for the sermon and wedding ceremony. The sermon was long but meaningful. When he was finished, Bishop Andy invited both couples to come forward. He placed a hand over the clasped hands of each couple. He gave them each a blessing; then the couples said their vows.

Bishop Andy spoke. "So then, may I say that the God of Abraham, Isaac and Jacob be with you and help you fulfill His blessing abundantly upon you, through Jesus Christ. Amen."

The bishop then pronounced Esther and David as well as Lizzie and Zack newly married. The newlyweds climbed into separate buggies and headed home for the wedding feast with William acting as hostler, or driver, for Zack and Lizzie while Lizzie's brother Luke drove David and Esther.

Zack turned to Lizzie as William drove them toward their destination. "*Hallo*, my wife," he whispered in her ear. He leaned in to kiss her, and she closed her eyes to the sensations that sent her spirit soaring. Zack sat back against the seat, smiling at her, as she opened her eyes.

"*Hallo*, husband." Lizzie gave in to the temptation to caress his jaw. His chin was warm and smooth—but not for long. Now that he was married, he would grow a beard along his jaw like those worn by other married men. Their life together would be a busy joy-filled journey. She realized that there would be bad times with the good, but she knew that with Zack by her side, they'd find happiness.

The buggy stopped, and William got out and opened the door for them. Zack and Lizzie stepped out of the vehicle and were greeted by their seven children and various other friends and relatives. Esther and David's vehicle pulled up behind them, and the preacher and his new wife alighted.

It was the children who had garnered Lizzie's attention. She was pleased to see all seven of them grinning at her and Zack.

"I'm hungry," Zeke stated suddenly, and Zack laughed, scooped him up into his strong arms and reached for Lizzie's hand. Then together he, Lizzie and the children entered the farmhouse to enjoy the festivities of their wedding celebration.

* * * * *

Dear Reader,

Welcome to the Amish village of Honeysuckle, Pennsylvania, the setting for the Lancaster Courtships series.

In my book *The Amish Mother*, you met Lizzie King Fisher, a nineteen-year-old widow whose late husband was a widower many years her senior. Lizzie has a bad hip and considers herself a cripple. She wed Abraham Fisher because her mother suggested that the sad, grieving man might be the only marriage prospect for a woman like her.

After her husband's death, Lizzie cares for Abraham's seven children while managing the farm. Suddenly her brother-in-law, Zachariah Fisher, arrives. Soon, Lizzie fears losing the children she loves and her home.

Zack's presence complicates matters for Lizzie. But you saw how feelings changed as love began to influence the lives of Zack, Lizzie and the children.

I hope you enjoyed *The Amish Mother* and that you had fun visiting with Ellen Beachey and her beau again from Emma Miller's *The Amish Bride*. You will get a chance to return to Honeysuckle, Pennsylvania, once again next month in Patricia Davids's *The Amish Midwife*, where you'll meet Annie Stoltzfus, the local midwife, who tangles with her aggravating neighbor, a dairy goat farmer, and wins the ultimate grace in life—love.

Happy Reading!

Blessings and light,

Rebecca Kertz

COMING NEXT MONTH FROM
Love Inspired®

Available October 20, 2015

A DOCTOR FOR THE NANNY
Lone Star Cowboy League • by Leigh Bale

When Eva Brooks finds a baby on Stillwater Ranch's doorstep, she'll have to go from kitchen cook to temporary nanny. Working with Dr. Tyler Grainger to take care of the infant could bring her closer to her happily-ever-after.

THE AMISH MIDWIFE
Lancaster Courtships • by Patricia Davids

Sparks fly when Joseph Lapp is forced to ask midwife Anne Stoltzfus for help in taking care of his infant niece. Will they be able to put their neighborly quarrels behind and realize that they're a perfect fit?

THE CHRISTMAS FAMILY
The Buchanons • by Linda Goodnight

Contractor Brady Buchanon loves Christmas—especially the home makeover his construction company awards each year. When single mom Abby Webster becomes the next recipient, can they see past their differences and build a love to last a lifetime?

YULETIDE COWBOYS
by Deb Kastner and Arlene James

In these two brand-new novellas, Christmas brings a pair of ruggedly charming cowboy brothers a chance to start over—and find love and family on their journey.

HER CHRISTMAS HERO
Home to Dover • by Lorraine Beatty

Single mom Gemma Butler is intent on revamping Dover's Christmas celebrations—despite Linc Montgomery's protests. But just as a storm threatens the town, they'll join forces to save the holiday—and to find a future together.

RANCHER FOR THE HOLIDAYS
by Myra Johnson

Seeking a fresh start at his uncle's ranch, Ben Fisher is drawn to help local girl Marley Sanders with her mission work—and finds himself falling for the pretty photographer. But could a secret from Marley's past derail their chance at happiness?

LOOK FOR THESE AND OTHER LOVE INSPIRED BOOKS WHEREVER BOOKS ARE SOLD, INCLUDING MOST BOOKSTORES, SUPERMARKETS, DISCOUNT STORES AND DRUGSTORES.

LICNM1015

REQUEST YOUR FREE BOOKS!

2 FREE INSPIRATIONAL NOVELS
PLUS 2
FREE
MYSTERY GIFTS

Love Inspired®

SPECIAL EXCERPT FROM

Love Inspired®

When an Amish bachelor suddenly must care for a baby,
will his beautiful next-door neighbor rush to his aid?

Read on for a sneak preview of
THE AMISH MIDWIFE,
the final book in the brand-new trilogy
LANCASTER COURTSHIPS

"I know I can't raise a baby. I can't! You know what to do.
You take her! You raise her." Joseph thrust Leah toward
Anne. The baby started crying.

"Don't say that. She is your niece, your blood. You
will find the strength you need to care for her."

"She needs more than my strength. She needs a
mother's love. I can't give her that."

Joseph had no idea what a precious gift he was trying
to give away. He didn't understand the grief he would feel
when his panic subsided. She had to make him see that.

Anne stared into his eyes. "I can help you, Joseph,
but I can't raise Leah for you. Your sister Fannie has
wounded you deeply, but she must have enormous faith
in you. Think about it. She could have given her child
away. She didn't. She wanted Leah to be raised by you,
in our Amish ways. Don't you see that?"

He rubbed a hand over his face. "I don't know what
to think."

"You haven't had much sleep in the past four days.
If you truly feel you can't raise Leah, you must go to
Bishop Andy. He will know what to do."

"He will tell me it is my duty to raise her. Did you mean it when you said you would help me?" His voice held a desperate edge.

"Of course. Before you make any rash decisions, let's see if we can get this fussy child to eat something. Nothing wears on the nerves faster than a crying *bubbel* that can't be consoled."

She took the baby from him.

He raked his hands through his thick blond hair again. "I must milk my goats and get them fed."

"That's fine, Joseph. Go and do what you must. Leah can stay with me until you're done."

"*Danki*, Anne Stoltzfus. You have proven you are a good neighbor. Something I have not been to you." He went out the door with hunched shoulders, as if he carried the weight of the world upon them.

Anne looked down at little Leah with a smile. "He'd better come back for you. I know where he lives."

Don't miss
THE AMISH MIDWIFE
by USA TODAY bestselling author Patricia Davids.
Available November 2015 wherever
Love Inspired® books and ebooks are sold.

LIEXP1015

SPECIAL EXCERPT FROM

 HISTORICAL

A marriage of convenience to rancher Shane McCoy is the only solution to Tessa Spencer's predicament. He needs a mother for his twins, and she needs a fresh start.

Can two pint-size matchmakers help them open their guarded hearts in time for Christmas?

Read on for a sneak preview of
THE RANCHER'S CHRISTMAS PROPOSAL
by **Sherri Shackelford,**
available in November 2015 from Love Inspired Historical!

"We could make a list." Tessa's voice quivered. "Of all the reasons for and against the marriage."

She had the look of a wide-eyed doe, softly innocent, ready to flee at the least disturbance. She'd been strong and brave since the moment he'd met her, and he'd never considered how much energy that courage cost her. For a woman on her own, harassment from men like Dead Eye Dan Fulton must be all too familiar. He felt her desperation as though her plea had taken on a physical presence. If he refused, if he turned her away, where would she turn to next?

A fierce need to shelter her from harm welled up inside him, and he stalled for time. "It's not a bad idea. Unexpected, sure. But not crazy."

These past days without the children had been a nightmare. Being together again was right and good, the way things were supposed to be. He hadn't felt this at peace since he'd held Alyce and Owen in his arms that first time nearly two years ago.

"We don't need a list." Her hesitant uncertainty spurred him into action. "After thinking things through, getting married is the best solution."

"Are you certain?" Tessa asked softly, a heartbreaking note of doubt in her voice.

"I'd ask you the same. It's a hard life. Be sure you know the bargain you're making. I don't want you making a mistake you can't take back."

"You're not a mistake, Mr. McCoy."

"Shane," he said, his throat working. "Call me Shane."

The last time he'd plunged into a marriage, he'd been confident that friendship would turn into love. Never again. He'd go about things differently this time. With this marriage, he'd keep his distance, treat the relationship as a partnership in the business. He'd give her space instead of stifling her.

She was more than he deserved. Her affection for the children had obviously instigated her precipitous suggestion. Though he lauded her compassion, someday Owen and Alyce would be grown and gone, and there'd be only the two of them. What then? Would they have enough in common after the years to survive the loss of what had brought them together in the first place?

"You're certain?" he asked.

Her chin came up a notch. "There's one thing you should know about me. Once I make up my mind, I don't change it. I'll feel the same in a day, a week, a month and a year. There's no reason to wait."

Don't miss
THE RANCHER'S CHRISTMAS PROPOSAL
by Sherri Shackelford,
available November 2015 wherever
Love Inspired® Historical books and ebooks are sold.